T0129412

Better Off Wed

Also by Susanna Craig

Better Off Wed

A Love and Let Spy Romance

By Susanna Craig

LYRICAL PRESS
Kensington Publishing Corp.
www.kensingtonbooks.com

LYRICAL PRESS BOOKS are published by

Kensington Publishing Corp.
119 West 40th Street
New York, NY 10018

All Kensington titles, imprints, and distributed lines are available at special quantity discounts for bulk purchases for sales promotion, premiums, fund-raising, educational, or institutional use.

Special book excerpts or customized printings can also be created to fit specific needs. For details, write or phone the office of the Kensington Sales Manager: Kensington Publishing Corp., 119 West 40th Street, New York, NY 10018. Attn. Sales Department. Phone: 1-800-221-2647.

Lyrical Press and Lyrical Press logo Reg. U.S. Pat. & TM Off.

First Electronic Edition: December 2021
ISBN: 978-1-5161-1061-2 (ebook)

First Print Edition: December 2021
ISBN: 978-1-5161-1062-9

Printed in the United States of America

To Anne,
for being both a friend and a fan

Acknowledgments

Focus, energy, and creativity are necessary ingredients for writing a book, and for me, they were in short supply during the pandemic. For this book's completion, I owe many, many thanks, especially to my editor, Esi Sogah, for her patience; to Amy, who coaxed this story out of me chapter by chapter; to my family, especially my husband, for unending support and encouragement; and to my readers, whose enthusiasm for this series kept me going.

Prologue

Lady Sterling had been born of darkness.

Not the darkness of night, though much of her work was done between dusk and dawn. No, her name had been forged in the dark souls of men— men whose lust for power extended beyond empires and crowns, beyond land and titles, beyond even trade and politics, into the comfortless garrets and cellars of their domestics, often mere girls, whose pleas fell on deaf ears and whose refusals meant nothing at all.

On behalf of those innocent victims, Lady Sterling let herself be branded a thief.

Tonight, her hunting ground was Vauxhall Gardens. Paper lanterns danced languidly in the breeze, and beneath them strolled smiling couples, eager young men, even families. The warm air was thick with their awareness that the pleasures of summer must soon come to an end. In the distance, she heard music playing and people chattering over their suppers of ham, sliced paper-thin.

But her eye was drawn to the unlit alleys where other appetites could be satisfied.

On the fringes of a crowd of gentlemen stood Lord Penhurst, ripe for culling from the herd. Painting a seductive smile on her lips, she tugged her bodice half an inch lower and strolled past.

He had been a difficult one to track down, preferring as he did the hallowed halls and balls of the haute ton, where he angled for a wealthy bride and where Lady Sterling had no right of entry at all. She could almost regret her success in finding him here tonight. She had enjoyed the challenge, the chase.

But she must think of Betty, who would soon be unable to hide her swelling belly, who had lost her position and the roof over her head, thanks to Penhurst's depravity. Well, those who danced must pay the piper, as the old saying went.

And tonight, she meant to present the baron with his bill.

She knew the exact moment he saw her—or at least her décolletage. She slowed her steps, the better to roll her hips. He would answer her silent summons. Of that, she had no doubt.

The only question was whether he would come alone.

"I say," drawled one of the men, not Penhurst, "that bird's ripe for plucking."

A shiver of uncertainty passed through her, but she disguised it by turning her head away from the other man's voice, displaying her slender neck, making the scarlet silk of her gown shimmer. With a backward glance, she boldly caught Penhurst's eye, then fluttered her lashes down.

"Aye," the baron agreed hungrily. "Not often one sees such a plump breast paired with such a fine tail."

The men were all already drunk. If she had not known it by Penhurst's unsteady steps toward her, she would have guessed from the comments his cronies exchanged behind him—ribald jokes about roasting spits and cream-filled sauces that evidently sounded quite clever to their ears.

Drink made some men easier marks. It made others mean. From what Betty had told her, she could guess the effect it would have on Penhurst. Another chill scuttled along her spine.

Then one of Penhurst's friends spoke to him in a low voice. "There's better sport to be had at Pandemonium, old man."

Penhurst waved him off with a laugh.

A blaze of satisfaction drove away her fear. Pandemonium was a notorious, high-stakes hell, and a man with Penhurst's reputation for failing to honor his vowels could not expect to gamble there on credit. If he had managed to scrape together some sum of money in preparation for tonight, he must have it somewhere about his person.

Of course, a fat purse could never make up for what Betty had suffered and would suffer. But even a thin one would satisfy the girl's immediate needs better than the pocket watch Lady Sterling had come to find.

Pleased by the additional prospect of bankrupting him, she did not even flinch when the baron's arm circled her waist to urge her along the shadowy path and his brandy-soaked breath wafted over her skin. "I've got a busy night ahead of me," he said, "but I'll give you sixpence for a quick spit and polish, dove."

Bile rose in her throat, but she swallowed it back. She had never yet had to make good on what men seemed to regard as the promise of her courtesan's garb. Tonight would be no different.

Unlike Lord Penhurst, she was clever, perfectly sober—and armed.

Fearing nothing so much as injustice, she turned and ran a palm over his fitted silk waistcoat, deftly snatching his watch as she passed. Even as she seemed to lavish her attention on him, her eyes were focused on that promising bulge lower down—the purse his friend ought to have advised him to guard. Her eager fingers drifted to his waist. "Ooh, gov. Me mouth's already waterin'."

It was not. But her eyes were. Why did gentlemen prefer dousing themselves in cologne to a thorough application of soap and water? Holding her breath, she leaned closer, clinging to him, curling her fingers against his chest, tracing the decorative stitching on his waistcoat.

As she had suspected, the purse was hooked to his clothes, probably by a loop of thread over a hidden button, so it couldn't easily be lifted by a pickpocket. Nevertheless, she managed to dislodge it when she pressed closer still and wrapped her arms around him. Though they were only just off the gravel path, hardly out of sight of passersby, his hands settled heavily on her shoulders, urging her toward the ground. Her body slid over his, obligingly, sensuously. By the time she was face-to-face with the front of his satin breeches, the purse was sagging free, visible below the hem of his waistcoat.

He gripped the back of her neck as she knelt before him. "That's it. I do like the sight of a girl on her knees."

That much Betty had already made clear.

Fighting the impulse to deal the man more than a pecuniary injury, she spread one hand over his thigh and dug her fingertips into his flesh. He hissed and tipped back his head in anticipatory pleasure. Now, while he wasn't looking, she made her most important move, leaving her calling card where the watch had been.

A necessary risk. Men—all men, as far as she could tell, but most especially ones like Lord Penhurst—were presumptuous, avaricious. Creatures of their appetites, yet sure of their superiority over the so-called weaker sex.

She wanted them to know the identity of the woman who had bested them, wanted them to understand who held their secrets, and their futures, in the palm of her hand.

Thanks to the reputation she had built, a simple rectangle of stiffened paper bearing the name LADY STERLING had the power to ensure that a man would think twice before continuing to tally victims.

With nimble fingers, she tucked the card into the slit pocket of his waistcoat, while with the other hand she pretended to fumble with the buttons of his fall as she slipped the purse from its hiding spot. When the little leather pouch landed on the damp leaves beside her, the weighty *chink* of coins was the blessed music of reassurance. Betty and her child would not be condemned to starve.

Penhurst froze, tightening his hand against the back of her skull. For a moment, she thought he too had heard the sound of his purse hitting the ground.

But no, his attention had been caught by another noise entirely: footsteps. Someone strolling along the path, coming from the opposite direction. The perfect distraction. Luck was definitely on her side tonight. She would not have to resort to her weapon to get free. Surreptitiously, she danced the fingers of her free hand over the dirt until she found the little leather pouch, and then drew back her head against the baron's hand, intending to rise.

Penhurst, however, was not to be so easily put off. "Go on," he ordered, jerking her by her wig and tightening his hold so that she could not turn toward the sound. "They'll pass by, if they know what's good for them." A grunt of laughter. "Unless they're the sort who like to watch."

They. A group of men, perhaps? Men who might conclude from her present position that she was more than willing to entertain…

For the space of several breaths, she feared she had pushed her luck too far.

Then she heard a man's voice say, "Let's turn back, Julia. We shouldn't have come this way." Relief flooded through her. The footsteps belonged to a man and a woman. Just a couple who had got into one of the darkened alleys by mistake—or intended to claim as much, if they were caught.

"But we're nearly to the end of this walk." The woman sounded young, though not a child. "See, the light's much brighter just over th—oh! Oh, my." Shock warred with curiosity in the young woman's voice. Easy to picture her craning her neck for a better look. "What *are* those people doing in the shrubbery?"

Lady Sterling didn't wait to hear her companion's reply. Instead, she seized her chance and shrieked. Startled, Penhurst released her, and she scrambled to her feet, gathering up her skirts in two clenched fists, the better to disguise her bounty. "How dare you, sir?" she shouted as she scurried back into the relative safety of the unlit walk, indifferent to the bite of gravel through the thin soles of her slippers. "He was trying to—to f-force—" she stammered to the couple as she darted past, intending to disappear into the night.

And she would have done if the man had not caught her by the arm. "Are you harmed, ma'am?"

She could make out little of his features in the near darkness, but she wanted to damn the solicitousness in his voice. If men truly cared about the fate of women, they would stop their brethren from doing to innocent girls what Penhurst had done to his parlor maid.

"Unhand me, sir." The shakiness in her voice was not put on. She had no more than a moment to get away. Even a notorious slowtop like Penhurst would soon discover—

"Why, you little—!" the baron exclaimed, the hedge behind her rustling as he fumbled with the buttons she'd undone. "Our business isn't finished yet!"

Expecting the other man's fingers to tighten around her upper arm in response to Penhurst's words, she did not at first realize he had released her. When she didn't move, he whispered, "Run."

For a moment, she remained frozen in disbelief. Her gaze skated over what little she could see of the stranger's face, the shadowy profile of a Grecian nose and glittering eyes whose color was indistinguishable. Then, tightening her grip on Penhurst's pocket watch and purse, she escaped into darkness.

Chapter 1

Even before Captain Jeremy Addison stepped into General Zebadiah Scott's study, he had some inkling of the trouble he must be in.

After all, being called before one's commanding officer was not ordinarily a good sign. Given that the general made a point of keeping his domestic affairs strictly separate from his military affairs, the order to appear at Scott's Audley Street home was even more ominous. Receiving said orders several hours before noon was worse yet.

But Jeremy had spent most of the past few weeks in the Underground, a network of subterranean offices that housed and hid the activities of some of the most skilled intelligence officers in the British army. General Scott's note had provided a welcome excuse to stretch his legs and clear his head, to escape a dungeon, grown musty with the stench of his failure. He had all but given up on cracking the cypher contained inside what appeared to be a French cookbook.

The moment Jeremy's booted tread passed from the marble tile of the foyer onto the plush carpet of the study, however—which was to say, the moment he found himself eye to eye with General Scott's speculative gaze—he knew a wiser man would have found any excuse to have stayed put.

Scott inclined his head in greeting. "Much obliged, Captain Addison. I wonder if you have been at leisure to read today's paper?" He gestured toward the copy of the *Times* spread across his otherwise empty desktop.

Only twice in nearly a dozen years of army life had Jeremy seen the inside of General Scott's office in the Horse Guards. Both times, the sight of the sloping, sliding mountain of books, letters, and maps on the man's desk had made Jeremy's palms sweat.

Somehow this—this blank expanse of mahogany, not even a blotter or an inkstand, only a small slice of the glossy wood covered by a single sheet of newsprint—was worse.

Officers in Scott's service had long speculated that the general was a first-rate actor. The genial, grandfatherly air. The haze of pipe smoke. The rumpled clothes and the forgetfulness and even the spectacles, perpetually perched on his forehead and usually too smudged to be an aid to vision. All props, so it was said, for a performance Scott directed with scrupulous care.

Jeremy had always had his doubts about such theories. Why would a man in Scott's position bother with theatrics?

Now, however, with the cleverly painted backdrop no longer disguising the stage's scaffolding, the dreadful truth of it settled over him. A man might fancy he had caught an accidental glimpse past the costumes and the greasepaint. But the fact of the matter was, he had seen those things only because Scott had invited him backstage.

And the show was about to begin.

Under Scott's watchful eye, Jeremy stumbled toward the desk, a reluctant understudy pushed from the wings. As he leaned over the paper, he thrust his hands behind his back and drew a steadying breath. Not a whiff of tobacco hung on the air.

A quick scan of the densely printed page revealed the item that must have caught General Scott's notice. The words struck Jeremy with all the subtlety of a swift poke to the eye:

> *Pandemonium! Sly Lady Sterling has struck again, this time vexing a visit to Vauxhall Gardens for the ordinarily penurious Lord P—, a plump pigeon plucked before he could play.*

Scott had dragged him away from his work, all the way across town, to read some prattle about a gentleman who had fallen victim to a pickpocket? Though his upbringing had been sheltered, army life had expanded Jeremy's vocabulary significantly. He was tempted to let fly with an impressive string of epithets in response.

But he settled for a glare in the general's direction. He knew exactly why Scott must have sent for him.

The unmistakable beginnings of a smile creased the corners of Scott's mouth. "Ah. I take it you have heard of the Lady Sterling?"

Who had not? Her scandalous career, seducing gentlemen of rank in order to steal their fortunes, had been fodder for gossips, in both high society and low, for months.

"My sister Julia finds the woman's exploits amusing and takes it upon herself to keep me apprised."

Wait until she learned that Lady Sterling had paid a visit to Vauxhall on the same evening they had. Julia had rambled excitedly for hours about that brief encounter with an unfortunate young woman fleeing from some rogue. What would she say to the possibility of a brush with Lady Sterling? She would be convinced their paths must have crossed, despite the crowd and the size of the park. She would speculate endlessly over whether she had been the woman in green or the one in blue. He would never hear the end of it.

Those telltale curves crept higher, into Scott's cheeks. "An interesting choice of alias for a thief, is it not? *Sterling.* Hints at excellence, trustworthiness. Purity—of motive, perhaps, if not of method."

Jeremy's gaze narrowed further. "I gather you didn't call me here over a trivial coincidence. Sir."

With a huff of exertion that sounded suspiciously like a laugh, Scott sat down behind his desk and motioned Jeremy into the chair opposite.

"Like your sister," Scott said after a moment, "I've been following the Lady Sterling's career with interest. She targets men whom I would call vulnerable in some way. Men with secrets they would like to keep. And while money may be one motivation for her exploits, I suspect it is not all she takes from these men."

In spite of himself, Jeremy was intrigued by the hypothesis. "She's gathering information, you mean?"

"Yes. Information that can be used for blackmail. Indeed, she may already be in possession of secrets capable of doing real damage—to the war effort, the King, even the nation. I need to know whose side she is on." Scott's fingers had been steepled in a contemplative pose. Now he slid them together and laid his folded hands before him on his desk. The paper beneath them crinkled softly. "So I'm sending *you* to find her."

Jeremy, who had been nodding absently as Scott explained his interest in the case, jerked to his feet. "*I?* But I—I don't—" He dealt with books and paper, not people. He choked back an outright refusal to follow orders and asked instead, "What am I to do with her if I succeed?"

"*When*," Scott corrected, picking up the newspaper and handing it across his desk to Jeremy, as if a gossip column could be mistaken for a set of orders. "And I should think the answer would be obvious, *Lord Sterling.*"

Jeremy narrowly avoided a shudder of surprise at the use of his title. No one in the army called him that. Occasionally, Jeremy wondered—nay, *hoped*—the men with whom he worked had forgotten he was also a viscount.

If only he could return to that state of blessed ignorance himself.

At seventeen, he had been unaware that his father had belonged to a so-called cadet branch of one of those grand families with lands, mansions, titles, and the like. Richard Addison, a rector with an antiquarian bent, would have delighted in the discovery, in tracing how the twig of his family tree intersected with the main trunk. But he had died the year before, leaving Jeremy next in line.

For a time, Jeremy had fantasized that the people in London who made determinations about the succession of titles would realize they had inadvertently turned two pages of their well-thumbed guide to the peerage and skipped over some more suitable heir.

His reluctance had only grown with the discovery that he had inherited not just lands and mansions, but also a stack of baize-covered ledgers in which the number at the bottom of the LOSSES column was always greater than the figure in the column headed GAINS. Jeremy—more than usually skilled in arithmetic, well-organized, responsible—had known instantly what those numbers meant: The property was mortgaged; Lord Sterling—*he*—was heavily in debt.

All his hopes to use the blasted inheritance to benefit his mother and sister, to allow them to live in not just comfort, but luxury, had flown out the window. After four days of quiet rage, Jeremy had set aside his plan to attend Oxford in the next term. By selling off what wasn't entailed and renting out what he could of the rest, he had scraped together just enough to buy an officer's commission instead, resigned to setting aside his studies in favor of bullets and bayonets.

But his true nature had eventually brought him to the notice of General Zebadiah Scott, the mastermind behind Britain's intelligence operation. For the past ten years, Jeremy had turned a gift for mathematics and wordplay into success as a code breaker, fighting enemies made of paper and ink, waging battles entirely of wits.

Until today, he had never had cause to regret the general's attention.

Now, Jeremy flinched when the paper landed with a thwack across his palm and Scott announced, "I want you to marry her."

For a moment, silence reigned, and the two men faced one another, impassive, though Jeremy's heart thudded in his chest, pumping blood to his limbs in an instinctive preparation for flight. After a long moment, he tipped back his head and managed to drag a laugh from his chest. "*Marry her.* Good one, sir. You almost had me."

Scott's smile widened, and his eyes twinkled with something that wasn't quite—or wasn't only—amusement. "Did I?" A chuckle. "But of course, my command does not extend quite so far as that, Captain Addison. Though I confess," he went on, "it *was* your title that suggested you for the assignment—the, er, *coincidence* of names, as you put it." He paused and tilted his head. "You see, I need someone to get close to her. Someone who can encourage her confidences. Find out what she knows—and whether she would be willing to ply her extraordinary gifts on behalf of the Crown."

As the nature of the mission grew clearer, Jeremy's fingers curled around the newspaper, wrinkling it past the point of legibility. All this, because Scott wanted the Lady Sterling to turn spy?

"And you think I am such a man? Wouldn't a field agent be better suited to the task?"

As Scott well knew, Jeremy's skill set lay elsewhere—which was to say, alone with his books.

Then again, he had been struggling to unlock a cypher that others had risked their lives to secure—the most important assignment with which he'd ever been entrusted.

Perhaps Scott had lost faith in his code-breaking abilities. Perhaps this strange new mission was intended as a sort of retraining.

"It will do you good to spend more time in the fresh air, Captain Addison," the general said, an oblique reference to the dark spaces and secret work of the Underground. "You're too pale. Besides, I haven't a field agent to spare." Scott fixed him with a pointed look. "They're being drawn into the greener pastures of wedded bliss at an alarming rate."

Fighting an unaccustomed urge to fidget, Jeremy instead smoothed and folded the newspaper until it was a neat square, no larger than a letter, and slipped it into his breast pocket. "No need to worry about me, sir," he said with a crisp bow of his head.

There would be—could be—no true Lady Sterling.

Not while he was alive.

And as for the one who called herself Lady Sterling? *Just a thief with a flair for irony.* Scott's order was a chance to unmask the woman, to put an end to speculation, gossip, his sister's teasing—and the sharp pang behind his ribs that accompanied every reminder that he was destined to end up alone. "I suppose I should begin by tracking down her last victim. Who is this Lord P— the paper mentions?"

"Roderick Penhurst. Resides on Brook Street, near Hanover Square. By all accounts, the man is pockets to let—and apparently desperate enough to gamble away what little he had left in the vain hope of improving his fortunes."

Though unfamiliar with Lord Penhurst, Jeremy had recognized the name of Pandemonium. The streets near the Underground were thick with gaming establishments, some reputable, most not. Not so long ago, he had been tempted to pay one or two of them a visit, given his skill with numbers. Only fear of a greater loss—the respect and trust of his mama and sister—had brought him to his senses.

Scott's lips parted, as if he were weighing his next words carefully. "You should also know that Penhurst has a reputation as a scoundrel—and I don't mean the sort of dashing chap one finds in the pages of one of my wife's Robin Ratliff novels." Another pause. "From what I can determine about her victims, Lady Sterling preys on predators, perhaps with the intention of making such men pay for their past crimes."

Purity—of motive, if not always of method. "A sort of avenging angel, you mean?" He made no effort to hide his skepticism.

Scott nodded insistently. "Just so. But that is only speculation—and Penhurst is sure to deny all wrongdoing. If you speak with him, you must be delicate in your handling of the matter. Subtle. Fools rush in, as the saying goes."

Jeremy bristled. "I'm no fool, sir."

"If you were, you would not be here," Scott agreed, rising.

Though he felt no clearer about matters than he had when the summons to Scott's home had arrived, Jeremy recognized the signs that their conversation was drawing to a close. "Colonel Millrose said you're leaving town, sir."

"Yes, first thing in the morning. I've promised my wife a long-overdue holiday in Brighton."

Jeremy tried to picture the general strolling along the strand in a straw boater. When his imagination failed him, he glanced around the spacious room instead: warm wood, dark green walls, deep leather chairs, neatly arranged bookshelves. Nothing at all like General Scott's office near Whitehall, yet a reflection of the man who inhabited it.

Whether a truer reflection, Jeremy would not at present hazard a guess.

When he had left the Underground, the morning sun had been almost painfully bright, but through a pair of velvet-framed windows he now spied darker clouds gathering on the horizon, a harbinger of autumn's gray skies and rain. He hoped the general's holiday would not be spoiled.

"I wish you and Mrs. Scott safe travels," Jeremy said with a deeper bow of leave-taking.

"Thank you, Addison—or should I say Sterling?" The hint of a smile that played about the corners of the man's mouth was indecipherable, even for a master code breaker. "And I wish you good luck, though I cannot think you'll need it."

"Thank you, sir." In spite of himself, his voice rose, striking a doubtful note. Whatever he felt in the moment, it was not gratitude. "I will try to reward your faith in me."

As he crossed once more into the foyer, he could've sworn he heard Scott chuckling behind him.

* * * *

The door of Penhurst House opened to his knock, revealing what was surely the gangliest footman in Mayfair, who stammered when he said he would have to see if Lord Penhurst was at home. After several minutes, the young man returned, told Jeremy that Lord Penhurst would see him, and led him to a study as unlike General Scott's as it was possible for two otherwise similar rooms to be.

In place of the more usual landscape, the mangy, stuffed head of an enormous stag hung over the fireplace. From one broken-tipped antler dangled a confection of lace and ribbon—a lady's garter, Jeremy realized, and jerked his gaze away. The mingled odors of cheroot smoke, whiskey, and sweat stung his nostrils. The drapes were tightly drawn, and it smelled like no one in the household had dared to open a window for some time.

From the center of the dimly lit room, slung across an upholstered chair that had seen better days, Lord Penhurst watched him survey the space. "Who're you?" he demanded, not rising. A cut-crystal tumbler dangled from the fingertips of one hand.

"Captain Jeremy Addison, my lord."

"Damn me." He looked Jeremy's uniform up and down with bleary eyes. "I'm in for it now, ain't I?"

"I haven't the pleasure of understanding you, sir," Jeremy answered, a reply that only served to muddle Penhurst's head further. "I'm here to ask a few questions about the events that transpired at Vauxhall last evening."

"Vauxhall." Penhurst spat out the word and then, evidently intending to wash its bitter taste from his tongue, lifted the tumbler to his lips. Finding it empty, he tossed aside the heavy cylinder in disgust, and Jeremy watched it bounce onto the stained carpet and roll beneath a table. "What's there to tell that the papers don't already know? That whore stole my purse and slipped off into the night, and I didn't even get the spit 'n' polish she promised."

A flush of embarrassment rose into Jeremy's cheeks, making him grateful for the darkened room. "Can you tell me anything that might help to identify, er, Lady Sterling?"

"The King's army's after her now, eh? Well, I wish 'em luck. Pity you didn't set about the job sooner," he grumbled. "I didn't see much—she set upon me in one of the dark alleys."

Those shrubbery-lined, lanternless paths perhaps had not been designed for lovers' trysts, but they were certainly used in that fashion. For that very reason, Jeremy had intended to steer Julia far from them on their visit to the pleasure gardens last night. Julia, pertinacious and almost always more curious than wise, had had other ideas.

If Julia ever discovered that the infamous Lady Sterling had not only been at Vauxhall but had secreted herself in one of those dark alleys to prey upon her latest victim…perhaps the *same* dark alley where the poor woman had run into Jeremy, evidently fleeing an assignation gone wrong…

The same? *Surely not…*

Nevertheless, the even trot of Jeremy's pulse shifted to an unsteady gallop. He drew a deep breath to calm himself, tasting the room's fetid air.

"Dressed like a fancy piece, she was," Penhurst continued. "An' she spoke in that throaty way—you know the sort. Made me hard enough to hammer nails, just to listen to her. Had her on her knees in a trice, you can guess. But before I could even drop my fall, there was a commotion a little way off, and she scampered. Ran smack into some bloke—I tried to hail him, but he let her go and got away himself before I could give him what for for ruining my night."

Jeremy's head began to pound to match his heart, every one of Penhurst's words another blow.

The woman in the shrubbery, the woman he'd held in his hands for the briefest moment, had been Lady Sterling? *The* Lady Sterling? And he had let her get away?

No, no, no

"Afterward, I realized she'd left this in place of my, er, valu'bles." From the pocket of his waistcoat, Penhurst plucked a small rectangular card and held it out to Jeremy between his first and second fingers.

Jeremy leaned forward to snatch it from him. In the semi-darkness, he had to squint to make out the words printed upon it:

the Lady STERLING
thief-taker

The sight of the name always held a jolt of discomfort for him, even when expected, and he skated over it as quickly as possible. But *thief-taker* was an eye-catching appellation: a curiously old-fashioned word, in these days of the Bow Street Runners. Still, in an ever-growing city, wrong-doers too often escaped apprehension, and there were certainly those who preferred the traditional methods of justice.

Thoughtful, he flicked the card between his first and second fingers. On its reverse, someone had inked two words in delicate script: *for Betty*. Did the handwritten message confirm Scott's suggestion that Lady Sterling's mission might be something other than the gossip pages made it seem? *Thief-taker*, the card read, not *thief*. The inscription *for Betty* suggested she had stolen Penhurst's purse on behalf of another woman.

Was she in fact some sort of female Robin Hood?

He held up the card but did not offer to return it to Penhurst. "My lord, who is Betty?"

Penhurst shrugged. "No idea." But even as he spoke, his gaze skittered away to a far corner of the room. *A lie.* "I hope to God she hangs for what she's done."

"First," Jeremy reminded him, "she must be found." For the first time since leaving Scott's office, he felt a flicker of grim enthusiasm at the prospect. "I thank you for your assistance in that endeavor, Lord Penhurst." With a crisp bow, the calling card still in his possession, he strode from the foul chamber and back into the comparatively comfortable entry hall.

The same footman waited there, near enough to have caught much of his master's conversation. From the scowl on his face, Jeremy could readily guess that the young man did not like what he had overheard.

Jeremy jerked his chin toward the front door, indicating that the footman was to open it, hopeful the noise from the street would give some cover to their conversation.

"Have you by chance heard your master mention an acquaintance named Betty?" he asked, low.

"She was a parlor maid here, sir." A muscle ticked in the young man's jaw. "She had the right misfortune to catch Lord Penhurst's eye, and when she turned up with child, he sent her packin'. No surprise he denied knowin' her. She might've starved, for all he cared—and the babe besides."

"What has become of her, do you know?"

The lad sent a quick glance around and dropped his voice lower still. "Every hired girl in London knows to call on Lady Sterling when things go bad. Gentlefolk call her a pickpocket, but if she is, she's only makin' 'em pay for what they've taken from girls like Betty." He paused, his eyes following a crested carriage as it lumbered past. "'Course, some things can't be made right again."

Jeremy thought of poor Betty, a victim of her master's depravities, perhaps one of many. Thought of Penhurst's insistence that *she* should hang—a reference to Lady Sterling, of course, but such a man would be equally quick to blame the maid for his present troubles.

He thought too of Penhurst's vulgarities with respect to Lady Sterling, his claim to have pushed her to her knees. Recalled the fear in the woman's voice, the trembling in her limbs when Jeremy had impeded her flight, and considered what might have happened, what Penhurst would have done, if Jeremy had held her arm a moment longer. Suddenly, he no longer regretted letting her escape.

Instead, his knuckles whitened where he gripped the calling card. Even as she stole from these men, what was being stolen from her?

"Do you know where Betty is now?" he asked, drawing another sharp breath through his nose—not calming, precisely, but focusing. Lady Sterling's well-being was not his concern.

"Aye. Lady Sterling found her a new place—leastways, until the baby comes. With a Mrs. Mildred Hayes in Clapham."

"And what of the other maidservants here? Are they safe from—?" He shot a glance over his shoulder.

"They soon will be." Jeremy's skepticism must have shown in his face, for the footman continued rapidly. "Lady Penhurst is sendin' her son to rusticate, she says. At the dower house in Cornwall, with only his valet to attend him."

"Because of Betty?" Jeremy asked, though he feared he knew the answer. The poor domestic, not the master, would have borne the brunt of her mistress's displeasure if they had been caught in a compromising position.

"On account o' Lady Sterling stole Lord Penhurst's watch and chain," he replied with a rough, humorless laugh at the pitilessness of valuing a timepiece over a serving girl's life. "Family heirloom, they say. Heavy gold piece with the letter *L* on the cover, all 'round swirlygigs an' the like."

Odd. Penhurst had said nothing about the watch, though it sounded like a valuable object. Distinctive, too. The sort of thing that might be easy to recover, if anyone knew to be on the lookout for it.

"Lady Penhurst was fit to be tied when he told her it was gone," the footman was saying. "Shouted him upstairs and down. Said she'd have his head if he steps foot out of his study, 'ceptin' to get in the travelin' coach."

He and Jeremy shared a grim smile, both of them knowing that it was at best a temporary reprieve for the maidservants of Penhurst House. No matter the value of what Lady Sterling stole, it would never be punishment enough to deter a man like Penhurst. Unless...

While money may be one motivation for her exploits, I suspect it is not all she takes from these men, General Scott had spoken of secrets, of vulnerabilities—was there some reason Penhurst had kept silent about the watch?

Jeremy once more glanced at the card and those two damning words: *for Betty.* The supposed pickpocket had gone to some trouble to remind Penhurst she knew the truth about him.

Now it was up to Jeremy to uncover the truth about her.

With a nod of thanks to the footman, he tucked the card into his breast pocket and started down the steps.

"Sir?"

Jeremy glanced over his shoulder.

"When you find Betty, sir, will you tell her that Walter sends his—" He paused, as if hesitant to reveal too much, and a flush of color highlighted his freckles. "Sends his best wishes? Tell her—tell her I'd still like that walk in the park, if she's a mind to it."

With narrowed eyes, Jeremy glanced down the street, which was growing busier as the morning advanced. Would the girl even be willing to speak to a stranger? "Why don't you come with me? You can tell her yourself."

Walter stared at him for a moment, slack-jawed. Then he glanced over his shoulder at the open door and the empty hall beyond, weighed his options for a moment, and shrugged. "Aye, sir. That's a capital idea," he said as he tugged off his curled and powdered wig and stuffed it in his pocket of his livery, and the two of them set out in the direction of Westminster Bridge.

Chapter 2

Standing before the window, her back turned slightly toward the room, Laura Hopkins withdrew the watch from her reticule, merely for the pleasure of tracing the pad of her thumb over the ornate *L* on its cover.

"My dear girl, that must be the tenth time you've looked at your watch this hour. Do come and sit down."

Aunt Mildred's eyes were unfailingly sharp, even without the lorgnette she sometimes wielded. With a half smile of reluctant amusement, Laura curled her fingers around the watch and went to the tea table. "It seemed to me your coach must be late."

"Nonsense. It's only quarter of one. Doesn't your new watch keep good time?"

"It's an excellent piece, Aunt," Laura reassured her, displaying the heavy gold circle on her palm.

"Rather masculine," was Aunt Mildred's firm opinion as she inspected the watch.

"I suppose," Laura agreed, once more rubbing her thumb over the monogram surrounded by a pattern of leaves and swirls. "But once I saw it, I felt it was meant to be mine."

Certainly she was as entitled to it as Lord Penhurst. And Lady Sterling's reputation was such that finding her calling card in his watch pocket should be warning enough, proof that she knew what Penhurst, and his mother, would prefer to keep hidden.

Ordinarily, the secrets Laura collected were less tangible, and she was forced to chart her triumphs by other means: the gossip columns' increasingly wild tales about Lady Sterling's exploits, and the gratitude of the unfortunate young women who came to her for assistance.

If Lord Penhurst's purse had been lighter, Laura might have looked for a way to pawn the watch and given the proceeds to Betty—though getting rid of such a distinctive item carried significant risk. But his lordship had proven unexpectedly...*generous*, especially for a man reputed to be penniless. Now that Betty and her unborn child were well provided for, Laura felt justified in keeping the watch herself.

Aunt Mildred's hand closed around hers, pressing the warm metal into Laura's fingers as she gave a comforting squeeze. The watch's steady *tick-tock* drummed reassuringly against her palm. "I wish you would reconsider coming with me, my dear. You look as if you have the headache again."

"Just a touch, Aunt." Laura raised her other hand to press her fingers to her temple.

Her head did ache—or rather, her scalp. Last night, in what might have been either eagerness or desperation, Lord Penhurst had grabbed her wig, tugging the pins that held it in place. Very little frightened Laura, but there had been a moment when she had wondered whether she would be able to get away from him without tearing out her own short curls by the roots. At the memory of it, she shivered.

"You see," scolded her aunt, taking the shudder that had passed through Laura's limbs as confirmation of her niece's incipient illness. "I'm sure the waters would set you to rights."

Laura smiled, having no intention of accompanying her to Bath. "I am never sick, Aunt," she declared.

"Then perhaps I ought to reconsider and take that new girl—what is her name? ah, yes, Betty—as a companion. The poor, wan thing. She could use some fresh air."

At just that moment, Betty stepped into the sitting room and dipped into a curtsy. "Your coach is here, Mrs. Hayes."

Betty's eyes were dark circled and red-rimmed, it was true—too many sleepless nights, for one thing, and even tears of joy and relief left their mark. But her cheeks were already brighter and plumper after just a fortnight away from Penhurst House.

"Betty is prone to carriage sickness, ma'am," Laura explained to her aunt. "I'm afraid the journey would be spoiled for the both of you. And besides, I should not like to stay here all alone," she added, favoring Betty with a conspiratorial wink.

In point of fact, Lady Sterling was wanted out of town.

"No, no," agreed Aunt Mildred, who had risen and turned toward the pier glass to adjust her bonnet, "I should worry about you every moment."

Guilt rippled beneath Laura's skin, but she shook it from her as if it were of no more consequence than an unwelcome crease in her skirts and rose to plant a kiss on her aunt's papery cheek.

Deception is protection, she told herself every time she donned the disguise of Lady Sterling, a maxim that applied equally well to the occasional fib told to protect her aunt's heart.

"No more conjuring dangers that don't exist, Aunt. You know I shall be perfectly safe, and my headache will be gone as soon as I can be sure you are following doctor's orders."

Though worry still clouded her expression, Aunt Mildred nodded. "Well, I suppose I'd best be on my way." She passed out the door onto the landing, and Betty followed, carrying her hatboxes. "I do hope we can outpace that storm," Laura heard her mutter on the stair. "I can feel the rain in my bones already."

From the window, Laura studied the dark clouds on the western horizon. She had been watching them gather for the past hour. She waited patiently as Aunt Mildred's carriage was loaded and waved when it finally rolled away.

Once it was out of sight, she opened the cover of Penhurst's watch again. "We shall have to hurry now, Betty," she said and went to fetch her pelisse.

"Your things are all set, miss," Betty replied, picking up a valise that had been stowed behind a chair.

"Thank you. Now," she explained as she tied the ribbons of her bonnet, "since I don't know how long I'll be gone, I've left letters in the drawer of my bedside table for you to send to my aunt at intervals, so she won't worry at not hearing from me. You'll find a variety, depending on the weather and whether she writes to say she is enjoying herself or complaining about the company. You must read her letters first and choose accordingly."

"Yes, miss."

In another moment, they were out the door of the sitting room, down the stairs, and onto the pavement.

Laura, who had come to live with her aunt at the age of twelve, did not think she would ever grow tired of Clapham, the only district in London where everyone had a cause. On any given day, the streets and churches were filled with the voices of those whom society termed "radicals"— men and women who opposed the slave trade and who believed children need not die regularly in mines and chimneys and who argued in favor of educating women and the poor.

For her part, Aunt Mildred attended lectures and made generous donations to a variety of causes and even, as on the present occasion, took in serving girls who had been unjustly dismissed from their posts.

She was far from immune to the fever of righteousness that permeated the very air of Clapham.

But she would undoubtedly have drawn the line at Laura's preferred remedy: namely, acquiring the dirty secrets of wealthy men and threatening to expose them if they would not leave their domestics in peace.

In the fight for justice, charm was Laura's stock in trade. She charmed wealthy ladies into giving more money than they had intended and taking on servants they didn't need. As Lady Sterling, she charmed men into situations that made it possible for her to punish their mistreatment of powerless young women as painfully as she knew how. She had little doubt she could have charmed herself into a most eligible match, if she wanted a husband. As she did not believe any man would suit her, however, she contented herself most often with charming her aunt into complaisance.

But she knew that her aunt's liberal mindedness would be strained past the breaking point if she ever learned of the dangerous situations in which Laura frequently found herself.

Journeying to Kent by the public stage to aid an unfortunate governess struggling to fend off the unwelcome advances of her pupils' father, for example.

The breathless sounds of Betty, hurrying after her with valise in hand, slowed Laura's ordinarily quick steps. But when the girl reached her side and gasped out, "You're ever so brave, miss," Laura wished she had not adjusted her pace.

She didn't feel brave. Not this time, anyway. London's vastness had provided a paradoxical sort of security. No matter the scrape Lady Sterling found herself in, there was always a hiding place. In the country, her every movement would be regarded with suspicion. If trouble befell her, she would know no one to call for aid.

Betty seemed to read her thoughts. "I know it's not my place, miss, but I can't like you going off by yourself, and your aunt none the wiser. Are you sure you'll be all right?"

"Of course I shall," Laura insisted. Lady Sterling always worked alone. She began to hurry toward the inn again; passengers were already taking their seats in the post chaise, and its driver would not tarry for anyone, not even if he'd known he was about to transport one of the most infamous women in London.

She secured the last place inside the coach, while one of the men took her valise from Betty and stuffed it between two trunks that were tied to the rear with ropes. As the post chaise lurched into motion, Laura raised her gloved fingertips in answer to Betty's encouraging wave and muffled that pesky inner voice, the one insisting she ought to have brought the maid along.

No need to endanger anyone else.

As they picked up speed, familiar shops and houses began to slide past the window in a blur. For the first quarter of an hour, she amused herself with a surreptitious study of her fellow passengers. On the rear-facing bench sat a trio of young men, the two youngest with ginger hair like her brother's, divided by a dark-haired man only slightly older. A tutor and his charges traveling somewhere, she decided, or perhaps returning from a sojourn in the capital. To her left, a portly squire of forty or so, clad in a tweed coat, soon began to snore softly. To her right, a woman, a widow by her appearance, nervously watched out the window. On her lap lay a small satchel, which she clutched in her gloved fingers tightly enough to signal to any observer that its contents had some value—an impulse Laura had long ago learned to recognize and exploit.

Before long, Laura caught herself tracing the shape of the watch through the heavy silk of her own little bag, fancying that she could make out the edges of the ornate letter *L*. But between the watch and her fingertips lay another barrier: a much folded and refolded sheet of parchment that no doubt crinkled at her passing touch, though nothing could be heard above the coach's rattling wheels.

She had read Miss Godfrey's letter so many times she had long since committed its contents to memory. She had no need to slip it from her reticule and read it again now, not with five pairs of strangers' eyes surrounding her. Though, of course, none of them seemed to be paying her any mind. The red-headed brothers peered steadily out their respective windows, while between them their tutor was engrossed by a small, leatherbound book of poetry. The squire snuffled occasionally but showed no further sign of wakefulness. And the widow's glass-eyed gaze was now fixed on the floor.

With a strict economy of movement, so as not to jostle her fellow passengers and draw their notice, she slid the letter free and unfolded it.

To the esteemed Lady S—

Will it surprise you to learn that your reputation as a warrior for mistreated women is known even in the country? The news travels on the breeze, lifting the spirits of every girl in service who has suffered at the hands of her master.

Each and every time she read those words, Laura pursed her lips into an expression somewhere between a smile and a frown. She distrusted flowery effusions of praise, no matter the honest sentiments that might underlie them.

She much preferred the more tangible reward she had received that morning: Betty's gasp of delight and daring hug of gratitude when Laura had handed her Lord Penhurst's purse and, with it, the means of avoiding the foundling hospital, the workhouse, or worse.

The stranger's letter, on the other hand, sent a prickle of apprehension down her spine with every fresh perusal.

> *Last spring, I was employed by Lady Thornton as governess to her three youngest children. My charges are not difficult pupils, and my time at Thornton Hall has been pleasantly spent. It may well surprise you, then, to see how my pen trembles in fear.*

Nothing surprised Laura. Not anymore. Even if she were not intimately familiar with the contents of the letter, she would have known what was coming next.

> *Though I heard no rumors before accepting this post, it seems Lord Thornton has forfeited his good character among his servants. The kindly housekeeper has warned me that when Lord Thornton arrives in the country this week, I must look sharp, particularly when he is in his cups. She would tell me nothing of what became of the last governess, but three maids, she says, were dismissed just last year, and through no fault of their own. I hope I make myself clear.*
>
> *I have hardly known a moment's peace since she spoke those words. I haven't even the means to flee the house, not yet having been given any wages. Without Lady Thornton's good word, how shall I ever find another post? You have succeeded in making such men pay for their crimes. But have you the ability to prevent Lord Thornton's depredations?*
>
> *Please, Lady Sterling, won't you help me—nay, not just me, for every female domestic here is in similar danger. Won't you help us?*
>
> *Emily Godfrey*
> *Thornton Hall, Kent*

Though her sympathy rose to the woman's plight, Laura would have refused Miss Godfrey's case under ordinary circumstances. She had come to accept, however grudgingly, that she could not help every poor woman who needed it. Kent was too far, the subterfuge required too great, for Lady Sterling to take the risk. Exposure—or worse—would render her unable to help anyone.

But the name *Lord Thornton* had reached out from the paper and arrested her.

Lady Thornton's personal maid had been one of Lady Sterling's first clients, but Laura, still inexperienced, had waited too long to corner the earl. Then, just this past spring, she had been approached by Lord Thornton's cook, hoping that something could be found to check the behavior a man for whom a cast-iron pan to the ribs had proved an insufficient deterrent. That time, Laura had secured something of value, but no secrets, no information with which she could threaten him, nothing that would keep such a man from continuing to exploit his servants.

Now, anticipation of Lord Thornton's arrival at his estate in Kent had struck fear in the heart of his children's governess—and all his female domestics. If Laura failed to stop him on her third attempt, how in good conscience could she go on calling herself Lady Sterling?

Her gaze rose to the window. Beyond, the sky grew ever more ominous. Laura's fingers wanted to tremble. But Lady Sterling's were steady as she refolded the note and returned it to its hiding place, alongside Lord Penhurst's pocket watch. Come what may, she was determined to see this case to its end.

Afterward, no one would need to tremble at the name of Lord Thornton ever again.

* * * *

The threat of rain and a cooling breeze had sent most of the residents of Clapham indoors. In more than a few windows, candles and lamps were already flickering to life despite the earliness of the hour. Walter grabbed Jeremy's elbow and nodded toward a maidservant who was just about to turn up a side street. "Well, I'll be. That's her. Betty!"

She paused but did not stop.

"Betty," the footman scolded, and she turned, first wary, then with surprised, eager eyes for the lad, and finally casting a mistrustful glance at Jeremy's uniform. She had the worn, wan look of a girl who had seen far too much for her years. He judged her sixteen at most.

"What brings you here, Wally? What is it you'd be wantin' with the likes of me?"

"Now, Bets," Walter protested, lovelorn and pathetic. "I've come all this way to speak with you." Joy flared into her face, restoring some of the girlishness Penhurst had taken from her.

"But, first, I'm afraid I have some less pleasant business," Jeremy said. "My name is Captain Jeremy Addison, and I had reason to pay a call on your former master this morning. I daresay you've heard that he was robbed at Vauxhall last night?"

At that, her gaze shuttered, and she turned away, with a pointed glance at Walter. "I'll be wanted at home."

"Wait."

She flinched, as if expecting to feel Jeremy's hand on her arm, arresting her movement. He reached instead into his breast pocket, withdrew the calling card, and showed it to her, first her own name, handwritten on its reverse, and then the name that had been embossed upon it. "Do you know where I might find the woman who left this card?"

She glanced from the card first to Walter and then to him. "What is it you want from her?"

He swallowed hard and forced himself to make some answer. "I've been ordered to—"

Marry her.

General Scott's jest had a way of sticking in his mind, though Jeremy had never felt less like laughing. He refused to let himself be intrigued by the woman, no matter the nobility of her cause. The more efficiently he dealt with the Lady Sterling problem, the sooner he could return to figuring out the cypher contained in that damned cookbook.

"To ask her a few questions," he finished. "I assure you, I mean her no harm."

Which was true, although he could not speak to Scott's intentions for the woman. Spying on behalf of the Crown was always dangerous business.

Now it was Betty's turn to hesitate. "I oughtn't to say anything—she risked her life for me."

"Come now, Betty," Walter prompted. "Captain Addison may be a gentleman but he's no friend to Penhurst and his sort. Can't you see it in his eye? Sure an' that red coat is enough to earn your trust?"

Once more, she looked Jeremy carefully up and down and passed a hand surreptitiously over her belly, though it had not yet begun to round.

"Well, that's just it, i'nit? Who knows better than I the dangers she might face? She—she's gone all alone to help a young lady," she offered at last, "governess to the children of Lord Thornton. An' oh, I'm afeared for her, sir."

The name *Thornton* was unfamiliar to him, but if Lady Sterling was involved, he could guess the sort of man to whom it belonged and the sort of danger she might be putting herself in.

"If'n you hurry, you might catch her," Betty urged, pointing down the street. He stared eagerly in the direction she indicated. Had Lady Sterling come in person to Clapham to deliver the stolen goods to the maid? He'd had her in his grasp last night. Could he once more be so close on the mystery woman's heels? "She's just left for Kent on the one o'clock stage."

His momentary flare of excitement fizzled like a damp squib. The public stage? Kent?

Jeremy was a planner, a thinker. He took notes. He made lists. Bad enough to have spent his morning darting through London, not knowing what he might find. The very idea of haring off across the countryside, the hound to Lady Sterling's fox, went against his nature. Why, any fool could see that his chances of overtaking her were slim at best.

But of course, he had to try. Because he was also the sort of man who did his duty.

Even when he would much rather not.

"Much obliged," he said with a nod to Betty and to Walter. "I'll leave you to your conversation. Something about a walk in the park, wasn't it?" No sooner had the words been spoken than the rain began to pelt down. As Betty grabbed Freddy's hand and dragged him into the shelter of a doorway, Jeremy flipped up the collar of his greatcoat and resigned himself to a miserable, pointless journey.

Chapter 3

When the storm began in earnest, Laura tried to ignore it. Its steady drumbeat on the roof only lulled the squire into a deeper slumber. The tutor too began to doze, leaving the brothers to engage in mostly silent wagers regarding the progress of raindrops chasing down the glass on either side of the coach.

Only the widow's face showed any sign of alarm as her gaze—indeed, her whole body—grafted itself to the window. Pressed close to her by the sleeping squire, Laura heard a low moan rise in the woman's throat and could just make out the words that shaped her lips: a muttered prayer.

This is England, Laura wanted to remind the woman, as her father had so often, and so unfeelingly, reminded her. Rain was to be expected, after all.

Time for a distraction. Laura mustered some of her usual charm and asked the woman whether she'd been visiting family.

"No," came the wary answer, but when Laura gave her an encouraging smile, the woman explained that she was on her way to visit her sister. "She lives near Dartford. She's been ill all summer, on account of that dreadful heat, but I wasn't able to leave my shop until now. I'm a milliner, you see."

"A milliner? I might've guessed from that lovely bonnet you're wearing," Laura replied, a compliment rewarded with a surprisingly lengthy dissertation on the season's most popular trims.

People loved to talk about themselves if given the slightest opportunity. Lady Sterling relied on it. No doubt bored by the talk of furbelows, one of the young men soon interjected to explain that they were on their way to Tunbridge Wells—"and eventually Hastings," added his brother—for a living history lesson with their tutor. The tutor, wakened by the lively discussion of hats and history, smiled politely at the milliner, apologized to Laura for his pupils' interruption and, at Laura's urging, enthused for a quarter of an hour or more about a new collection of poems by some fellow called Wordsworth.

Their voices eventually woke the squire, who proclaimed himself a Mr. Richardson, of Aylesford, who had been attending the wedding of a cousin in Wembley. "I had to wish him well, you know, though if he should be blessed with a son, I suppose I shan't inherit that pretty little manor house of his."

Thus the rain and Lord Thornton and all manner of unpleasant things were forgotten until the coach stopped at Dartford and the milliner and the three young gentlemen descended and went their separate ways.

The rocking coach and gray afternoon soon had Mr. Richardson dozing again, and Laura slid closer to the window, tempted to follow his lead. Last night's visit to Vauxhall had kept her up quite late, as she never dared either to leave or reenter the house until she was sure Aunt Mildred was sound asleep.

Whether it was the jarring lurch of the carriage or the coachman's shouted curse that woke her, she was not sure. She only knew that when she opened her eyes, her cheek was still pressed against the cool glass, while Mr. Richardson, who had been on the opposite end of the seat, was once more snug against her left side—because the post-chaise was listing sharply to the right.

He snuffled and grumbled and tried to restore a proper distance between them, scrabbling about in the shadows for something to hold onto, making the body of the coach sway with his movements. Once he'd lifted himself away from her, Laura drew a deep breath and tried to take stock of the situation. Outside, she could hear the voices of the coachman and the postilion arguing. Had they steered the carriage into a ditch? That would certainly explain their present angle on the world.

One of the men outside rapped on the door that pointed almost skyward. "Are ye hurt?"

Mr. Richardson, suspending himself by one of the leather straps above the window, peered toward her.

"I am unharmed," Laura insisted, ignoring the tenderness in her right arm where it had been jammed against the unforgiving wood.

"All safe and sound," the squire reported.

"Praise God," came the voice from outside. "The carriage slid off the road on account of all this mud. A pile of rocks stopped us, but one of 'em broke the wheel an' that sent us arse over ears an' almost into the ditch— beggin' your pardon, ma'am. Once the horses are unhitched, you'll have to climb out through this door," he ordered, slapping it with his palm and making the coach tremble.

Working against gravity, the squire and the coachman managed to get the door open. Cold rain began to pelt against Laura's upturned face. After some debate, the two men decided that if the squire could make his way out first, the carriage might tilt back a few degrees and allow Laura to make a safer descent.

Mr. Richardson managed to hoist himself through the partly open door on his second try and wriggled out, falling onto the wet ground with an oath. The coach, which had creaked and shaken alarmingly with his every motion, rocked back into a more upright position, as everyone had hoped, though it was far from stable.

Two pairs of hands reached to help her down. Perched at the edge of the door, Laura breathed a sigh of relief at the sight of the muddy roadway soon to be beneath her feet. Just one little jump...

Though she was slight of build, the shifting of her weight caused the carriage to tilt—not much, just enough to disrupt her already precarious balance. A manageable leap of perhaps three feet suddenly became a far more precarious one of almost five and in her eagerness to get free of the coach entirely she fell, her hands slipping from the men's wet grasps. She tumbled onto the ground, taking the coachman with her.

She scrambled away from him and onto her knees, swiping rain from her eyes with the back of one muddy, gloved hand while clutching her reticule to her chest with the other.

"Are you all right, ma'am?" Mr. Richardson asked, bending forward and gripping her elbow to help her rise.

Before she could answer in the affirmative, he had set her on her feet. Pain knifed through her ankle. Startled to discover the injury, she made no attempt to stifle the little cry of pain that rose to her lips.

"Seems like the answer's no, squire," said the postilion from where he stood farther off, a pair of horses gripped in each hand.

The coachman leered at her, his face close enough that she could smell the whiskey on his breath. "Can ye walk, happen half a mile or so?"

She gritted her teeth. Shifting her weight, she tested her ankle once more and nearly lost her balance again when it refused to hold her.

Before she could form an answer to the coachman's question, the squire stooped, slipped a hand behind her knees, and lifted her into his brawny arms, prompting another squeal of surprise from her. She had not recovered from that shock when he gave her another, depositing her unceremoniously her on the broad back of one of the coach horses. Rain drizzled down her neck and dripped from the limp trim of her bonnet.

"Now, which way to a warm fire and a pint, lads?" Mr. Richardson asked, grasping the horse near the bridle and preparing to lead it away from the wreckage.

"My valise?" she asked, trying to blow a damp feather away from her face and spattering herself with rainwater in the process. Grumbling, the coachman rescued her bag and plopped it in front of her. The horse shivered its withers as if trying to cast off the additional burden, forcing Laura to grip the valise's wooden handle with the same numb fingers that clutched her reticule.

When the horse began to move, she swallowed back yet another shriek, wound the fingers of her free hand in its mane, and said nothing more, not even as the promised half mile stretched far beyond its usual length, the icy rain ran in rivulets down the back of her neck, and the squire's breath huffed in little clouds. Summer seemed a distant memory.

Never had the glow of candles in a window been more welcome, though they revealed nothing more than a small, low-ceilinged pub, rather than a posting inn. Mr. Richardson helped her to a chair near the fire, at the far end of a long, rough-hewn table, then scraped one of its benches across the floor and sat down beside her. A serving girl, looking harried by the new arrivals, thumped a mug of ale down in front of him and promised to bring her tea. But there was no offer of hot water or towels, and no rooms to be had. The coachman and postilion, busy about the horses, could be accommodated in the stable. Mr. Richardson had already demonstrated his ability to sleep anywhere. Laura knew she must prepare herself to pass a miserable night.

She peeled off her muddy gloves and laid them aside with her bedraggled bonnet.

Miss Godfrey was not expecting her. She had at present no means of sending word of her whereabouts to anyone. And with an injured ankle, she stood very little chance either of reaching her destination or returning home anytime soon. She had charmed her way into and out of any number of scrapes, but what she needed right now was closer to a deus ex machina, an unlooked-for and improbable rescue late in the fifth act...

Before her tired mind could concoct any sort of plan, the door of the pub banged open, and a pair of men strode inside.

The first swept off his hat, revealing fair hair thinning a little at the crown, and made a show of shaking off the rain, though the many capes of his greatcoat were still dry and his boots shone despite the weather. He walked with the familiar strut of a man who expected others to give way before him and who would not hesitate to make things uncomfortable for anyone who did not.

The owner of the dingy little pub hustled out from behind the bar and made a servile bow. "My lord. To what do I owe the honor?"

The man sent an accusatory glare around the room. "Who is responsible for leaving that wreckage strewn across the roadway? My horses were nearly tangled up in it! As it is, I fear the paint on one of my wheels was scraped."

Despite her discomfort, Laura sat up a little straighter. When his cold eyes found her near the fire, she realized she knew the man—not just his type: the callous indifference, the supercilious air—but the man himself.

Lord Thornton.

Her instincts warred with one another. Drop her gaze, as he so obviously expected? But he had never even glimpsed Lady Sterling. He had no reason to recognize Laura, and thus she had no reason to fear him.

To meet him with a defiant stare might attract undue attention, however. So she compromised by reaching into her reticule, which lay nestled on her lap, and withdrawing the heavy gold watch, as if to check the time. She let that object absorb her attention until she felt Lord Thornton's gaze move on.

"But *you* are unharmed, my lord," the pub owner ventured to observe, a gentle reminder that others might not have been so fortunate.

"No thanks to the driver of that ramshackle coach," Thornton spat out. "I suppose he was drunk. Where is he?"

Laura gripped the watch harder and squeezed her eyelids shut. Lady Sterling's previous efforts to call the man to account for his selfishness and cruelty had failed. She flicked her thumb across the watch's cover, but her hands were too numb with cold to feel the engraving. Instead she turned it this way and that, letting the firelight catch the ornate *L* and set it aglow. How could she possibly ensure that the third time would be any different? What valuable secrets did he keep? Why, she might never even have the opportunity to—

Her musings were interrupted by the sound of the second man clearing his throat. When she looked up, she found him studying her, his expression not exactly unreadable, but something for which she had no single word. Surprise, fascination, even disapproval, all bound together by sheer exhaustion.

When the two men had entered the pub, she had assumed they were traveling together, but now she saw her error. Lord Thornton's coat and hat had been marred by no more than a few drops of rain, barely dampened on his dash from the door of his carriage to the door of the pub.

The second man was wet through, head to toe, hardly less bedraggled than she. He had obviously been traveling on horseback, and from the mud spattered over his boots, riding at speed despite the storm, eager to reach his destination, or—or—

The slightest frown notched between his dark brows as he studied her, the blue of his eyes evident even from across the room.

Or perhaps in pursuit of someone?

In pursuit of her?

She tried to shake off the very idea. What could this stranger have to do with her? She did not recognize him, and she never forgot a face. Particularly not one like his, all sculpted angles, rain dripping from his perfect Grecian nose. Beneath his piercing gaze, her pulse danced nervously. Unable to hide, she did the next best thing and busied herself with tucking the watch away.

Or trying to.

It slipped from her grasp and went skittering down the length of wood that divided her from the stranger. At the far end of the table, he stopped the watch with one gloved hand, picked it up, and looked from it to her with the same surprising intentness. A breath shuddered from him.

"My God," he murmured. "Lady Sterling."

The name knifed through her, cold, sharp, and deadly. How did he know her? Had she somehow forgotten a past target?

But he didn't look angry. In fact, he was doing a remarkable impression of someone who had just smacked his forehead against a low-hanging beam. Stunned, and more than a little pained.

Everyone in the room swiveled to look at her, and their gawking faces were all the proof she needed that the London gossip had made its way into the provincial broadsheets. These people knew Lady Sterling, or imagined they did, and by their expressions, she could only hope that the ones who regarded her as a sort of folk hero would prevent the rest from stringing her up.

"What did you say?"

She had been so arrested by the stranger's words, so conscious of the curious disapproval radiating from the local villagers, she had momentarily forgotten the greatest source of danger in the room: the man with friends to whom the name *Lady Sterling* was far more than a mention in the papers.

The silkiness of Thornton's voice belied the coldness in his eyes as he turned and sized up the stranger. "Did I hear you aright, sir?"

"Indeed you did," replied the stranger. "This lady is—is—"

That slight stammer of hesitation gave her hope. Whoever he was, however he knew her, he evidently had not meant to blurt out her identity to Lord Thornton.

But she did not dare wait to discover how he intended to finish that sentence. She needed to take control of the situation, and now.

Praying the stranger would be willing to play his part at least until the earl went on his way, anything to get her out of the bind he'd put her in, she spoke first.

"His wife."

At that, both Lord Thornton and the stranger turned toward her, Thornton wary and the other man incredulous.

"We were wed just this morning," she explained to Lord Thornton, the weariness in her voice promising a somber tale. Her aunt's love of the theater had saved Laura more than once, providing fodder for tales that were just believable enough. "I can see by your expression that the name of Lady Sterling conjures no pleasant association for you." The earl grumbled his assent, and the rest of the pub was quiet enough that the hiss and crackle of the fire behind her seemed almost unbearably loud. "I may say the same for myself. When my brother proposed the match between myself and this gentleman," she explained, tipping her head toward the stranger, praying he would be willing to take up the role in which she had so abruptly cast him, "I had no notion I would be forever linking my reputation to that of a—a—"

"Thief," Thornton readily supplied.

Laura conjured a wry smile, grateful he hadn't chosen something worse.

"Having been raised by an aunt who did not permit me to read the scandal sheets or listen to gossip," she continued, "I knew nothing of the existence of such a person until this morning. Then, at the wedding breakfast, a friend of Lord Sterling took the liberty of informing me—"

"A friend of mine?" the stranger broke in.

The nervousness she felt as she shifted her attention to him was not feigned. She was not accustomed to performing with a partner. Much rested in the man's hands, and she did not yet know whether he meant well or ill.

"A *former* friend, you may be sure." His voice was firm. "You needn't have run away."

Her breath stuttered in her chest. He was going to play along?

"I—I was mortified," she ventured.

"You must have known I would follow." He took three steps closer, convincingly hesitant, as if he feared to frighten her away again. "I blame myself," he said, casting a glance over his shoulder to Thornton before focusing once more on her. "But to whom were you flying?"

"A school friend." The excuse rose to her lips without thought. "Near Margate."

"A long, dangerous journey on the public stage," Thornton declared. "Especially for a lady."

Her supposed husband stepped closer still to her, dropped down on one knee, and reached for her hand. This was a degree of commitment to the role she had not expected. Despite the mud on her sleeve and the iciness of her bare fingers, and the fact that he was a perfect stranger to her, she seemed to have no choice but to surrender it to him. "Were you injured in that accident, my dearest?" The pad of his thumb swept across her knuckles, chafing warmth into her hand.

My dearest? Those two words from the stranger's lips were almost as unwelcome as *Lady Sterling* had been. It was one thing to pretend to be married, quite another to pretend affection.

"I twisted my ankle," she said, freeing her hand from his grasp to gesture toward her foot, "jumping from the wreckage of the coach."

"Right brave about it she's been, though," Mr. Richardson stepped into the conversation. The stranger—Lord Sterling, as he would have it—listened but did not take his eyes from Laura's face. "Can't walk a step on her own, now. I put her on one of the carriages horses myself and carried her inside, I did," the squire finished, puffing out his barrel chest.

"I am much obliged for your care," the stranger said, rising. "But we must call for a doctor to look at her injury."

"I'm—"

I'm fine, she had intended to say, and thereby dismiss any further need for assistance. But as she pushed to her feet to prove it, pain shot through her ankle, and she abruptly sat down once more.

Lord Thornton had the audacity to laugh at her struggle. "Here's what I propose, Sterling," he said, turning toward the stranger. "You'll not find a bed in this establishment. At least, not one suitable for your, er, wedding night."

At those words, heat rushed into her cheeks, and into the stranger's too. The flash of color only made him more appealing.

As quickly as the unwelcome thought rose in her mind, she tossed her head, trying to dislodge it. She needed to keep her wits about her.

"Thornton Hall is only another twenty miles or so," the earl continued. "I think you'd best come with me."

Her mouth popped open. She had wished for a rescue, and here was one tailor made. A nod, a few words, and she would find herself yet at her destination.

But as rescues went, this one carried with it more than its share of drawbacks. The last thing she had wanted was to attract Lord Thornton's attention—at least, not before justice had been served. And having to pretend to be married—to any man, let alone a man she did not know, a man who had nearly exposed her identity—made matters even worse.

Lady Sterling worked alone.

When the stranger's lips parted to speak, she found herself leaning slightly forward, wondering what he meant to say. He'd played along so far, it was true, but what possible motive could he have for continuing the charade? Any that occurred to her were not worth contemplating for long. Did she want him to say yes, or no?

Either way, a word or two from him would change everything.

Thornton too was all impatience. "Well, then?"

"You are too kind, sir," the stranger said at last. "Don't you agree..." When he turned those lapis lazuli eyes to her again, she could have sworn he saw through to her very soul. "Lady Sterling?"

Pinned beneath that gaze, she had to make an effort to nod, to shake off the sensation of his perceptiveness. Whoever he was, he was just a man—and men were simply not that clever.

"Very good. My coach waits just outside the door." As Thornton spoke, he moved toward the exit. "Once we've arrived at Thornton Hall, I'll send for the physician to tend to your wife, and you may travel on from there as soon as she's fit."

"Th-thank you," she stammered, her mind busily at work weighing how to use the earl's unexpected hospitality to bring about his downfall.

"May I be of some help?" Mr. Richardson spoke up, gesturing toward her as if she were a cumbersome piece of luggage.

The stranger looked from her to the squire and back again. "Thank you, my good fellow. But I'm quite sure I can manage."

There was nothing of brawn about the man, but he nonetheless bent and lifted her into his arms with ease—and none of the huffing that Mr. Richardson's similar efforts had required.

She tried not to gasp at her sudden awareness of the solidness of his chest, the surprising strength of his arms. "My valise?" she managed to ask, channeling her quickened breath into words.

Mr. Richardson picked up the bag and indicated with a gesture that he would follow them to the coach. She found an odd sort of comfort in his presence, although she suspected he was drawn only to the spectacle. "What of your hat and gloves, my lady?"

She eyed the sodden pile lying at the table's edge, suddenly conscious of the ways in which even kid gloves and useless little bonnets were a sort of armor, shields behind which a woman might hide at least some small part of herself. Her hand was pale against the stranger's coat. "My wedding finery, ruined," she replied with a sigh. "Leave them."

As her imposter-husband moved to follow a few paces behind Lord Thornton, she squirmed slightly in his embrace. "How did you—how *do* you know who I—?"

"Later." The word came soft and low at her ear, and his arms firmed, drawing her closer to his chest. "Quickly, while Thornton is out of earshot, tell me your real name. A husband would know it," he prompted when she hesitated.

"Laura," she breathed against his neck, feeling the chill of his rain-damp skin against her mouth. "And yours?"

From below, she watched his lips quirk, only partly with amusement. "Lord Sterling."

Chapter 4

Laura.

Jeremy had recognized her the moment he'd walked into the pub, though the accident had left her disheveled, and it had been nearly a year since he'd seen her.

Miss Laura Hopkins.

Quite a contrast from how she'd looked then, clad in a gown of demurest white, her hair a riot of burnished gold curls; vivacious and pretty, charming everyone at the holiday entertainment for some of the officers in Scott's service. Though young ladies had been scarce that evening, he'd been too diffident to fight his way through a sea of red coats for an introduction. He certainly did not expect her to recognize him tonight.

Lieutenant Hopkins's sister.

He knew Fitzwilliam Hopkins only as a genial junior officer, the up and coming field agent who had found the book that had subsequently made Jeremy's life hell. Despite the tenuousness of their connection, Jeremy had been prepared to approach and offer his assistance, seeing a family member of a fellow officer alone and in obvious distress. Certainly, he hoped another man might do the same for Julia, if the tables were somehow turned.

And then Hopkins's sister had pulled a watch—a gentleman's watch—*Penhurst's watch*—from her reticule, and the little gears and springs in his own head had momentarily jammed. Miss Hopkins was—?

No. Absolutely impossible.

But once again the facts were persistent. Less than a mile from here, he'd passed a coach lying in a ditch, the coach in which Lady Sterling had left Clapham on her way to Thornton Hall. Of course, Miss Hopkins could have been aboard that same coach, but he saw no sign of any other female passengers. And while it was possible that Lady Sterling had exited the coach earlier, it seemed unlikely. According to Betty's information, her next victim stood less than an arm's length away from him, as she pretended to check the time on a watch remarkably like the one Penhurst's footman had described.

Certainly, he had not meant to speak her alias aloud. Even less had he expected Miss Hopkins to claim the title, to proclaim herself his wife.

For a long moment, Jeremy had not known what to do next.

When those little gears and springs that made up his otherwise reliable, occasionally even formidable, intellect had begun to click and whir once more, their motion had echoed in his head, sounding alarmingly like General Scott's knowing chuckle.

I should think the answer would be obvious, Lord Sterling.

Had Scott somehow known—had he planned this encounter?

Of course not. How ridiculous even to think such a thing.

Nevertheless, Jeremy's choice was clear. He had endangered her, very nearly exposed her. If he played along with her scheme to smooth over his mistake, she could still end up at Thornton Hall tonight, despite the accident and her injury, just as she had set out to do.

And he would be able to observe her in action, see just the sort of woman Lady Sterling really was.

So, he'd taken her hand in the pub and called her *dearest*, telling himself he was only following Scott's orders to get close to the woman.

He ought to have considered just how close he was willing to get.

Last night had been one thing, an accidental embrace in the dark. At present, however, she had one arm curled around his neck, the very picture of a trusting bride about to be carried over the threshold. When they stepped into the cold, drizzling rain, she tucked her face against his shoulder, almost inviting him to drop a kiss on her damp hair.

Would that be forgetting himself, or playing his part with conviction?

Thankfully, they were meant to be at odds, she running from the man whose very name...*oh, he was almost tempted to laugh*...had exposed her to gossip and scandal.

Gently, he lifted her into the carriage and placed her on the forward-facing bench, then hesitated a moment over where best to seat himself. He could not like the idea of forcing Miss Hopkins to endure several hours in close proximity to Thornton; the look in Betty's eyes as she'd spoken of the man's reputation was burned into Jeremy's memory.

Then again, he saw nothing like fear in Miss Hopkins's present expression, and nothing like welcome for himself.

In the end, Jeremy took the seat opposite, thinking it better to pretend deference to his host. The position had the added benefit of making it easier to study his, er, wife.

Despite the plush, well-sprung seat, her stiff, awkward posture reflected her discomfort, though he could not judge whether pain or embarrassment caused the larger share of it. Even in the shadows of the carriage, her practical traveling costume of tobacco-colored wool was still a few shades too light to mask the mud caking her hems, her knees, and the edges of her sleeves. Because she'd abandoned both her muddy gloves and bedraggled bonnet in the pub, nothing now disguised the way her golden curls framed her face or hid the nervous motions of her pale hands, absently winding the ribbon of her reticule around her first finger, allowing it to unspool, then starting over again.

Lady Sterling had been an entirely shadowy figure in his mind, the mere outline of a woman, featureless, faceless. Despite the vagueness of his mental sketch of the notorious thief, however, the present picture of Miss Hopkins was entirely incongruous with it. For one thing, she was young—twenty-five, or thereabouts, he guessed; her petite frame and heart-shaped face made her look younger still. Scott's speculation and Penhurst's account of the events at Vauxhall had led him to expect someone more mature. Someone who did not look so...innocent.

So in need of protection.

The carriage rocked as Thornton ascended the steps. The motion seemed to startle her, perhaps calling to mind the accident, and her wide, gray eyes raked over Jeremy in passing as she jerked her attention to the door. She seemed to resent having been rescued—or, more accurately, she resented needing to be rescued.

Yes, even aside from the injured ankle, the lady was quite obviously miserable in her made-up marriage.

And Jeremy, who had been so reckless as to laugh dismissively at General Scott's order, was hardly less so.

Thornton swung inside. "All set, then?"

She nodded, even as she drew back further against the opposite wall when the man seated himself beside her.

"A nervous bride is nothing new," Thornton mused, looking her up and down, "though I can't say I've heard of many who actually took the trouble of running away. I hope this little adventure has taught you a lesson, Lady Sterling?"

The direct address still startled her—or else she feigned it well. "Indeed, my lord. It has been a day of"–her gaze flickered briefly to Jeremy– "discoveries."

"And soon to be a night of them, eh, Sterling?" Thornton joked in a low voice, favoring Jeremy with a ribald wink. "When the doctor arrives to check on that ankle, I'll see that he gives your bride something for her nerves, too."

The less-than-subtle meaning of those words shuddered through Miss Hopkins with all the force of a blow, and her eyes flared and darted to Jeremy's face, apprehensive of his reaction. From the tinge of fury in her expression, he could guess that fear was an emotion she generally managed to keep at bay.

"A sedative might be in order," Jeremy agreed, mustering his best aristocratic drawl. "I daresay what my wife needs most is a restful night. Uninterrupted."

Thornton made a noise of bemused astonishment in his throat and folded his arms over his chest. Evidently, it had never occurred to him that a man might not wish to force his attentions on an unwilling—even unconscious—woman. "As you wish."

Though she still radiated wariness, Miss Hopkins's shoulders settled a notch lower. She fixed her attention on the window and the ever-darkening sky beyond. The storm had cloaked late afternoon in the gloom of dusk. They would be fortunate to reach Thornton Hall by nightfall.

Thornton settled into a similar posture, gazing out the opposite window. Jeremy seized the quiet moment to arrange his thoughts into some less haphazard order. After all, he was meant to be a highly trained intelligence officer.

But instead of answers, his brain seemed only capable of generating more questions.

What would happen when they arrived at Thornton Hall?

What explanation was he prepared to offer Miss Hopkins, once they were alone? Should he reveal his mission, his name, his knowledge of hers?

How far would they have to go to convince others they were truly husband and wife?

"Sterling," Lord Thornton muttered, and the frantic pace of Jeremy's mind once more skidded to a halt. Thornton did not turn from the window, but out of the corner of Jeremy's eye, he noted the slightest shift in Miss Hopkins's posture, an unexpected stillness inside the jostling coach. She was listening too. "Your family seat is in…?"

"Wiltshire, though I have a tenant for the manor. I live in town. Or I did—before my, er, marriage."

Hardly an unheard of arrangement, for an unmarried gentleman to prefer to spend his time in London. Jeremy only hoped that his anticipatory explanation meant that Thornton would not probe further, into details about Everham even Mama and Julia did not know.

"A pleasant enough part of the country." Another reflective pause. "Your father must have spent a great deal of time there, though. I do not recall ever having met him."

Jeremy weighed the answer he must give. "My father never held the title, sir. I was still in mourning when it came to me from a distant cousin, quite unexpectedly."

The speculative lift of Thornton's brow, the quirk at the corner of his mouth were visible even in profile. "A welcome surprise, I'll wager."

In spite of himself, Jeremy's jaw tightened. He could guess the sort of mental calculations Thornton was now performing. The worth of his inheritance. What degree of gentleman Jeremy had been before becoming a peer. "A surprise, yes."

At last Thornton turned to face him, and Jeremy forced himself to sit impassive beneath the other man's scrutiny. "I recollect the story, now. Wasn't the previous Lord Sterling in some trouble?" he asked at last. "Some debts—?" he began, then caught himself with a sideways glance toward Miss Hopkins. "But I'm sure that's all been settled."

Jeremy couldn't decide whether the intention was to reassure his supposed wife, or whether Thornton assumed the matter was not fit for a lady's ears. Perhaps he imagined that Jeremy had entered into marriage solely for whatever wealth his bride had brought, which might further explain said bride's reluctance.

Well, let him go on thinking it. People married for money all the time. Such matches were generally regarded as practical and respectable, if far from romantic. If he ever were to marry—which he had no intention of doing—he would have to make just such a choice.

Besides, as an explanation for the obvious tension between Jeremy and "Lady Sterling," a loveless marriage arranged purely for financial motives sounded far more reasonable than the truth.

"Thankfully," offered Miss Hopkins, pulling her gaze from the rain-speckled window, "wealthy merchants supply daughters and dowries enough to meet even the most penurious nobleman's needs." The softness of her voice made it almost possible to overlook the sharpness of her words.

"Merchant or no, if I were your father, you can be sure you would feel my displeasure for behaving as you have done," Thornton declared, "running off instead of being grateful for the fine lot you have drawn." He tipped his head to indicate Jeremy.

"I suppose you are right, sir," she conceded. "Better to be married to a handsome stranger"—from beneath a fringe of lashes, her eyes swept boldly over Jeremy, then blinked innocently up at Thornton—"than be at the mercy of some gouty old man."

The implication could not have been clearer, though Thornton displayed no obvious signs of gout and, at five and forty or thereabouts, was not precisely *old*. The earl's disgruntled *harrumph* provided excellent cover for the snicker Jeremy narrowly disguised as a cough.

Not that he was surprised to discover the woman who masqueraded as Lady Sterling was quick-thinking and spirited.

He just had not expected to admire her for it.

Despite her injured ankle and her disheveled state and her vulnerable position—trapped in a carriage with two men, one she intended to rob and another who might be friend or foe—she refused to cower. He wondered whether Thornton would still be in possession of his purse and pocket watch when he arrived home.

"Still," Miss Hopkins continued, "it *was* rather a shock to find his—er, *my* name linked with scandal. From the stares at the pub, I gather I can now expect impertinence at every turn."

"You must trust your husband to answer anyone who presumes to act on such a ridiculous connection," said Thornton.

"Trust my husband?" she echoed, a skeptical note in her voice. "I suppose you're right, my lord." She shifted her attention back to Jeremy. Beneath her assessing gaze, the knot of uncertainty in his chest unspooled, like the ribbon of her reticule, then wound painfully tight again. "What other choice do I have?"

He thought he understood now how she gained the confidence of the men whose purses—and secrets—she stole. Those eyes had the power to make a man weak, willing to give up…everything.

He dragged his own eyes back to the window, watching eagerly for any sign of their approach to Thornton Hall.

Or rather, *pretending* to watch eagerly. He was not actually eager to be alone with her. He didn't trust her, any more than she trusted him.

Only a fool would take pleasure in being the object of Lady Sterling's regard, and he was no fool—he'd insisted as much to General Scott earlier today.

Jeremy's sigh left a circle of steam on the glass.

Perhaps if he made the assertion a few more times, it would actually prove true.

* * * *

As Laura turned to the window, she let a soft curse escape her thoughts, though not her lips. She had been so deliberate in her selection of an alias, wanting a name associated with wealth and worth. Something to weigh against the power of the men she sought to punish. *Sterling* had been such a clever choice—or so she had thought.

Why hadn't she consulted a guide to the peerage?

At first, she had assumed the stranger was lying about his title. But the more Thornton probed, and the more the other man revealed, the more persuaded she became that he was telling the truth. Regrettably, he must actually be Lord Sterling.

Even more regrettably, the very real Lord Sterling was neither ancient nor feeble, and not entirely dull-witted. He had the potential to cause her a great deal of trouble.

Under different circumstances, his handsome face might at least have been a pleasant diversion; earlier, the feel of his arms around her had kindled a flicker of warmth in her chest that still kept the creeping combination of cold and pain at bay.

She snapped off the thought like a brittle twig, before it could grow branches or take root. She could not allow herself to be distracted by anything, especially now.

Besides, the more she saw of him, the more inclined she was to reject the adjective. *Handsome* he was not.

His face was like something from a painting of an angel, all perfect lines and angles. A flush of color crested his sharp cheekbones; in the dim interior of the carriage, she could not determine whether it was another blush. Dark hair, just a shade shy of being truly black, swept over his brow, framing a pair of startlingly blue eyes.

Beautiful was surely the better word for such a face, though she supposed most men would object to it. He was not any less manly for it, though. He had carried her effortlessly from the pub, and he answered Thornton without servility, though he was considerably younger than the earl, not yet thirty, she thought. As sham husbands went, a young lady might certainly do worse.

But Laura did not want any sort of husband, pretend or otherwise.

She must focus her mind on more pressing business. How had he recognized her? And what were his intentions toward her? Perhaps he sought to avenge a friend on whom Lady Sterling had been asked to pay a call. Or perhaps she had inadvertently concocted a partial truth. Had his betrothed or perhaps his mother—*oh, dear*; men could be quite irrational when it came to their mamas—been mortified by Laura's masquerade and insisted he find a way to put a stop to it? She knew something about what the desire for vengeance could drive a person to do.

Then again, if that had been his game, he might have exposed her to Thornton many times over in the last hour. She might even now have been in the custody of the village magistrate.

Of course, Lord Sterling's present silence on the matter hardly guaranteed her safety. Her efforts to help innumerable young women had taught her that men generally reserved their most dangerous and debauched behaviors for occasions when there would be no witnesses to their depravity. She certainly must avoid whatever tonic Thornton's physician might prescribe, anything that would muddle her thoughts or leave her more vulnerable still.

Yet it was difficult to persuade herself that Lord Sterling meant to set upon her the moment they were alone. He certainly had not agreed with Thornton's vile hint that she would be in no fit state tonight to deny him his husbandly prerogative. He didn't even seem to like Thornton much. In fact, she could almost believe he had accepted Thornton's hospitality for her sake alone. Almost as if he had known her destination and intended to help her reach it…

Ridiculous. How could he? No one but Betty had known. Not even poor Miss Godfrey had expected her.

The coach skidded as it turned sharply off the main road and her fingers scrabbled for purchase on the highly polished strip of wood beneath the window as a gurgle of terror squeezed from her throat.

Thornton seemed to find her lingering trauma amusing. "Did you think you were still in that rattletrap stagecoach, Lady Sterling? I assure you my driver better knows how to manage a little mud."

Lord Sterling said nothing, though his eyes narrowed as they contemplated Lord Thornton for a moment before shifting to her and softening slightly. Under other circumstances she might have called his expression compassionate, though there was still something cool and keen in those blue depths. As though she were a riddle he was trying to solve.

"My dear Laura has never had much fondness for rain," he said, holding her gaze. "Her mama took ill after a being caught in a storm, and sadly, never recovered."

An icy shard of fresh panic slid into her chest and lodged itself behind her breastbone. The memory of her mother's death was painful enough, but how—*how?*—could this stranger know anything of it? She pressed back against the squabs, placing as much distance between them as possible within the confines of the carriage.

She had built her reputation on the premise that knowledge was power. Lord Sterling knew entirely too much for comfort.

Thornton murmured something that might have been condolence. "We're nearly there, now."

Laura pressed her fingertips to the glass, grateful for an excuse to look out the window, away from Lord Sterling. But a quarter of an hour at least passed before she saw any sign of gatehouse or parkland or lights in the windows of Thornton Hall. Ample time for apprehension to spread and send its tremors into her limbs.

Not nearly enough time for her to plan how best to respond when the coach at last rolled to a stop before a stately Elizabethan manor and Lord Sterling indicated his intention to gather her in his arms again.

Chapter 5

"Ikin mange ahminown."

Jeremy frowned, trying to sort out the meaning of those sounds, ground out from between clenched jaws. At present, pressed into the corner, spine stiff, she put him in mind of a frightened cat that had backed its way into a crevice and was now spitting and hissing to prevent its rescue. He had hoped she would unbend a bit when Thornton exited the coach, but at present it was more than clear that his own hand was equally likely to get scratched.

At last she pried her teeth apart—light cast from the house made it easy enough to see that her jaw and lips were trembling; whether with cold or fear or fury, he was less sure—and spoke again. "I said, I can manage on my own."

He curved his lips into a thin smile, all the while silently cursing General Scott. "I'm sure you believe that, ma'am. But if you put weight on that foot and injure yourself further, you—we—will be stranded in Kent for a month. So I'm going to have to insist you accept my assistance."

"*We.*" The venom in the word nearly made him flinch. "And who are you, my lord? How do you know anything—everything—about me?"

In nearly two hours of travel, Jeremy had reached no conclusions about how much to reveal about himself or his mission. But it was obvious that his attempt to reassure her by revealing that he knew *her*, not just the fictitious Lady Sterling, had offered no reassurance at all.

Wishing he had not repeated Lieutenant Hopkins's offhand comment about his sister's dislike of rain, Jeremy coaxed his features into what he hoped was an encouraging expression, tilted his head, and stretched forth his hand despite the risks. "If we stay here a moment longer, it will only raise more questions. I promise I'll explain, just as soon as I can be sure we won't be overheard. Come, now."

After a moment, she unbent herself enough to slide along the seat, closer to him. With a grimace, she lifted herself onto her good foot and tipped forward, into his waiting arms.

Certainly he had never anticipated that half a lifetime of carting Julia around on his shoulders and catching her whenever she took a mind to launch herself from a tree branch or the top of a stile had been preparing him for his work as a secret agent.

Then again, hoisting his little sister out of various scrapes was really nothing like cradling Laura Hopkins against his chest.

He paused while she arranged her skirts to cover her legs, then encircled his neck and shoulders with one arm. "I do not like to be a burden."

"You're no burden," he insisted, and it was—in the most obvious sense—perfectly true. She could not be much more than five feet tall or weigh more than eight or nine stone. Granted, she would have been easier to carry if she were not holding herself stiff as a corpse, but he chose to attribute that to cold and pain.

The real burden was knowledge, or the lack thereof.

Knowing his mission did not make it any clearer how he ought to proceed.

Knowing her true identity did not make her intentions any less mysterious.

Knowing that if she ever relaxed her rigid posture, her body would fit perfectly against his was more dangerous than knowing nothing at all.

Thornton had already begun to ascend the steps, and the door swung open to admit him. Light and voices spilled from the house, and Jeremy followed dutifully in the path they created. Miss Hopkins's body quivered with something that sounded suspiciously like a wry laugh. "I hadn't planned on entering Thornton Hall via the front door," she said.

In a low voice, he replied: "Consider yourself lucky. When I woke up this morning, I hadn't any notion I would be entering it at all."

The entry hall was high-ceilinged and walnut-paneled, dark despite the branches of candles lining the walls and large enough that the half-dozen or so people awaiting Thornton's arrival were nearly lost in the space.

A footman stepped forward first, to relieve Thornton of his greatcoat and hat. He was followed by a middle-aged woman, presumably Lady Thornton, murmuring a steady litany of complaint and concern about the damp air. Three children stood behind her, two girls on the brink of awkward adolescence and a boy of about six, none of them looking particularly eager to greet their father.

Thornton stepped to one side to give his wife a better look at their unexpected guests. "I found these strays in a pub east of Dartford. Coaching accident. Couldn't very well leave them in the rain, could I?" he declared with the sort of laugh that invited no one to join him. "I give you Lord and Lady Sterling, newlyweds."

From the shadows came a soft gasp, drawing Jeremy's attention to a young woman he had previously overlooked—a young woman hoping to be overlooked, if her ill-fitting gray wool dress and downcast eyes were any indication. No one else seemed to have heard.

"Oh, dear," exclaimed Lady Thornton, coming closer. She struck Jeremy as the sort of woman who liked having someone to fuss over—or, more accurately, liked for others to perceive her as the sort of woman who enjoyed fussing over people. "Were you injured? But obviously you must have been," she corrected herself, her close-set eyes darting over Laura's form in his arms. "Poor dear. Can you walk at all?"

Miss Hopkins's head scrubbed against his shoulder. "I think I'd best not try, ma'am."

"Send for Phelps," Thornton ordered the footman.

At the same time, Lady Thornton spoke to the young woman in gray, only half turning her head. "Godfrey, take the children to the winter parlor, then tell Mrs. Tenney to have the green bedroom prepared for Lord and Lady Sterling."

"Would not?"—Miss Godfrey began, astonishing both herself and Lady Thornton with her boldness—"would not the blue bedroom be preferable, my lady?"

Lady Thornton considered the suggestion. "I suppose you're right. It is closer. Go on, then."

"Yes, my lady." Miss Godfrey gathered the three children with a sweep of both arms and ushered them toward the wide, curving staircase at the back of the hall. At the landing, she paused and sent a hopeful look over her shoulder. Suddenly, Jeremy remembered: according to Betty, Lady Sterling had come to Thornton Hall for the sake of the governess.

Lady Thornton herself showed him up the stairs to the blue bedroom, lavishly appointed with draperies and bed hangings of precisely the shade one might have expected, but of course, only one bed.

Its four mahogany posters and plump mattress dominated the room. At least so it seemed to Jeremy, to whom Lady Thornton had to speak twice before he even saw the dainty, damask-covered sofa before an empty fireplace. He deposited Laura on its cushions as instructed, heaved a

grateful sigh, then lifted his shoulders twice in quick succession and tried
to shake the feeling back into his arms.

Something like amusement twinkled in Laura's eyes, though it did
not erase the shadows of pain and worry. "I thought you said I was no
burden, my lord."

Before he could think of a suitable retort, the room was bustling with
servants: a pair of maids to dress the bed in fresh linens, another to light
the fire, while Lady Thornton promised the imminent arrival of the
physician and hurried off as if to ensure it. A second wave of servants
appeared shortly after the countess's departure, and it soon became clear
that his vow to explain himself to Miss Hopkins would have to wait for
some time. A footman brought her valise and Jeremy's satchel, then carried
away Jeremy's muddy boots and greatcoat to be cleaned. Mrs. Tenney, the
housekeeper, sailed in with a tea tray held high, while still more footmen
carried canisters of hot water and a copper tub.

It was a parade of ostentatious hospitality that left Jeremy equal parts
suspicious, grateful, and jealous. Everham could no more have provided
these ample, instant comforts than the pub outside Dartford. But he also
knew enough about the way men like Thornton managed their business
to guess how such luxury was afforded. Just for the moment, however, he
was quite prepared to luxuriate in the warm glow of the fire, a cup of hot
tea, and the promise of a bath.

As if to the manor born, Miss Hopkins watched the spectacle unfold
about her, tilting her fair head graciously when the housekeeper offered
her a cup of tea and wincing apologetically when one of the maids knelt
to peel off her muddy shoes and stockings.

That glimpse of bare foot and ankle ought not to have elicited any
response in Jeremy, other than perhaps pity—it *was* rather bruised and
swollen-looking. But it was too easy to imagine that ankle's ordinarily
well-turned proportions. He knew he hadn't any business noticing such
things—they weren't actually newlyweds, after all—but every bit of her
drew his eye, as charming as he remembered, and as difficult to ignore.

He needed to exercise caution. According to Penhurst, she was not above
using her wiles to lure a man to his doom if he gave her cause, and though
he could muster no sympathy for Penhurst or others like him, he had no
intention of ending up as another of Lady Sterling's victims.

For that reason, he eagerly absented himself from the room when one of
the maids shyly indicated a plan to help his wife out of her muddy traveling
clothes and into a bath. In the relative privacy of the chillier dressing

room, he undressed without assistance and made do with the water in the washstand and one small, rough towel.

He was grateful for several reasons that he'd made a brief stop at the Underground after leaving Clapham. There, he had shed his uniform, the better to retain his anonymity; packed a few necessities, though too few for what he feared might be a protracted stay in Kent; and arranged for a horse fit enough not to collapse under the strain of a lengthy gallop.

Once clad in a fresh shirt and stockings, face washed and hair combed, he had only to wait for Miss Hopkins to finish her ablutions. As there was no door between the dressing room and the bedchamber, he could hear—and imagine—far more than he liked: the splashing and trickling of water over her flawless skin, a scattering of feminine giggles—Lady Sterling, he felt certain, never giggled, but he very much feared that Miss Hopkins might—and, when a flannel nightdress was produced from the valise, a tittering debate between the two maids about proper attire for one's wedding night, in which Miss Hopkins thankfully did not participate beyond a few inaudible murmurs.

No sooner had one of the maids advised him that he might return to the bedchamber than Mr. Phelps, the physician, arrived. From the doorway near the bed, Jeremy could see that Miss Hopkins was once more seated on the little damask sofa, decently covered with a dressing gown and a woolen blanket, her hair brushed so that her close-cropped golden curls shone in the firelight, which lent them a reddish glow.

"Come closer, please," called Mr. Phelps, a small, balding man with spectacles. "You are the husband?"

"I, er—"

"He is," said Miss Hopkins calmly.

Jeremy wondered whether it was possible to be both grateful for her quick tongue and dismayed by the ease with which she lied.

Then again, he was an intelligence officer. He of all people knew that no one always told the truth.

She was sitting with her left foot on the floor, the injured right leg lying along the seat of the sofa, a plump pillow beneath her foot. Speaking soothingly to her as he worked, Mr. Phelps raised the hem of her dressing gown, folded it to mid-shin, and examined her ankle, moving it gently this way and that, while she dug her teeth into her lower lip.

"A mild sprain" was his diagnosis before he applied some pungent smelling liniment and then wrapped the ankle snugly with a length of linen. "You must keep it elevated as much as possible for the next few days, my lady. I understand you are a new bride. You must allow Lord Sterling to wait on you. Nothing strenuous," he said, shooting Jeremy a stern glance.

Jeremy felt heat rush up his chest and into his cheeks. "Of course not, sir."

"Now," said the physician, turning back to Miss Hopkins, "how does that feel?"

"Better," she said, and Jeremy thought it might be true. Some of the color that had left her face during the examination was returning. "The bandage helps a great deal."

"And this will help still more," he said, reaching into his bag and offering her a tiny glass bottle: a tincture of laudanum. "Just a drop or two, every few hours."

For a moment, he thought Miss Hopkins meant to refuse it. But after the slightest hesitation, she tucked it into her palm and gave the doctor a nod of thanks.

"I shall speak to Mrs. Tenney on my way out," he said, closing his bag. "Lady Thornton has ordered her to bring whatever you require. You are fortunate in your hosts, my lady."

This time, Miss Hopkins was the one at a loss for words.

"We are indeed," interjected Jeremy, resting a hand along the back of the sofa, almost but not quite touching his supposed wife. If he did not at least sometimes act like a lover, surely it would raise suspicions.

She turned to look up at him and, for just a moment, he thought she meant to lean her cheek against the back of his hand in a convincing impersonation of wifely adoration. Then she said in a cool voice, "My luck cannot be all bad."

Jeremy knew too much about mathematical probabilities to entertain the notion of luck, either good or bad.

But he had no rational explanation for what had transpired over the last twenty-four hours, the series of improbable events that had brought him to this moment.

He looked toward Mr. Phelps just in time to catch a flicker of uncertainty chase through the man's benevolent smile. "I'll pop in the day after tomorrow, to check on the patient. But for now, I'll show myself out."

When the door latch clicked, they were at last alone.

Miss Hopkins turned away again, exhaled—in relief? exasperation?—and flicked both her skirts and the blanket back into place. "Well?" she demanded.

Clearly, she was not in so much pain that she had forgotten his promise of an explanation when he was assured of not being overheard. Jeremy glanced toward the door, almost hopeful of another interruption.

No knock came. No sound at all, but the crackling of the fire. Altogether too domestic and cozy.

Instead of speaking, he stepped around the little sofa to the tea table. Mrs. Tenney had kindly crammed every inch of it with food to tempt the weary travelers, but he had no appetite. Fortunately, the housekeeper had also included a decanter, not quite half full of some amber liquid.

He plucked the stopper from the bottle and lifted it to his nose. Brandy. *French* brandy. No surprise that the sort of man whose mistreatment of his domestics had led to Lady Sterling's involvement was also the sort of man who did not scruple about contraband liquor. Jeremy poured a generous swallow into the glass that had been provided, feeling less guilty than he ought. The tea had grown tepid and would, in any case, have been inadequate to the purpose.

"Is that brandy?" Miss Hopkins asked, peering around him. "I should like some."

He turned fully around to face her. Pain still pinched her features. "You ought to have a few drops of that laudanum instead." Her knuckles whitened around the little bottle hidden in her hand. "Please pay no mind to what Thornton said in the carriage. I wouldn't—I won't—"

She fixed him with an assessing look, her gray eyes as sharply intelligent as if Homer had composed the poem with her in mind. "I believe you. But I'd still prefer the brandy."

He twisted the cut-crystal tumbler between his fingers, studying the play of light through the liquid, before extending the drink to her. "There's only one glass."

He had not expected her to demur. Not really. Nor had he expected her to toss the brandy down her throat with nary a cough nor a wheeze, to sigh a self-satisfied sigh with eyes closed, and then, after a moment, to tip her head forward and bring him once more into focus.

"All right. I think I can bear it now," she said, handing the glass to him. The brandy had made her voice husky. "Tell me how you know who I am."

Chapter 6

Laura watched him return to the table, examine the lone teacup with its residue of sugar and tea leaves, and then refill the tumbler from the decanter. His back was still to her when he raised it to his lips and tipped back his head; that hasty swallow was followed immediately by sputtering noises and shaking shoulders as he tried to prevent himself from choking.

Thornton's brandy was smooth and mellow, some of the best she'd ever had. Clearly, Lord Sterling did not imbibe often. A rarity among gentlemen, in her experience.

After he had regained his composure, he set the tumbler on the table and perched on the seat of an overstuffed chair with striped upholstery. He crossed his legs, then uncrossed them, all the while avoiding her eye. She sensed that the intimacy of the moment—the shared glass, she clad in a dressing gown, he in his stockinged feet—made him uncomfortable.

Against her better judgment, she found it almost endearing. She did not often encounter men who were so easily, so innocently embarrassed.

"Lord Sterling?"

For a moment, her voice seemed not to have penetrated his thoughts; then he started and finally met her gaze. "Oh. Yes. I was only considering how best to…I don't really use the title, you see. I'm unaccustomed to being addressed as…"

She wanted to ask what sort of nobleman didn't use his title. But when she considered what Lord Thornton had forced him to reveal in the carriage, the fact that the title had been not only unexpected but perhaps even unwelcome, she let that question go unasked.

Her others were more pressing.

"Have we met before, my lord?"

The question, intended to coax him into admitting something, anything, instead seemed to alarm him. He leaped up and began to stride back and forth in front of the fire. "We have not been introduced, no," he replied after a moment. "But I—I am acquainted with your brother, Fitzwilliam, Miss Hopkins."

Blood thundered in her ears. "Ohhh." If not for her injured ankle, she would join him in wearing out the hearthrug. Never had she so envied a man's freedom of movement. So that was the explanation for the stranger's interference. "I might have known that Fitz would find some way to keep his eye on me."

Lord Sterling smiled weakly. "I too have a sister. I certainly understand your brother's concern for you, especially given how you—that is, your—" Evidently finding no word that satisfied him, he abandoned the search. "But I do not think he—that is to say, it was not he who—"

Hardly hearing him, she narrowed her eyes, once more probing his face for some familiar feature. She was relieved to know he was not the sort of man to have any prior dealings with Lady Sterling. But new questions rose immediately to her mind. When had he seen her? Where? In whose company?

"That's how you knew about my mother."

He nodded. "May I say how sorry—?"

"But that doesn't explain how you know Fitz," she continued, brushing off his expression of condolence. At present, she couldn't afford to be distracted by memories of another life entirely.

"I'm Captain Jeremy Addison."

"Captain Addison," she echoed, not attempting to hide her surprise. "As in, the army?" His build, his bearing...he was nothing like any of the brash young officers she'd had occasion to meet. Nevertheless, it was as plausible an explanation as any other her tired brain could conjure. "I suppose next you'll tell me that you and Fitz are members of the same division, or regiment, or whatever it is?"

Something like amusement flickered into his eyes. "Whatever it is, indeed. And yes, we are. Last winter, you attended an officers' dance with your brother. Such entertainments are a rarity for men like us, and you were so...so..." With one long-fingered hand, he sketched an aimless circle. "Suffice it to say, you are not likely to have been forgotten by anyone who was in attendance, ma'am." A fresh flush of color rose to his cheeks. Much more of that and she was in danger of being flattered in earnest. "That night I glimpsed you only from a distance, so when I saw you tonight at the pub, I didn't trust my eyes. That's why I stepped closer. And then you…dropped the, uh—"

"The watch," she finished for him, tugging her reticule from behind the pillow on the sofa where she had secreted it earlier. She loosened the drawstring on the little silk purse, slipped a hand inside, and withdrew the timepiece. The gold gleamed dully against her palm.

"I am sorry," he said, and there was sincerity in his voice. "When I saw it, I was caught off guard. I had never considered there might be a connection between someone I knew, however slightly, and the famous—"

"Surely you mean infamous?"

"Lady Sterling," he finished with a sidelong glance at her mischievous interruption. "The name slipped out before I could think of the consequences to you, or to"—now his eyes swept the room; she knew the precise moment when they landed on the bed—"us."

"And are you really also Lord Sterling?"

A muscle ticked along his jaw. "I am."

He had offered his military rank with far more confidence and pride than he confessed his title. But both were undoubtedly his. She was too accustomed to ferreting out facts to doubt it.

Until that moment, he'd been forthcoming, surprisingly so. But it seemed she and the stranger each possessed a pair of names and identities they preferred to keep separate, even secret.

"How did you come to connect this to me?" she asked, hefting the watch. When he extended a hand, she reluctantly surrendered it to him again. Her fingers brushed against his as she slid the watch onto his palm.

"It was…described in the newspaper," he said, turning the watch toward the firelight and making it gleam. "The report said Lady Sterling had stolen it. From Lord Penhurst. Last night at Vauxhall."

He was a poor liar, thankfully. But even if that series of tiny hesitations had not given him away, she would still have been suspicious. "Which paper?"

His gaze was once more directed at the carpet as he began to pace along the hearthrug. "I, er, I don't remember. Someone had left a few pages lying about, and I only had a glance at it."

No newspaper had carried a description of the watch, because Lord Penhurst and his mother would not want one bandied about. Of that, she felt certain.

Time, perhaps, for Lord Sterling to understand that Lady Sterling was no ordinary thief.

"The newspapers do report that Lady Sterling picks gentlemen's pockets," she said. "What they don't know is why. Too many men—rich men, powerful men, yes, but even ordinary men—consider themselves entitled to women. Entitled to women's time and attention. Entitled to their persons. Any woman might struggle to free herself from a man who holds himself in such high esteem and the so-called fairer sex in contempt, of course, but women in service are particularly vulnerable."

He listened intently, but said nothing, so she went on. "Imagine if you had a sister who, through no fault of her own, was forced to seek a post as, say, a governess in a house like this one, with an employer who persisted in speaking of lewd matters before her, merely because he liked to see her blush—merely, in other words, to remind her of his power over her."

"Such a man ought to be horsewhipped for his impertinence." Lord Sterling's fingers curled tighter around the watch chain. As he moved, the watch dangled from his hand, swinging erratically. "And as it happens, ma'am, I do have a sister. But I assure you I would not have to be related to a young woman in order to understand the difference between right and wrong."

Laura did not try to hide her irritation. She was tired of being surprised by him—even agreeably. "Far too many men can only be bothered to remember women's humanity when it is placed in relation to other men. To them, a woman's true value is as a man's sister or wife or mother, and if she is none of those, then what worth has she? Very little, in their eyes. But even women with male relations often lack resources or are rejected by their families when they find themselves in circumstances such as I have described. Many have nowhere else to go. Even the law is against them, for all that they are victims of a kind of robbery. No one to listens to their tales of woe…except Lady Sterling."

His gaze distant, he nodded his understanding.

"Lady Sterling believes that gentlemen who behave in such a fashion ought to be repaid in kind. So, she takes something from them: something of value, yes, something to help the poor, displaced domestics, but also something that makes each man feel as vulnerable as the woman, or women, he's assaulted. And she leaves with him a reminder that she is the one in power now, because she knows something about him he would much rather she did not."

Just as I now know about you, my lord.

"You threaten to expose their behavior." His cheeks were pink with a sort of secondhand embarrassment.

For a soldier, he really was too entirely sweet and naïve. "Sadly, too many of your fellow men would sooner brag about their lechery than feel chagrined by its discovery. But such men invariably have some other... foible, shall we say? Something they wish to keep secret from the world."

At the mention of a secret, his pacing footsteps quickened.

"For example, that watch," she said, nodding toward it. "It was stolen, but not by me—at least, not first. It belonged to the Duke of Langerton, who married Penhurst's cousin a dozen years or so ago, much to the dismay of her aunt, Lady Penhurst—she was kin but not kind, as they say, and appalled to see a poor relation elevated so high. Soon thereafter, the duke, who was positively ancient, died. His son, the present duke and a most unpleasant man, raised a great fuss and tried to disinherit the young duchess. All signs point to the fact that Lady Penhurst stole the watch, hoping to make matters even worse for her niece. It is indeed a family heirloom—just not Lady Penhurst's family."

As she spoke, Lord Sterling resumed studying the timepiece from every angle, as if it could somehow confirm her story. "A dozen years ago. You would've been a child. How can you know all this?"

"When a potential client asks Lady Sterling to intervene on her behalf, I make it a habit to learn all I can, the better to plan. I have read, researched, interviewed, even spied. I have disguised myself as a maid, an old woman, even a lady of pleasure." She paused, sensing dismay in his reaction to those words, though he held his tongue. "Whether Penhurst himself knows the provenance of that watch, I cannot say," she continued. "But he knew his mother would be furious with him if she discovered something had happened to it. That's why he never pawned it to settle a gaming debt or used it to pay for some other illicit pleasure. I doubt even he was foolish enough to reveal that it was missing—certainly not to someone who could have put its description in the papers."

Lord Sterling swung the watch upward and caught it in his fist, making the chain *chink* softly against the cover. "However it came about, his mother knows," he said after a moment. "And she was furious with him. Furious enough to berate him about its loss within earshot of the servants."

Lady Penhurst's reputation among her servants was hardly better than her son's. Laura could easily believe the woman had revealed too much in a fit of temper. And what a foul mood she would have been in, for early that morning, the baroness had also received a calling card—Lady Sterling was nothing if not thorough—and a note hinting that if her son's behavior did not improve, she would find the resulting scandal quite distasteful.

But why had Lord Sterling been speaking to Penhurst's servants? Was he conducting his own investigation about the watch, perhaps even hired to find it by Penhurst himself?

Then he said, "As a consequence of its disappearance—and, I now understand, what certain revelations about it might mean for the family—Lady Penhurst has put her son on a tight leash, and she's keeping the female domestics out of his reach, too."

A flush of heat—warmer than either the brandy or the fire—spread through Laura's veins, momentarily displacing her concern. *Success.* Lady Sterling had done it again!

"Tell me," she said, pride straightening her spine, "do you think my brother will be surprised by what you tell him of his sister's exploits?"

Lord Sterling cleared his throat, as if the burn of liquor still troubled him. "I cannot say, Miss Hopkins. As I tried to tell you before, it was not he who asked me to find you."

As quickly as it had come, the warmth fled. "Who, then?" she managed to whisper; her own voice seemed equally inclined to disappear. *Surely not Penhurst?* Had her pride led her straight into a trap?

Lord Sterling gave a weak smile, which nevertheless had the power to make something in Laura's insides stir. "Someone who found it amusing to send Lord Sterling in pursuit of Lady Sterling."

The little joke, if it was a joke, did not amuse her. "Am I meant to be relieved?" she asked drily. "I suppose if this mysterious person had instead sent Captain Addison, I should have to wonder whether the whole British army was soon to follow."

His answering laugh was hesitant, and his second attempt at an explanation was no more satisfactory than the first. "Let us say, then, that I am here on behalf of someone who wishes to have a better understanding of Lady Sterling and her intentions."

"Despite what you may believe of me, sir, I do not enjoy riddles," Laura replied with a frown bordering on sternness, bemused by his sudden reticence.

"I'm afraid, ma'am, I cannot give a more satisfactory reply at present." He turned away from her in the course of his perambulation before the fire. "For the moment, you will have to content yourself with knowing that it is someone who means you no harm—unless, of course, you mean harm to others."

"I mean harm only to those who deserve it," she tossed back, lifting her chin.

At the far end of the hearth now, Lord Sterling paused and shot a look over his shoulder. "Such as Penhurst."

He shifted the watch to his other hand, then fished into the breast pocket of his coat. Even at this distance, she recognized the calling card he produced. One of her own. The one she had tucked into the fob pocket of Penhurst's waistcoat. For written on its reverse...

"Betty," she breathed. The missing piece in the map of this man's quest to find Lady Sterling.

How could the girl have been so careless, so ungrateful as to have betrayed Laura to a stranger?

"Penhurst denied knowing anything about the maid on whose behalf Lady Sterling claimed to have visited him—rather unconvincingly, I might add, and much to the dismay of a certain footman named Walter, who still nurses tender feelings for the young woman. It was he who took me to find her in Clapham, where I understand she is now in the employ of a Mrs. Hayes."

Laura gave one sharp nod to hide her distress at having been tracked down so easily. "My aunt."

"You mustn't think ill of Betty for telling me where you'd gone," he insisted. "She was worried about you." His lips curved as his gaze flickered over Laura. "She seemed to think you might need some looking after, out in the country."

Feeling utterly exposed, Laura tucked the wool blanket more securely around her. From the beginning, people had speculated about the identity of Lady Sterling. But she had always believed herself clever enough to avoid being caught.

Now, she had to figure out how to manage what distance remained between her and Lord Sterling. Even if doing so required drawing him closer still.

"Perhaps Betty was right." She glanced toward her ankle, then returned his smile, making sure her own was ever so slightly chagrined, and thoroughly disarming.

Lord Sterling, however, appeared to be oblivious to her charms. Lost in thought, he flicked her calling card against the thumb of the hand holding the watch. "Thornton is equally, er, deserving?"

Resigned, Laura straightened the tilt of her head and flattened her smile. "More so. He forced his attentions on his wife's maid while Lady Thornton was making calls and was in the habit of summoning his last cook to his chambers to address his...*appetites*."

"But I thought—the governess—?"

"Oh, yes. Miss Godfrey is among the recipients of his unwelcome attention, or fears she soon will be." She patted her reticule where it lay in her lap, making the folded paper inside crinkle. "She wrote to Lady Sterling and asked for help."

"You have not tried before to—?"

"I have," she said, the words clipped. "And I have failed." Once more, she found herself tracing the edges of Emily Godfrey's letter through the silk purse. "In Lady Sterling's storied career, Lord Thornton has been the lone adversary who cannot be bested, the villain who reappears just when all seems well."

"Such characters are usually defeated in the end, are they not?" When she looked up at him sharply, he lifted his shoulders in a sheepish sort of shrug. "My sister has a decided fondness for the theater," he explained. "Even the melodramas."

"As does my aunt," she admitted eventually. She raised her forefinger to her forehead and pressed the space between her eyebrows, realizing she had furrowed her brow in surprise at his confession—and the discovery that they had something in common beyond her assumed title and his real one. "But don't you often feel that the retributions of the final scene must be small consolation to the victims who were sacrificed in acts one through four?"

His head tilted, as if he had never considered the matter before now. "I daresay they would prefer to be avenged, even belatedly, than forgotten."

"Vengeance is easier said than done. Why, even with careful study and preparation, Lady Sterling's campaigns sometimes go awry." Hearing the confession from her own lips startled her. She need not strive to match Lord Sterling for honesty. "For example, in the present case, I had intended to spend a few days in the nearest village, gathering information. After I had formed a plan, I would've sent Miss Godfrey a note and asked her to meet me on her half day."

"Surely being right inside the house is an advantage?"

"Oh, yes, yes," she agreed, rolling her eyes. "Creating a stir with one's entrance, drawing the notice of every family member and servant in the place..."

"Thanks to that entrance, Miss Godfrey not only knows you are here to help but was able to specify your very room—this room," he said, gesturing calmly around him, "and not another. Surely she must have had a reason?"

Had Miss Godfrey suggested the blue bedroom for some reason other than its proximity to the great hall? Laura could not say which surprised her more: the fact that she had not considered the possibility, or that Lord Sterling had.

Clearly pain was addling her thinking.

"And that's another thing," she continued, tossing a scowl at her injured ankle. "I've failed to best Thornton when I had the use of all my limbs. How am I to manage anything now?"

Slowly, he stepped toward her, one hand extended, and returned both the watch and the card to her possession. She curled her fingers around them, noting the contrast between the cool paper and the metal, warmed by his touch. "Perhaps you just need a little assistance," he suggested as he took up the nearby chair once more.

"Absolutely not. Lady Sterling works alone. I cannot—"

He raised a peremptory finger to silence her. If he had been just a little closer, she might well have snapped it between her teeth. *How dare he?*

"We're not alone anymore," he mouthed, tipping his dark head toward the door.

Laura strained to listen. All was quiet except the crackle and hiss of the fire. Her lips popped open to issue a reprimand, but before she could speak, those words disappeared beneath the *tap-tap-tap* of a quiet knock.

Lord Sterling cocked his brow and lifted one shoulder as if to say, *See?* Pushing to his feet, he cleared his throat once more. "Come in."

Chapter 7

When the person behind the door did not immediately enter, Jeremy considered whether the proper thing was to repeat his invitation or open the door. His concern about how much of his and Miss Hopkins's conversation had been overhead could only be eased when he knew who had been listening.

He had taken three steps toward the door before the quiet creak of the hinge revealed the governess, Miss Godfrey. Against the rich walnut paneling, she looked almost colorless in her gray gown, with her ashen complexion.

Behind him, he heard Miss Hopkins stir on the sofa. "Miss Godfrey! Do come in."

The governess appeared more inclined to accept that second invitation, apart from a chary glance in Jeremy's direction. She crossed the floor and took the chair he had vacated, nearest to Miss Hopkins's head. He might have taken the one opposite, by her feet, but he instead elected to stand, leaning one shoulder against the mantel.

Miss Godfrey turned in the chair toward Miss Hopkins. "How are you feeling, my lady?"

"Considerably more comfortable than I was. Mr. Phelps seems to think the ankle will be better in a few days."

"Oh, I am glad to hear it," she said, looking anything but as she wrung her fingers in her lap. "How could I live with myself if I were the cause of your injury?"

"Should not the blame be laid on the driver who nearly overturned the coach?" Jeremy ventured, genuinely baffled by the governess's overdeveloped sense of guilt.

She started at his voice but did not raise her eyes to his face. "If I had not written and begged Lady Sterling for help, she would have had no cause to come into the country…"

"And if Lord Thornton were a different sort of man, you would have had no cause to write." Miss Hopkins's words were gentle but firm. "As we know precisely the sort of man he is, we may dispense with this game of conjecture."

"Yes, my lady," Miss Godfrey replied.

"Has he harmed you?" Jeremy asked.

The question earned him a sharp look from Miss Hopkins, but no direct answer. "I—I did not know you were married, Lady Sterling," Miss Godfrey stammered, looking to her for reassurance.

"It is a recent development. But being a married lady has its advantages. Far greater freedom of movement, for one," his supposed wife explained, with no touch of irony.

At the utter absurdity of the situation, a laugh rose in his chest which he only narrowly managed to turn into a cough.

The sound caused the governess to turn her eyes toward him again. "In answer to your question, my lord, I am perfectly well. I had never laid eyes on Lord Thornton until tonight. He spends most of his time in town, even when Parliament is not in session. Lady Thornton hired me in the spring, and we have been alone here in the country all summer. The children and I get on well, and I was most content in my post. Until Lord Thornton's return was announced, that is, and I began to overhear the whispers among the maids. Even that, I should have dismissed—I abhor gossip as a general rule," she defended herself. The knot into which she had twisted her fingers looked painful. "But Mrs. Tenney took me aside and advised me to look sharp. She says we must expect a houseful of his friends 'ere long, and to keep on my toes until they decide that someone else's birds will provide better targets."

Jeremy wondered whether the birds in question were of the sporting variety or the more metaphorical sort. The very thought of the women of the household forced to steel themselves against the men's expected behavior made something twist in his gut, a sort of sick feeling, a mingling of disgust and pity, and another sensation altogether outside his previous experience: a burning desire to curl his fingers into a fist and plant Thornton a facer, followed by each one of his so-called friends.

"Oh, I see now," Miss Godfrey said suddenly, brightening. "You aren't injured at all, are you, Lady Sterling? You knew Lord Thornton had a preference for male company and decided that a gentleman's assistance was required in the case. Your ankle is just a ruse, to get Lord Sterling into the house. Brilliant!"

Though he would not claim to know Miss Hopkins well, he had experience enough with military matters to recognize the battle brewing behind her eyes. Her determined independence was prepared to lead a charge against the unwelcome assumption that she required assistance from anyone, let alone a gentleman. He half expected her to leap to her feet to prove her fitness, as she had tried to do in the pub.

But she was also susceptible to Miss Godfrey's flattery, or—as she no doubt preferred to think of it—was astute enough to see that the governess's explanation for his presence could prove useful. Her lips had been parted to speak, but after a moment's hesitation, she closed them instead and gave a rather regal-looking nod of acknowledgment. "Gentleman do, on occasion, have their uses," she said, glancing at him almost dismissively.

In spite of himself, he bristled. "Other than a means of acquiring a title, do you mean?" When Miss Godfrey's eyes snapped to him, he forced a laugh. "That's my clever wife. But it strikes me that you are also clever, Miss Godfrey," he said. "In fact, I suspect you had some reason for suggesting that Lady Thornton put us in the blue room, did you not?"

Slightly behind her, Miss Hopkins rolled her eyes.

"I—well, perhaps I will have misjudged, for in the green bedroom, you would have been closer to Lord and Lady Thornton's chambers. But I did think…"

"Yes?"

"You're closer here to the servants' stairs."

"Ah," Miss Hopkins said. "That will indeed make it easier to get from place to place without being seen."

"The schoolroom and the nursery are just above, so I can slip down here more easily without drawing attention to myself, should—should my help be required," she added, sounding surprised by her own boldness.

"And what is below?"

"Lord Thornton's study."

The slightest frown wrinkled Miss Hopkins's brow as she lifted a finger to her lips and tapped thoughtfully. She offered no explanation for her meditative pose, and in another moment, the skin of her forehead smoothed.

"You should go, Miss Godfrey, before you are missed."

"The children are with their parents this evening," she made the excuse, even as she got quickly to her feet. "I am unlikely to be wanted."

"Until Lord Thornton decides it is necessary to make a visit to the schoolroom," Miss Hopkins reminded her, her head tilted in a sort of gentle scold. "But wait," she said just as Miss Godfrey stepped toward the door. "Have you a hatpin, Miss Godfrey?"

The governess looked as bewildered by the question as Jeremy felt. "No, my lady."

Miss Hopkins reached for her reticule and fished inside, eventually withdrawing an object which she displayed on her palm.

Miss Godfrey leaned forward to see it, temporarily blocking his view. "Oh!"

When she stood upright again, he saw a pretty jeweled pin, the bauble on one end larger than the sort favored even by dandies, and the stick itself almost a hand's breadth long. The point was blunted by a small ball of wool, rather like an absurd pincushion, out of all proportion to the pin. With nimble fingers, Miss Hopkins unsheathed the pin from the cushion; the sharp tip gleamed in the firelight.

"One of my preferred methods of self-protection, Miss Godfrey. Easy enough to have about when one is wearing a hat, of course, but as you can see, I make sure never to be without a weapon. Take it," she said, reaching out her arm toward the governess. "Put it under your pillow tonight and find some way to have it at hand tomorrow and in the days that follow. And for God's sake, if Thornton approaches you, use it."

Miss Godfrey leaned away from the proffered pin in alarm. "Stab him, you mean?"

"Yes, indeed."

"Good heavens! Where?"

"In whatever soft spot he is ungentlemanly enough to expose to you."

Though he felt no pity for Thornton or his ilk, Jeremy could not entirely suppress a wince.

With some trepidation, Miss Godfrey palmed the hatpin, curtsied to Miss Hopkins and belatedly to him, and hurried to the door.

When they were alone again, he asked, "Are you regularly in the habit of handing out hatpins and doling out such advice to your clients? If so, it's a wonder there is a still a man on this island foolish enough to put a hand where it isn't wanted."

Her answering laugh held a patronizing note. "If men were capable of being deterred by the pain of others, *Captain Addison*, war would be a thing unknown. Now, do sit down. I am in discomfort enough without incurring a crick in my neck."

He sat down where Miss Godfrey had been sitting, aware once again as he closed the distance between them of the uncomfortable fact that they were alone together in a cozy bedchamber, presumed by everyone around them to be husband and wife.

Trying to seem nonchalant, he crossed his legs and was reminded of the indignity of appearing in his stockings, one heel carefully mended by his mother. "You seemed interested in what Miss Godfrey had to say about the location of Thornton's study," he said, placing both feet on the floor. "Were you considering the possibility that you might overhear something important from up here?"

"An interesting suggestion. One never knows in these old houses." Her lips quirked. "You show promise as an assistant, Lord Sterling. Why, you might even prove useful for coaxing Lord Thornton into confessing all sorts of things over a..." Now her mouth twitched, suppressing a laugh. "Over a glass of brandy, perhaps?"

What, he wondered, had made her so hard? Obdurate as polished stone—if that stone had been fashioned into the head of an arrow, ready to slip between plates of armor and lay a man low. And why was she so determined to display that side of herself to him? As if there was some danger of him forgetting her cleverness, or falling prey to her charm...

With every passing moment, he felt more certain that Scott should've sent someone else on this mission—and oddly grateful the general hadn't. Being locked away with books for weeks on end could grow a trifle dull.

There was nothing dull about Miss Hopkins.

"I don't make it a habit to muddy my head with strong liquor, ma'am—as I'm sure you already surmised from my reaction to a swallow of brandy," he answered with a self-deprecating smile. "Are you not fearful that with a tumbler full, I would spill my own secrets instead?"

She studied him for a moment, her head tipped to the side. Her eyebrows rose and fell in a flare of mocking interest. "Now *that* might be something more worth hearing." She slipped her fingers into her reticule and withdrew the watch again. "Lady Sterling has two goals with every case: first, to secure something of purely monetary worth, with which a wronged domestic might support herself once she escapes; and second, to find something of less tangible value, like this watch. Oh, it would also bring a pretty penny in some less than reputable pawn shop, I have no doubt." He watched as she swept her thumb back and forth across the ornate *L* on the watch's cover, as she had done in the pub. "But as long as it remains in my hands, I have the means of reminding Lord Penhurst, and his mother, that their crimes have not gone unnoticed."

Jeremy nodded. He well knew the value of secrets but also the difficulties of unraveling them. "You engage in blackmail."

Her lips twitched in distaste. "Such a crude word makes me think of greedy politicians or a gang of petty thieves."

"Whereas you are just one thief."

"Thief-*taker*, my lord," she corrected him evenly. "I assumed you read my card." The watch once more disappeared into the depths of her reticule. "I want to ensure that justice is served. In the past, Thornton has posed a particular challenge. When his wife's maid came to me, she was too distraught to be of much assistance, and I too inexperienced to know how to get the sort of information I required to stop the earl. I was forced to report back to her empty-handed."

"What became of her?"

"She died." A breath shuddered from Miss Hopkins's slender frame but did not ease the heavy guilt that suddenly weighted her shoulders. "She walked into the Thames, her pockets filled with stones."

At that revelation, Jeremy found himself momentarily frozen by an increasingly familiar combination of unexpected grief and cold fury at the damage Thornton and men like him had done. "My God. And the—the cook, I think you said?"

Miss Hopkins's shoulders lifted a little. "Mrs. Croft fared some better: fifty pounds and a new post. But still, nothing I could use for the larger purpose."

Everything she had told him confirmed General Scott's theory about Lady Sterling's motives and abilities, and these days at Thornton Hall promised to provide the necessary proof. She was smart, determined, and more concerned with justice than law—just the sort of asset Scott would relish acquiring, if she proved willing to turn her talents to espionage.

Would it matter, *should* it matter, that the mysterious avenging angel was a gently bred young woman and Lieutenant Hopkins's sister?

He was afraid he already knew the answer.

"What is your interest in Thornton's study, then?" he asked instead.

He followed her gaze as it traveled the room: the landscape in oils above the fire, the old-fashioned table on which the tea tray rested. "Thornton is a collector. Antiquities. Rarities." She paused for a moment, and he half expected that she would add *vulnerable women* to the list, but she did not. "There must be something in this house that he shouldn't have, and the library is an excellent place to begin looking for it."

"What if there isn't?"

She wavered. Just a slight wobble of her chin. If he hadn't been studying her face for hours now, he would have missed that telltale sign, that glimmer of doubt.

Almost before he could be sure of what he had seen, she firmed her jaw. "There will be."

Her behavior, a weary sort of determination, struck a familiar chord. At various times, including recently, he had been so convinced that the solution to a particularly stubborn encryption was just around the corner, he had foregone sleep and even sustenance. Wordlessly, he rose, went to the tea table and prepared two plates of whatever looked most tempting. She was ready to refuse when he handed one to her, but he shook his head. "You need food. And rest. We both do. The contents of Thornton's study will have to wait until tomorrow."

She took the plate with a defiant sigh, but in a moment, she was picking at the food with her fork. Another moment found her devouring every morsel with indecorous, almost dangerous, haste.

He smiled around a mouthful of bread and butter. "You see? Better already."

"I'm surprised Mrs. Tenney hasn't sent someone for the tray, or to see if we need anything else," she observed, licking salmon mousse from the side of her thumb.

"I suspect they don't want to disturb the, ah, newlyweds."

Something—a bite of fish, an epithet better left unspoken—lodged momentarily in her throat, and she began to cough. Was the color that rose to her cheeks the result of almost choking or a flush of mortification?

He returned to the table and poured her half a cup of cold tea. "You haven't forgotten this marriage was your idea, have you, Lady Sterling?"

Steely eyes met him over the rim of the cup.

"Right, then." He returned to his chair. "I shall assume you wish to carry on as we began in the carriage: cool and distant. The furthest thing from a love match. You will send me scathing glances I'll pretend not to see; I will make tepid jokes about how fortunate it is that you sprained your ankle, so you can't run away from me again; and everyone will laugh nervously."

Her face twisted, not in annoyance, but as if something about the suggestion intrigued her. "Did you see *A Scandalous Marriage* at the Haymarket last year?" she asked, handing over her empty plate.

"That outrageous French farce?"

"Yes! About the elegant lady who pretends to be head over heels in love with her husband to prevent anyone from discovering her affair with the footman, who is really her husband in disguise."

"Meanwhile, the husband is carrying on shamelessly with the parlor maid—"

"The lady herself, naturally, in an atrocious wig," she interjected.

"In order to keep everyone from suspecting he's in love with his own wife?" Jeremy nodded sheepishly. "My sister found it most amusing... unfortunately."

"The same with Aunt Mildred." She held up two fingers, indicating they had attended the performance twice.

He offered what he hoped was a sympathetic expression, though he knew it was tinged with disbelief. Miss Hopkins did not strike him as the sort who would be led anywhere against her wishes, not even by her aunt. "But what does our shared suffering at the theater have to do with our present dilemma?"

"Really, isn't it obvious?" Her color was bright and her expression animated. The food seemed to have revived her spirits, and he was no longer entirely sure that was for the best.

"Ah. Well..." After a moment's rumination, he was forced to admit defeat. "I'm afraid not. I hope you're not suggesting that I pretend to nurse a tendre for Thornton—or his footman?" he joked.

"Certainly not," she said with another roll of her eyes. "Unless... No, I don't think it's very likely that Lord Thornton would be flattered by your attentions, handsome as you are. Though, of course, you are at perfect liberty to do whatever it takes to encourage him to tell you any secrets he might be keeping."

"Perfect...liberty..." He shook his head again, this time more vigorously, in a vain hope that he could either rattle her words about until they made sense or drive them out of his mind entirely. "Miss Hopkins?"

"You really ought to practice calling me *Lady Sterling*, though *Laura* will also be acceptable on occasion. And of course, you shall be *my darling Jeremy*, especially when I am most likely to be overheard."

"But you..." At a loss for words, he rose to return their plates to the table. "I don't—"

"In front of the servants, for example," she went on, ignoring him. "Or when Lady Thornton is almost out of earshot, but not quite. They will assume I am quite besotted with you."

"Quite besotted. While I...?"

"Well, of course, you must behave with cold reserve toward me in public, just as in the play. We shall disregard that tender scene at the pub in which you called me *dearest*. The key thing is for our performance to overshadow any prior association people here may have with the name of Lady Sterling. Everyone in the household should be drawn to the unfolding drama between the newlyweds, while behind the scenes..." She twirled her fingers, bringing them together at the end in a snap, as if she had caught something in her grasp. Her face gleamed with triumph. "Just the thing to distract them from what's really going on."

And what is really going on? he wanted quite desperately to ask. He rubbed his eyes and pinched the bridge of his nose and prayed a silent prayer that when he looked about himself again, he would be surrounded by the slightly mildewed walls of the Underground.

He opened his eyes to find Miss Hopkins…Lady Sterling…*Laura* studying him, a birdlike tilt to her head. "Do you see?"

When Penhurst had described Lady Sterling's attire and behavior so crudely, Jeremy had thought he understood the lengths she was willing to go to trap one of her victims. He had been utterly unprepared for…this.

"Wouldn't it make more sense," he began, aware even as he said the words that *sense* was hardly relevant, "if the roles were reversed? You're meant to have run away from me, after all."

"Perhaps," she conceded. "But of the two of us, I am unquestionably the better actor. Today, a petulant runaway, tomorrow a new woman who wakes to find herself conquered by love."

"Conquered by…" He ran one hand through his hair. "And what exactly is meant to have changed overnight?"

She blinked at him, lips parted, incredulous.

Realization dawned. "Oh. That. Well, under the circumstances, wouldn't it be better *not* to draw attention to ourselves, or invite speculation about our…relationship?"

Her answering half smile was undeniably patronizing. "I can understand how someone with very little experience in this sort of thing might think so."

This sort of thing.

Love affairs?

Deception?

Spying?

He could feel another ill-advised laugh building in his chest. "Tell me, do you often rely on bad plays for inspiration?"

"On occasion, yes. My work as Lady Sterling is a sort of theater. I promise men what they think they want, some little distraction or transitory pleasure, which in turn allows me to take what *I* want without them even noticing—at first, anyway—that anything is gone."

The last word was muffled behind her fingertips, the vowel stretched almost beyond recognizability as she fought to disguise a yawn. Certainly if the other activities of the day had not tired her, her dazzling display of acrobatics ought to have done the trick—and he wasn't thinking of the leap from the overturned carriage.

For his part, he could not remember ever having felt either so exhausted—or so entertained.

"I think we could both do with some rest," he said, stepping toward her. "Shall I help you to the bed?"

She craned her neck to see behind her, then back to face him, wearing an expression he could only call pleasantly scandalized. "Why, Lord Sterling!"

"I shall of course make do with the floor of the dressing room," he said stiffly.

"No, no. That won't do. What if the servants come in in the morning and find we're sleeping apart?"

"I thought…I thought I was supposed to be keeping myself cool and aloof?"

"Well, yes, but remember the rest of the play. Despite the way the husband behaves in front of others, he's really quite desperately in love with his wife."

"Ah. Yes. Well, let us say then that I desperately love you enough to let you sleep undisturbed while you recover from your injuries."

That perfectly reasonable explanation earned only a moment's pause. "But wouldn't you be worried that I might require your assistance in the night?"

"Are you—are you asking whether *I* will actually worry, or whether your husband would?"

"For the next few nights, I'm afraid, those two gentlemen are one and the same. Now, Jeremy darling, take me to bed." She smiled benevolently as she stretched her arms upward, her reticule clutched in one hand and the bottle of laudanum in the other.

If she continued to refuse Phelps's tonic, perhaps she would be willing to spare him a drop or two? His temples were beginning to throb.

Uncertain what else to do, and recognizing that further protests tonight would be a waste of breath, he hoisted her into his arms, making the uncomfortable discovery that her pliant body fitted to his just as perfectly as he'd feared. More so, in fact, for now she was wearing no corset or mud-stiffened gown, only nightclothes.

He carried her across the room, to the side of the enormous bed where the linens had already been turned back, and placed her atop it, giving her a moment to arrange herself before he covered her loosely, so as not to strain her injured ankle.

Once she was comfortable, he would go around to the other side of the bed. Just a few steps farther, and he would be safely in the dressing room. She was in no condition to stop him—

She patted the blue coverlet, indicating the space beside her.

"Miss Hopkins," he said after drawing a breath to steady himself, "whatever role you pretend, you are in fact an unmarried lady with a reputation to guard, and I—"

She cut across him with an exasperated sigh and shook her head. "Thank goodness we have had this time to rehearse."

"*Rehearse?* My God. If word of this charade gets out, the gossip—"

"Exactly. The gossip. Oh, for pity's sake," she cried when he stared at her, uncomprehending. "This is why Lady Sterling works alone. Don't you see? The drama will only be enhanced when the servants speculate that your indifference to me is really all an act, because they have seen—"

"Seen what?" Alarm made his voice rise.

"Only what we wish them to see," she reassured him, with the sort of exaggerated gentleness he generally associated with speaking to small children and dull-witted men. "But we can't very well persuade them that you made me fall in love with you from the dressing room floor."

"This is madness. You are mad."

"All over England tonight, people with minds filled by tomorrow's worries and no desire for anything but sleep, people who don't even like each other, will climb into the same bed and lie side by side for a few hours," she said, in what she no doubt imagined to be a reassuring tone. "Surely, for the sake of Miss Godfrey, we can do the same? As to my reputation, I am perfectly indifferent. And as to concern for my person, well…" Her gray eyes twinkled, and she gave the reticule a little shake, rattling the contents. "Are you certain I haven't another hatpin?"

In a sure sign he had succumbed to madness, he laughed outright this time. And blew out the brace of candles on the bedside table. And shed his coat—but not, definitely not, his breeches. And lay down atop the soft, luxurious bed, careful not to jostle her foot, or any other part of her.

"See? Was that so difficult?" The linens rustled as she settled herself more comfortably. "Goodnight, Jeremy darling."

He could picture the smile he heard in her voice. "Goodnight, Miss—er, Laura."

He stared into the darkness for what might have been an hour, listening to the muffled ticking of Penhurst's pocket watch and, soon enough, the soft, even breathing of the sleeping woman beside him.

People who don't even like each other will climb into the same bed…

She was difficult and changeable and a practiced liar. Not to mention fit for Bedlam. Oh, and creative and filled with righteous wrath and really, impossibly lovely.

Not liking her wasn't the problem.

Chapter 8

Laura stirred, not immediately sure what had woken her: a noise, the pain in her ankle, or the sudden awareness of finding herself in a strange bed.

Yesterday's carriage accident, the arrival of Lord Sterling, her plan to ensure that the household believed them to be newlyweds…all of it came rushing to her before her eyes were fully open.

But not before she realized she was alone in that bed.

This is madness, he'd said. *You are mad.* No faith at all in her scheme. Why, he'd probably risen the moment she'd drifted off and…and what? Gone to sleep in the dressing room? Left Thornton Hall entirely?

Ruined everything?

She dared to peek from beneath a mound of bed linens. At the far end of the room, two maids were busy about their work, both brown-haired and near in age, one sweeping out the ashes while the other gathered up empty dishes and put them on the tray. Neither of them had been part of the cadre of servants who had assisted her the night before.

As they worked, they spoke to one another in low voices.

"Do you suppose it's her? The Lady Sterling from the papers?"

A huff of skepticism from the one at the hearth. "And why should she come all this way?"

"To help us?"

"If that Lady Sterling exists, she i'n't likely to be lyin' in that bed, now is she? You heard Mrs. Tenney—that lady is a new bride who got a bit skittery, ran away from her man, an' got hurt."

The girl dawdling over the tea table got a faraway look in her eye. "Have you seen 'im? *I* wouldn'ta run."

With little effort, Laura too conjured an image of Lord Sterling, his raven-dark hair and arresting blue eyes, the perfect angle of his jaw shadowed last night with a hint of scruff.

"Dinah!"

"You're just jealous," came the saucy reply. Laura no longer had to strain to hear the exchange. "You might've laid eyes on him if you'd been in the breakfast room this morning."

"Some of us have work to do," sniffed her counterpart, rising and dusting off her hands.

"An' wasn't I there on Mrs. Tenney's orders? You're just fussed because she don't trust you not to break things. Anyway, I saw 'im when I was gatherin' up dishes, same as I am now, an' I heard 'im thank Lord Thornton for the offer."

"What did 'is lordship offer 'im, then?" asked the other girl, wary.

A shrug. "The loan of a gun, maybe? James Tucker says he saw 'em leave the house together, dressed for shootin'."

The first girl turned to the window and pushed open the drapes. Gray morning light starkened her skeptical expression. "You're the one who told me not to trust 'is lordship. Nor 'is friends—no matter how han'some."

Laura found it a commendable retort. Experience had taught her that handsome gentleman were just as likely to commit atrocious acts—perhaps more so. And the worst behavior of all was mostly possible because other men countenanced it, or at least looked the other way.

"Fair 'nough," Dinah conceded. "But Mrs. Tenney seems to think Lord Sterling is all right, not like t'others. Said he were right polite to her this mornin', thanked her for this here tray"—the dishes rattled as she hoisted it onto her hip—"an' asked her to make sure his lady had everythin' she needs."

The other maid gave a low, knowing laugh. "The way she's sleepin', I'd say he took care o' that last night."

Dinah giggled and dropped her voice to a scandalized whisper. "I overheard Mrs. Tenney tell Cook that if she were married to a man who looked like that, she'd never get off her back again."

At Dinah's words, heat plumed in Laura's belly, or perhaps a little lower, then spread into her chest, up her throat, until it reached her cheeks. When concocting her plan, she had failed to consider how it might feel to overhear the servants' earthy speculations about her supposed marriage.

She turned her head into the pillow, seeking its coolness as a remedy for the unwelcome heat, and was met with the subtle, spicy scent of Jeremy's shaving soap.

Evidently, he'd lingered by her side longer than she had imagined. Despite her injury, she had managed to work her way across the bed over the course of the night. At the faint memory of seeking his warmth when the room had grown colder as the fire died, she stiffened a little and pushed herself more upright against the pillows.

The movement drove a grunt of pain from her lungs, and she bit the inside of her cheek. The discomfort was not as bad as yesterday, thank heaven, but bad enough to make her wish she had stayed still.

One of the maids gasped in surprise.

"Beggin' your pardon, milady." The first maid set down her bucket of ashes before curtsying.

Dinah's eyes were downcast. "We weren't to wake you."

"No, no," Laura insisted. "I'm usually an early riser. I can't think what's come over me."

After taking in Laura's pink cheeks, the other maid pursed her lips, as if fighting back a smirk. "Happen it's that sore ankle, milady."

"Where is my husband?" Laura made the question breathy, tentative, though of course she already knew the answer.

"Gone out shootin' with Lord Thornton, milady." The maids—sisters, she thought, now that she had a better look at them—exchanged a knowing glance. "Said he thought you might need your rest."

"I'll just take this tray down to the kitchen an' be back in a wink to help you up, milady," promised Dinah, and the pair of them left the room, hardly able to contain their giggles until they reached the corridor.

Once the door was closed behind them, Laura permitted herself a self-satisfied smile. Everything was coming together just as she had hoped. Jeremy was playing the part of the polite but distant husband. He'd also taken steps to befriend Lord Thornton. And the servants were too busy with gossip about the newlyweds to expend much energy wondering over the name Lady Sterling.

So why, as she swept her palm over the cool linens on the empty half of the bed, did she feel strangely dissatisfied?

Lady Sterling works alone, just as she had told Jeremy last night.

In a matter of moments, the maid returned bearing a breakfast tray and introduced herself with a curtsy. "Now, milady, I'll help you up. Don't you worry about leanin' on me. I can take it."

Laura accepted Dinah's assistance to stand, and then tested her injury. She was still several days from walking without assistance, she feared, but at least the slightest brush of her toe against the carpet no longer sent pain shooting through her ankle.

"Don' overdo, milady," cautioned Dinah. "We'll just make our way to the dressing room, nice and slow."

Laura found no evidence that Jeremy had fashioned a makeshift bed in the adjoining room. Someone—one of the bevy of maids that had attended them last evening, she presumed—had hung the spare dress from her valise in the clothes press beside a pair of fresh men's shirts. Her linen and Jeremy's lay in companionable piles on a nearby shelf. The arrangement of their things felt surprisingly intimate, given the fact that the two of them had lain side by side in the same bed.

After Laura had performed her ablutions, Dinah helped her dress. While Laura brushed her hair, the maid bustled back into the room to straighten the bed, whistling softly all the while.

"That's a pretty tune," Laura complimented her.

"Thank you, ma'am. But Mrs. Tenney would scold me somethin' fierce if she'd heard me."

"Have you been here long?"

"Almost two years."

Long enough, then, to have heard tales of, witnessed, perhaps even experienced Lord Thornton's ill treatment. Then again, such men could be careful when they wished to be, and Dinah was young. Thornton might have some limits, and he surely would not want to drive away every female domestic in his employ.

"Thornton Hall seems a beautiful old place," Laura observed a moment later, determined to keep her interrogation casual. "You must be happy here?"

"Oh, aye, milady."

A truthful answer? Laura fancied she heard a little hesitation. And the other maid's words suggested that Dinah had received warnings from the housekeeper about things other than whistling.

When Laura's curls were arranged, Dinah helped her rise and served as a willing crutch as she hobbled back into the bedchamber and made her way to the little sofa by the hearth.

"Breakfast for you, milady." The maid brought the tray closer once Laura was comfortably seated, with a pillow atop a footstool propping up her injured ankle. "Shall I light the fire? It's a damp, drear day—more like November than the start of September, if you ask me."

"Thank you, Dinah. I would like that." A fire would help to cement her place as a sympathetic invalid.

"Be there anything else, milady?" Dinah asked when the fire was crackling merrily. She was red-cheeked from the exertion and really quite pretty. Good God, but Laura hoped the girl had little occasion to cross Thornton's path.

"No, thank you. Unless…" She remembered suddenly the part she was meant to be playing. "Unless you have some notion of when the gentlemen might return from their sport?"

"No tellin' that—his lordship's been known to tromp through the woods all day."

It was excellent news, really. Jeremy would have more time to gather information that might prove valuable to her cause. But as a new bride, of course, she must pretend disappointment at being left alone. "Oh. I suppose I should not—" A strategic pause, as if she feared she had said too much.

"Ma'am?"

She let a small, mournful smile slide onto her lips. "I was so cool to him during our courtship. I suppose I should not be surprised if the tables are now turned."

As she'd hoped, Dinah's eyes widened as she took in Laura's expression and words, no doubt storing them up for relating below stairs. Not knowing what to say in reply to such a confession, however, the girl curtsied to signal that her work was done. "Lady Thornton has said she will come see you this morning, if you wish it."

How much did the countess know about the man to whom she was married? Lady Sterling had, on occasion, found unhappy wives to be most useful, if occasionally unwitting, allies to her cause. Others, unfortunately, blamed their husband's victims for their own unhappiness.

"Please tell her a visit would be most welcome."

When Dinah left, quiet fell over the room. Wondering about the time, Laura glanced behind her at the bedside table, where both Phelps's vial of laudanum and her reticule still lay. She despised her lack of mobility, her near helplessness. But, most of all, she disliked the fact that she found it genuinely unsettling to be alone.

Missing Jeremy was supposed to be an act.

An eternity later, a tap on the door signaled the arrival of Lady Thornton and her two daughters, who evidently had accompanied their mama to practice their company manners and to learn how to display ladylike compassion for the less fortunate. Lady Eleanor and Lady Margaret were sallow-faced girls of twelve and fourteen whose rather petulant expressions made Laura pity Miss Godfrey afresh.

Half an hour's vapid conversation with their mother, in which Laura was forced to conjure details of Lord Sterling's proposal and yesterday's wedding ceremony, left Laura pitying herself.

It was an opportunity of which she ought to have been glad, a chance to engage these strangers' sympathy and interest, to help them forget any previous association they might have had with the name Lady Sterling. And since it was unlikely that Lord Thornton had spent the morning quizzing Jeremy along similar lines, she need have no fear of exposing inconsistencies in their stories.

But she was beginning to resent the time she was required to spend thinking of her supposed husband. Hearing parlor maids sigh over his good looks. Watching a grown woman who ought to have known better grow misty-eyed over his made-up request to be made the happiest of men.

An almost inaudible tap on the door brought the visit to a merciful close. Miss Godfrey opened the door. She looked, if possible, more wan than she had last night, a timely reminder that Laura must use whatever resources were at her disposal to prevent Lord Thornton from crushing the poor governess's last spark.

"My lady," Miss Godfrey said, curtsying to Lady Thornton. "I came to fetch Lady Eleanor and Lady Margaret for their geography lesson."

"Oh, is it one o'clock already?" Lady Thornton said, rising. Her daughters followed suit, though displaying no enthusiasm for a return to their schoolwork.

"Will the gentlemen stay out all day, Lady Thornton?" Laura asked, catching Miss Godfrey's eye, hoping to convey encouragement.

"Why, I couldn't hazard a guess," said Lady Thornton.

"Papa is a great sportsman," declared Lady Margaret.

Miss Godfrey cleared her throat, then looked stricken by the attention that slight noise brought her and the subsequent expectation that she was about to speak. "The gentlemen returned more than an hour ago," she said at last. "I happened to see them from the east window in the schoolroom."

An hour? Laura let a sharp sigh escape her lips, though she refused to feel actual disappointment, particularly not when Lady Thornton's next words were, "Then I daresay they shall spend the rest of the day in the billiards room—or perhaps Thornton's study, if your Lord Sterling is the sort of man willing to listen to endless stories about the acquisition of this treasure or that." Jeremy had been given another excellent opportunity to gather information about their host.

But Lady Thornton's fond smile at her husband's self-indulgence spoke volumes. Laura knew too much about the sort of gentleman who bragged about his conquests, of whatever variety. She knew something, too, of the sort of people who let them. In that instant, she felt sure that the female staff of Thornton Hall could expect little support from their mistress.

She glanced toward Miss Godfrey, thought of Dinah. She needed to act, and quickly.

Instead, she was trapped in this bedchamber, left to hope that Jeremy was the man her imagination had painted him to be.

Chapter 9

Like the blue bedchamber, the library was paneled with warm wood and darkly furnished, making the large space feel cozier than it was. After several hours striding through the cold, damp woods in Thornton's uncongenial company, with absolutely no interest in whatever prey they were meant to be stalking, and no desire to shoot it should it be cornered or made to take flight, Jeremy had been grateful when his host had called for them to return to the house, and even more grateful when he ordered a fire to be lit.

But when a maid arrived to light it, rather than a footman, he instantly wished he had told Thornton not to bother. His own comfort was nothing. The stout, brown-haired girl cut a wide berth around the earl as she crossed to the hearth, he noted. But not wide enough to keep Thornton from casting an assessing eye over her backside when she bent to her work.

Jeremy stood. "Tell me about this," he asked Thornton, gesturing toward the nearest item to hand.

Thornton dragged his attention from the maid's figure to his desktop. "The inkwell?"

Only now did Jeremy look where he had pointed. An inkwell? Good God, the thing looked very little different from what might be purchased in any stationer's shop. "Er…yes?"

Thornton approached the desk, his thumbs hooked in his waistcoat, the maid at least momentarily forgotten. "You have a good eye, Sterling. That was used by one of Charles the Second's mistresses to pen some rather daring love poems—I won it in a hand of cards, from a chap who claimed to be descended from the woman's cousin."

"Fascinating piece," Jeremy said, hoping his tone did not betray his skepticism. Then again, Thornton struck him as too avaricious to be easily taken in. He remembered what Laura had said about having tried twice before to trick the man into giving up something of value. Looking about the study, he understood now that the problem was made more complex by the sheer number of valuables in Thornton's possession—which was an item he could not bear to part with? Which was an item he wanted no one to connect with him?

The maid had completed her task and very nearly managed to escape the room when Thornton turned and pinned her with a glance. "You're new here."

The girl sank into a curtsy and looked as if she wished she could go right on sinking, through the floor. "Aye, milord. Dora Pratt, milord. Mrs. Tenney hired me last Lady Day, on my sister Dinah's word."

"Pratt...Pratt..." He readily took the opportunity to look her up and down again as he mulled the name. "The butcher's girls?"

An almost imperceptible nod.

"Have Mrs. Tenney send up coffee," he ordered and turned back toward the desk.

Every butcher Jeremy had ever seen had arms like anvils. He wondered whether the image of such a man, the idea of what the girl's father might feel should he discover how Thornton had looked at her, had given Thornton pause. But of course, the girl's treatment ought not to hinge on the existence of male relations, just as Laura had pointed out. And either way, the earl had power far beyond fisticuffs. As if to prove it, Jeremy heard him murmuring "Dora" under his breath, committing the name to memory.

Cataloging another treasure.

Thornton was a product and a creature of the world of men: a fair shot, a gossip (so long as that gossip could be passed off as politics), and a braggart. He knew he could do and say as he pleased, and he spared little thought for others who were not similarly situated.

Under the best of circumstances, Jeremy would've found the man's company boring. Under the present circumstances...well, he had bitten his tongue and unclenched his fists more times today than he could count, trying to remember that he was meant to be working his way into Thornton's confidence.

Despite the morning's unpleasantness, however, Jeremy had been glad of an excuse to go out and clear his head. Waking with Laura snuggled up against his shoulder, her unruly golden curls tickling his cheek, had been... overwhelming. So he had slipped out of bed, found his freshly polished boots waiting outside the door, and gone downstairs, not sure of what he sought, only knowing that he did not dare hope to find it in Thornton Hall's blue bedchamber.

You are mad, he'd told her. But he'd gone along with her scheme last night, nonetheless.

He wouldn't abandon it now, no matter how distasteful he found Thornton. "Do you mind if I have a look around?" Jeremy asked.

The words startled Thornton from his reverie, and he grunted his assent as he began to shuffle through a large pile of correspondence.

As he wandered around the library, Jeremy took in the expected items: antique furniture, artwork, books by the hundreds on every subject imaginable. He also saw a number of objects that raised his eyebrows and sent his thoughts skittering off in untoward directions. Paintings that looked perfectly unexceptional...until he tilted his head at a particular angle. Marble statuary that rightfully belonged in some far-off temple to a pagan goddess—of fertility, if the bosomy curves and jutting phalluses were anything to judge by. Metal and jade pieces about whose function he did not intend to hazard a guess.

Since the man obviously entertained guests in this room, at least on occasion, one might think he would have qualms about some of the pieces on prominent display—if he were the sort of man capable of feeling shame. Laura had expressed her doubts on that point, and Jeremy was increasingly inclined to agree with her.

He strolled onward, careful not to indicate any special interest by pausing in one place too long. Thornton continued with his correspondence, pausing to peruse the occasional letter, flicking most of them aside half unread.

His back was to the door, so he did not see the maid return, tray in hand. Fully absorbed by the contents of the last letter he had opened, he did not hear Dora's silent footsteps across the thick carpet. "Coffee, milord," she said as she moved to place the laden tray on one corner of the desk.

"Bloody hell," the earl cried in surprise, his obvious displeasure making Dora flinch. The tray wobbled in her hands. From halfway across the room, Jeremy watched the event unfold as the silver urn tipped and coffee sloshed across the desktop.

Jeremy hurried forward as a furious Thornton shouted, "You clumsy c—"

"An accident, clearly," Jeremy said, momentarily forgetting his part and speaking across whatever horrible aspersion Thornton had been about to cast on the frightened girl. Calmly he righted the urn, and with his handkerchief, he began to mop up the spilled coffee.

Thornton snapped shut his jaw and scrambled to rescue his papers from the spreading pool. Dora's efforts to help only made matters worse by shuffling together the letters he had separated. Coffee creeped across the polished mahogany, following the edges of the leather blotter, until it reached a blank sheet of foolscap. As the dark liquid soaked into the paper, words began to appear.

Jeremy had learned that trick in his school days, long before Scott's service. Words written in lemon juice, white wine—"even piss, in a pinch," Robby Firth had sworn—made the page look empty, until heat or some other substance was applied to reveal the print. Then, it had been the means of playing boyish pranks, but in more recent years, he had seen the method put to far more nefarious uses.

Why in God's name was Thornton getting letters written in invisible ink?

The answer to that question could be just the sort of damning information Laura sought.

Jeremy had the sense to look away as Thornton tossed aside the other papers he had gathered and snatched up the mysterious letter. Dora was sobbing. "Out," Thornton roared, and she fled without a backward glance.

With studied calm, Jeremy finished wiping up the spilled liquid. "Not such a disaster," he said, tossing his ruined handkerchief onto the tray, then pouring a cup of coffee and handing it to Thornton. "The letters will dry if you spread them out."

Thornton grunted and began to lay them out face down in a line. Most were only dampened along the edges. As far as Jeremy could tell, the letter written in invisible ink was no longer among them. Thornton must have tucked it into his coat when Jeremy's head was turned.

It might have been anything, of course. But the sort of men who encrypted their secrets were no secret to Jeremy.

"I ought to turn that wench over my knee," the earl declared, sinking into his chair.

Jeremy's pulse pounded, his ears ringing with Laura's insistence that he must earn Thornton's trust. He poured a second cup for himself, knowing there was but one reply to make to such a man. Fortifying himself with a sip of the bitter brew, he mustered a sly, knowing smile and said, "Be honest, Thornton. You wanted to do that before she dropped the tray."

Thornton's answering chuckle was not the slightest bit sheepish. "Who wouldn't want to see those pretty cheeks blushing?"

Was this the sort of life field agents lived? Pretending to share some despicable vice in order to gain the confidence of a target?

Unable to meet Thornton's eye, Jeremy sent a pointed glance around the room instead. "My own tastes run to…less arcane pleasures."

Thornton shrugged and took a noisy slurp. "To each his own."

Not a thought spared for *her*—the lady's maid, the cook, poor Dora. Jeremy was not so naïve as to imagine Thornton couldn't find a willing partner who shared his proclivities. No, the man seemed to be indifferent to, perhaps even spurred on, by a woman's unwillingness.

Disgust choked Jeremy, the hot coffee insufficient to burn it away. "You will dismiss her?" He struggled for a tone of apathy, hoping for Dora's sake that Thornton's answer would be yes.

"Not yet." Thornton settled the cup in its saucer, then laid the saucer on his desk. "How long until Lady Sterling is on her feet again? I have friends coming in a few days for some shooting, and other…amusements. You are welcome to stay. You might find you enjoy"—one brow arced—"*arcane pleasures,* after all."

Jeremy forced a thin smile. "A generous offer, I'm sure. But I think Lady Sterling would protest."

"Ah. I forget what it is to be a newly married man. But the last time you gave her her head, she ran away. She must learn that you are in charge."

Do whatever it takes to encourage him to tell you any secrets he might be keeping.

"Excellent advice, Thornton." Standing, Jeremy placed his cup and saucer on the tray, hoping the rattle did not betray his true emotion. "You can bet she will."

With a bow, he left the library and returned to the blue bedchamber, where he found Laura sitting once more on the little sofa, a book open on her lap, her gaze directed to the window, though from her position, he doubted she could see anything but cloudy skies.

She started when the door shut and the latch clicked. "Oh, there you are. At long last."

There was no mistaking the reproving note in her voice. He lingered by the door. "Believe me when I say I would have preferred to spend the day in pleasanter company."

He expected defiance or self-pity or perhaps the assumption that he had been hinting at a desire to spend the time with her. Instead, she visibly deflated, which was somehow far worse. "I know. I'm sorry. It's only…"

"Is your ankle giving you much pain? Where's that bottle Phelps left with you yesterday?"

She gave a half-hearted wave of one hand, indicating the far end of the room. He spied the tonic on the bedside table. "But it isn't that," she insisted. "I am not accustomed to sitting and waiting and doing nothing."

"I wouldn't call it nothing. Healing is something," he said, crossing the room and seating himself on the chair closest to her. "Plotting is something. But from what I know of masterminds, it does involve an unfortunate amount of waiting."

That earned him a dubious smile. "Do you know many masterminds?"

"A few."

Her smile deepened. "Thank you."

He could not decide whether she was thanking him for breaking her gloom or because she assumed the compliment had been directed at her. Both possibilities brought an answering smile to his own lips, easing the tightness that had settled into his jaw during the hours with Thornton.

"So," she continued, closing the unread book without even the pretense of marking her place, "have you learned anything of use today?"

"Whether it will be of use, I hesitate to say." He leaned back in the chair and crossed his ankles, his feet resting close to hers. "But certainly I have had my eyes opened to Thornton's...well, I hesitate to call it *taste*."

"Worse than we suspected?"

Why did that single word, *we*, warm him more than the embers of what had been a roaring fire in the nearby hearth?

"I might have forgiven him for the insufferable hours in the woods—I've spent time with bores before—but then we adjourned to his study."

She glanced downward, as if hoping the floor beneath them had suddenly become transparent. "And?"

"He possesses a substantial collection of artwork and other items having to do with..." Heat suffused his face. After flailing for words he could bring himself to utter in front of her, he settled at last on "... marital relations."

Laura laughed and mischief twinkled in her eyes. "I suspect most of the relations in question are *extra*marital, are they not?" Then she sobered. "Did you see anything in that room that could be used to expose him?"

"Exposure would require him to be capable of feeling shame, and with such a display..." He shook his head. "He seems to think he has nothing to hide."

"Outrageousness can itself be a distraction," she said, still staring thoughtfully at the floor. Then she raised her eyes to him, her expression knowing. "Just as we, with our little charade, intend to distract the household from divining our true purpose here, he may hope to shock or amuse with the contents of his library shelves and walls, in the hopes no one bothers to dig deeper, to uncover something he is determined to keep secret."

Such as a letter, written in invisible ink?

Jeremy shook off the thought. He had grown too used to searching for a hidden meaning in things. It was likely nothing of significance, a note from some equally depraved friend who liked to play games.

Now that he had found Lady Sterling, his mission at Thornton Hall was clear: discover how far she was willing to go to see justice served.

"And even if Thornton's proclivities in art and entertainment *are* the crux of the matter," she was saying, "I intend to find a way to make him regret indulging them. Limited to women who share his vices, they would be harmless enough, I suppose, though one must spare a pitying thought for her ladyship, who does not strike me as the adventuresome type." Again, something that might have been wry amusement played around the corners of her mouth and quickly disappeared. "But I cannot and will not ignore the exploitation of his employees."

Jeremy hardly knew how to respond. Was Laura herself *adventuresome*? Instinct told him that she knew at once too much and too little for her safety. For his part, he wished he knew even less.

"He seemed disturbingly eager to, ah, discipline the young maid who brought us coffee, even before she had the misfortune of spilling it on his desk." The words were difficult to coax past his clenched jaw. He would rather not know of such things, and would much rather not speak of them.

Absently, Laura's fingertips traced the embossing on the cover of the book. "By discipline, I take it you don't mean dismissal?"

Never in a thousand years could he have imagined having such a conversation with anyone, particularly not a gently bred young woman. "I had the distinct impression he did not intend to let a defenseless girl get away so easily. Particularly not when he expects to be entertaining his friends by the week's end."

"A house party of rakehells," she mused. "Miss Godfrey mentioned as much in her letter, and the maid hinted at it when she came to our room this morning to clean the hearth. I suppose Thornton's friends are cut from the same cloth?"

"One assumes." He pushed to his feet, unable to keep from pacing. "And we should be long gone before they descend on this house." A shudder passed through him as he imaged Lieutenant Hopkins's face if he ever discovered what his sister had seen and heard while under Jeremy's—good God, he hardly knew what to call it. Surely not *protection*.

"Did he invite you to stay?" Her pose was eager.

"Yes, but—"

"Then stay we must, my dear husband. The Lady Sterling intends to see that Lord Thornton has made his last threat. If other fish slip into the net while it is cast, so much the better."

"Laura."

Did he intend to plead, to scold?

Either way, her name rose to his lips with astonishing ease.

"That's it, my lord," she said, that maddening smile once more firmly in place. "You spoke my name with a perfect blend of exasperation and... dare I say, longing?" Her eyebrows arched most provocatively. "And you must also have managed to persuade Lord Thornton of your sympathies to him. Bravo! Your acting talents are better than I would have supposed. But now," she said, waggling her fingers to shoo him away, "you must go and dress for dinner and make up some excuse for our staying on until the others arrive."

He should put a stop to this plan right now.

Why, he wasn't even sure it deserved the name of *plan*.

Then he thought of what Thornton had said and threatened to do. Last night, he'd wanted confirmation of Lady Sterling's accusations, and today's events had given it to him in spades. He thought too of Miss Godfrey and the nameless others at Thornton's mercy. His own sacrifices of time and dignity were nothing. He couldn't, wouldn't abandon those women to their fates.

But as he strode to the dressing room, past the bed, he was forced to admit that his purpose in staying would not be entirely noble. He could not shake the image, the sensation of Laura's golden head slumbering against his chest, nor stamp out the selfish, treacherous hope it might rest there again tonight.

He liked some parts of this game of pretend very much.

And what sort of man did that make him?

Chapter 10

For some time after Jeremy closed the door behind him, Laura had held out hope of a visit from Miss Godfrey to dispel the evening's boredom. Surely, the daughters were of an age to dine with their parents, and if the boy was not, he might be left with a nurse. But the door remained shut as the room's gloom deepened.

The maid who brought up her tray—neither Dinah nor Dora, to Laura's grave disappointment—was obliging enough to light two lamps. After eating what she could of an excellent dinner, Laura resigned herself to the abandoned book, an account of someone or other's travels in Ireland.

Inadequate to the purpose of keeping her thoughts from straying to Jeremy.

He'd left clad in a dark blue coat and charcoal breeches that were not his. Perhaps they belonged to one of Thornton's elder sons; certainly they had never fit the shorter, stockier earl, though Thornton's valet had brought them earlier that afternoon.

Even in clothes untailored to his slender figure, Jeremy drew the eye.

Drew *her* eye, at least.

And that was the problem. Laura, who well knew the value of a distraction, never let herself be distracted while on a case. One as complicated as Thornton's required extra diligence.

Yet here she was, alone again, and contemplating the ways in which the blue of the coat had complemented Jeremy's extraordinary eyes.

Eyes. Yes, and ears. Legs too. Until she was back on her feet—er, foot—she had no choice but to rely on him to see and hear what she could not. He was a device. A means to an end.

For the half dozenth time at least, she dragged her attention back to the question of what Thornton might be trying to hide behind a façade of lurid paintings and bawdy sculptures, and whether the threat of its disclosure would be enough to put a stop to his abuse.

But to answer that question, she needed more information, information she would not have until Jeremy returned from dinner. Which meant she had no choice but to wait. Wait and watch the door.

It was not as if she were waiting for *him*, she reminded herself as she stared at that unmoving panel. She was not merely wanting him to return and bear her company. Certainly she was not anticipating the hour in which he would lift her in his surprisingly capable arms and bear her to...

She glanced toward the bed. Perhaps it had been unwise for her to insist on carrying their newlywed performance quite so far. Although really, what had they done but lie side by side in a space big enough for half a dozen to sleep comfortably?

It was not as if they'd sunk into the plush feather bed, tangled in a passionate embrace, and—

She snapped her eyes shut, dismissing a mental picture that she feared might put the artwork in Thornton's study to shame. But before her lids closed, her restless gaze snagged the reticule lying on the bedside table. *Penhurst's watch.* She might at least discover the hour and how much longer she had to wait.

Gripping the arm of the sofa to steady herself, her fingers digging into the plush upholstery in anticipation of pain, she lifted her injured ankle from the pillowed footstool and rested her toes on the floor. It still hurt, but she needn't put any weight on it. Not much, really. With a crutch or a cane, she thought she could have managed quite admirably.

But absent either implement, she was forced to hop along on one foot, steadying herself by the back of the sofa, the edge of the table, the chair. The chasm between the sitting area and the end of the bed, devoid of furnishings on which to lean, gave her pause. Last night, it had seemed but a few steps.

After sucking in a determined breath, she hopped across the carpet, fearful that if she stopped for long, she would lose her balance and topple over. At last, she could lay a hand on the bed's carved post, then grip the blue counterpane. Finally, a few hops more, and she was at the bedside table. Leaning against the bed, out of sorts from the effort such a little journey had required, she jerked the watch from her reticule.

Miss Godfrey's letter slipped free with it and fluttered to the floor beneath the bed.

Time was, such an annoyance might have brought an unladylike epithet to her lips. But now, to her utter humiliation, tears sprang to her eyes. Oh, she hated, hated, hated helplessness. It was more than just a loss of control over her life—which would, in all conscience, have been bad enough. Certainly, she had had plans go awry before, and events had not always unfolded as she had hoped. Lately, almost always related to her dealings with Lord Thornton.

That realization made her grit her teeth, more determined than ever to see him not just hindered in his ability to do harm, but genuinely made to face justice.

She sank down, dragging the coverlet half off the bed in the process, the slippery silk offering little to counterbalance the graceless slide of her body. But at last she was kneeling on the floor, then lying on her belly, half-hidden beneath the bed, muttering under her breath, and straining first with one arm and then the other to reach the letter that taunted her from just beyond her fingertips.

"Lady Sterling?"

She had not heard the door open or the sound of footsteps crossing the floor. Startled, she jerked upright, struck the back of her head on the bed frame, and saw stars. To cap off the absurd scene, the silk counterpane slid obligingly off the bed to smother her.

"Good God, what's happened? Are you all right, darling?" Jeremy was kneeling beside her. "Did you fall out of bed?"

"No." Her voice sounded weak, muffled, even to her own ears. Experimentally, she shook her head, which only made the room spin harder.

With the care and strength and decency she had come to expect, he disentangled her from the counterpane and guarded the back of her skull from another encounter with the solidly made bed as she slowly wriggled her way back to freedom. At last she could sit up, eyes closed, and rest her head against the edge of the mattress. "I didn't fall," she explained. "I had an attack of...ennui." Lord, what an embarrassing confession. "I wanted to know the time, so I hobbled my way over here to fetch that blasted watch. But then I—I dropped Miss Godfrey's letter and it..." She gestured vaguely with one hand.

"And I startled you." Jeremy's voice was comfortingly contrite. "Can you look at me?"

After a few blinking attempts, she opened her eyes and brought his face—his handsome, worried, altogether too-perfect face—into focus. What was it about that face that looked so familiar? His blue eyes searched hers from just inches away as he crouched beside her. "I don't think you're concussed. But say something clever so I'll know for sure."

"And what makes you a suitable judge of my cleverness?"

That cross answer earned her a lopsided smile. "See? Right as rain."

She meant to smile back. Or perhaps offer a skeptical, scolding frown. Instead, more tears sprang into her eyes and, to her utter humiliation, this time began to leak from the corners of her eyes and trail down her cheeks.

"Oh, my dear, don't cry. You're all right." He produced a handkerchief and swiped away the evidence of her humiliation. The warm square of linen carried that same subtly spicy scent. Perhaps it wasn't his shaving soap. Perhaps it was just...him.

"I'm fine," she agreed, snatching the handkerchief from his hand and blowing her nose. "If you don't count my ankle, or my head, or my complete inability to do what I came to Thornton Hall to do. Lady Sterling may never live down this ridiculous—"

Rather than listen to her complaints or try to coax her out of her near-hysteria, he rose and disappeared from view. In another moment, he returned bearing a glass of water. "Here."

She accepted it from him with a hand that wasn't quite steady. "I'd rather it was brandy."

"I know."

She groped toward the bedside table. "Where's Phelps's tonic, then?"

With damnable effortlessness, he snatched up the little glass vial before she could reach it. "Are you certain that's wise?"

"It's for pain, is it not? Well, I have a headache."

His gaze narrowed, and his dark brows knit together. After a long moment, his reluctance plain, he uncorked the little vial, then cupped her hand to steady the glass as he tipped two measured drops into the water. She watched, mesmerized, as the two liquids swirled together, while he stoppered the bottle and slipped it into his pocket. "Go on, then. And when you've had another moment to rest, I'll help you up and call for a maid to—"

"No!" Caught mid-swallow, she spluttered out the refusal. "Lady Sterling has a reputation to protect, and I would not let Dinah or one of the others see me in a moment of weakness."

Something like humor twitched at the corner of his mouth at the mention of Lady Sterling's reputation. "But isn't the whole purpose of this ruse to keep them from suspecting you're *that* Lady Sterling? I expected you to seize on this opportunity to garner sympathy—won't they assume your awful husband has said something to break your heart?"

"N-n-no one thinks you're awful," she sobbed as the tears welled up again, and the glass tumbled from her nerveless fingers.

He caught it before the last drops spilled. "Well, then, I suppose I shall have to try harder," he teased as he set the tumbler on the tabletop. "I daresay Thornton's little house party will provide ample opportunity."

She hiccupped. "You got another invitation?"

"It wasn't difficult. Thornton seems downright eager to show off the depths of his depravity. Now," he said, reaching for her, "let's get you up and into bed before that laudanum takes hold."

"I c-c-can't sleep in this," she said, gesturing toward her already disheveled gown. "It's the only thing I have that isn't mud-stained. You'll have to help me undress first."

The humor fled from his eyes. His pupils flared, and his hands stilled. "I don't think that's wise."

"We left *wise* behind in a pub east of Dartford. Now, let me just undo my stockings before I stand up." When she leaned forward slightly, a wave of dizziness washed over her, forcing her to lay her hands palm down on the prickly carpet. "Oh. Well, never mind. I can—"

"I'll do it."

Was it her imagination, or had that reply come through gritted teeth? She could no longer see his face as he bent to his task, made easier by the fact that her skirts were already rucked up to her knees.

With fingers that fumbled only a little, he reached beneath her hems to untie her garters and gently rolled down first one stocking, then the other, sliding the first from her left foot, and finally easing the second over her tender right ankle.

"How does it look?" she asked.

"Beautiful. Er, I mean to say, it looks to be healing beautifully. The swelling's gone down from last night."

She had closed her eyes, bracing for discomfort that never came, but now her eyes popped open. "Last night? I didn't know—"

"I, er, I was watching when—that is, when Mr. Phelps was examining the injury, he called me over." She watched him ball her stockings nervously in one hand, then apparently discovering belatedly what he'd done and uncertain what to do with them, he stuffed them into the same coat pocket in which he'd stashed the tonic. Finally, he raised his eyes to her face, and she saw a telltale flush across his cheekbones. "Do you not recall?"

The laudanum must already have begun to work, for her breathing felt suddenly shallow, uneven. She could not speak, only managing to move her head in something that must have passed for a nod.

He pushed himself to a half-kneeling position. "Right then. Let's get you up."

His hands at her waist, lifting her, steadying her when she wobbled, turning her to face the bed—it was only the familiar strength and firmness, the same hands that had carried her the night before. Nothing had changed.

If his touch seemed different now, gentle, almost reverent, it was only because she had so little experience with the hands of men, and almost all of it limited to the sort of grasping and groping Penhurst had done that night at Vauxhall.

Still it would be easy to make too much of the way his fingers loosened the fastenings of her gown—was that a tremor of nervousness? or something else entirely?—and unknotted the laces of her corset. His fingertips never brushed her skin, yet her flesh tingled with awareness.

He'd been right to call this unwise.

"Tell me," she said, though it required clearing her throat twice before the words would come, "what was discussed at dinner."

"Oh, nothing of particular interest. Lady Thornton wanted to hear more about our courtship. Apparently my proposal of marriage was...what did she call it? Ah, yes. 'Heart-stoppingly romantic.'"

His proposal? Oh, dear God. They'd been caught in a lie, and Jeremy didn't even know it.

Instead of stopping, Laura's heart, which had been beating too fast already, began to hammer against her ribs, threatening to break free of what had heretofore seemed a sturdy enough cage. Surely he could feel it pounding?

He'd paused in unlacing her as he searched for the word, but now he resumed drawing the sturdy silk cord through the eyelets, at each step a quiet *zing*. "I pretended modesty, of course, and told her I'd been so nervous I could hardly remember your answer, let alone what I might have said that prompted it. Her eldest daughter was generous enough to offer a few hints." *Zing*. "For a moment, I could not think why such a speech would sound familiar, then I recalled where I had heard it: from the lips of Kean himself in *Love's Crooked Arrow* last season. Evidently the story is a great favorite with your sex; my sister insisted on seeing it three times."

Had she stolen the idea from the play? Fortunately, Jeremy's memory was better. "Did anyone else recognize it?"

Zing. "No. I do not believe Lady Thornton ventures much into town, and if Thornton attends the theater, I doubt he goes to hear the play." *Zing, zing*. "I must say, I'm surprised you were willing to give your husband such eloquent words. Any real ones a man might offer would be lackluster in comparison."

Her corset began to gape, and she tried not to wonder about the condition of her shift. Until that moment, she had never worried much about undergarments that no one ever saw. "Honesty is always preferable to a rehearsed speech, I think."

"I am glad to know our fine English actors have not left you jaded." One last *zing*, and then, out of the corner of her eye, she watched him lay the coil of corset lacing on the bedside table. "Shall I fetch your nightgown?"

"No, I'll just…manage…" Shyness was not a condition with which she was ordinarily afflicted. But now, positioned between Jeremy and the enormous bed, longing for something she was reluctant to name, she no longer knew what to do. She had not considered the dreadful possibility that pretend emotions might become real. Shaking free of her dress and corset, she clambered onto the bed without assistance, heedless of either aching head or injured ankle, and pulled the sheets up to her chin.

The sudden series of movements seemed to startle Jeremy, who took a step back and developed an unexpected interest in the ornamental molding on the ceiling. "All set, then?"

"If you could…cover me…" She gestured toward the blue counterpane draped half off the bed and onto the floor.

"Yes, of course." He bent to straighten the bedding, then kept going, until he was kneeling beside her. His dark hair gleamed like a raven's wing in the lamplight.

"Jeremy, I—"

When he looked up, the pounding of her heart became something perilously close to anticipation. Then he rose again, clutching her discarded clothes in one hand and a folded piece of paper in the other. "Miss Godfrey's note. Wouldn't want to forget that."

Mortification flushed into her face. She was in danger of forgetting a great deal more than that. "Burn it, please," she instructed him, certain the heat of her cheeks would be sufficient to do the job. "I should have done already."

He nodded, strode to the fireplace, and flicked the note into the glowing coals. "There. Now it won't cause any more trouble."

If only. "Strange the upheaval a single slip of paper can cause."

His head tipped to one side, as if the remark required a great deal of thought. "Yes. I suppose it is." Then he disappeared into the dressing room.

Determined to get the better of her foolishness and steer what remained of the evening onto safer ground, she called after him. "What else was discussed over dinner?"

"Nothing of consequence." Through the doorway, she could hear the rustling of clothes being removed and the splashing of water in the washbasin. "Even after the ladies withdrew, Thornton was remarkably subdued. Seemed to have something on his mind. While he nursed a glass of port, I made mention of the expected guests. He was quick to extend another invitation to join them, so I took it. The others will begin to arrive on Friday."

The days—and nights—between now and Friday stretched before her, much like the expanse of the bed on which she lay. "I wonder if it wouldn't have been better to—"

"How's that?"

He appeared in the dressing room doorway, scrubbing a towel over his jaw. He'd shed coat and waistcoat and unwound his cravat, and the sight of dark hair on his chest, revealed by the open neck of his shirt, somehow had the power to ratchet her pulse even higher. All she could manage was a mute shake of her head.

Last night, shock must have prevented her from understanding just how foolish it would be to behave as if they were really married. But tonight, what excuse did she have for being willing to court this danger?

She could not bring herself to blame two drops of laudanum in a swallow of water.

"Are you certain you wouldn't rather I slept in the dressing room?" he asked, approaching the bed, seeming to sense her sudden rash of nerves. "Or by the hearth? The sofa isn't long, but I think I could manage on the—"

"No." Her voice was strangely husky. "What silliness that would be," she insisted, after clearing her throat. "Why should you be uncomfortable? Surely two people—"

"Who don't even like each other," he interjected with a wry smile, echoing her words of the previous night.

"I shouldn't have said that. I don't even know you."

One corner of his mouth kicked up a little higher. "Almost like a real society marriage, then."

She wanted to laugh with him, but a question rose to her lips instead. "Was someone in the corridor when you came into the room tonight?"

Confusion flickered into his eyes at the non sequitur, and he paused to think back. "No. Why?"

Because you called me darling *when no one was around to overhear.*

"Why are you helping me?" she demanded, ignoring his question even as she chided herself: *He's merely doing what you asked him to do.* "You—you clearly had your own reasons for following me into Kent, and you must have other demands on your time, but now you're...we're..."

He smiled outright. "Do you doubt that I was eager to lay aside my usual, boring work in favor of a breakneck ride through the country after a pickpocket?"

With the nail of her first finger, she drew an aimless shape on the counterpane. "Not when I'd so thoughtlessly stolen something from you already."

"The title, you mean?" One shoulder lifted in a show of indifference. "Much like Penhurst's watch, it hardly qualifies as theft to take something from a man he ought never to have possessed."

She puzzled over his meaning—could regret over his father's death have left such a long shadow on his inheritance?—but said nothing more as he set about dousing the lamps.

In the velvety-soft darkness, she felt the bed dip as he climbed onto it, heard the rustle of sheets as he settled himself beside her, felt the warmth of his body, though they did not touch.

"What I've seen and heard in the last day has made me realize the importance, the necessity of Lady Sterling." His voice was little more than a whisper now, and the intimacy of it made her shiver with delight. "I do not want Miss Godfrey and Dora and the rest to end up like Lady Thornton's maid. By the bye," he added as he turned away from her, evidently preparing for sleep, "what did you take from Thornton that brought in fifty pounds for the cook? Knowing might help me figure out where to direct my attention."

"A—a book." His focus on business was admirable, sensible. How silly of her to imagine there might be anything else between them. "A French cookbook. Mrs. Croft told me she had once seen him perusing it. When she asked if he wished for her to prepare something from it, he acted rather strangely and hid it away instead. His behavior ignited my suspicions, so I disguised myself as a parlor maid, intending to find out his secret. Unfortunately, the book turned out to be nothing more than it purported to be on the cover and therefore, nothing I could truly use. I took it anyway, hoping it might have some value, but I did not leave Lady Sterling's calling card in its place, as I knew my work was not done. Later, my brother happened upon the cookbook at my Aunt Mildred's, and when I told him it had been a donation to one of her charities, he offered to take it 'round to the shops on my behalf, to see what could be got for it.

A few days after that, he brought me the money, which I passed along to Mrs. Croft. More than a year's wages meant a great deal, of course, but I *had* hoped for something more..." She paused in the telling to find that his breathing had grown shallow and even, and he made no other sound. "Jeremy?" Still nothing.

He'd endured a long day of Lord Thornton's company on very little rest. Of course he must be exhausted. And she ought to be grateful he would offer no further temptation to do something other than sleep tonight.

With a huff that came alarmingly close to the sound of disappointment, she rolled onto her side, facing away from him, and closed her eyes. Despite the laudanum and her best intentions, however, she could not shake her awareness of the man beside her, and sleep refused to come.

Chapter 11

Finding himself torn between conflicting desires, Jeremy steadied his breathing and pretended to sleep, though his mind raced.

The first of those desires—to roll toward Laura and gather her in his arms—was so far beyond the pale he could hardly bring himself to acknowledge it.

But there was no denying it, either.

Christ above, what had possessed him to agree to any part of this scheme? Not the false marriage, nor the flowery proposal. Not undressing her, inch by exquisite inch. And definitely not sharing her bed.

Neither a silent recitation of his catechism, nor a detailed recollection of every cricket match he'd ever played was sufficient to keep his cock from hardening as he'd unfastened her gown and unlaced her corset. If the process had revealed anything more than a crescent of flawless skin at the tops of her shoulders, he might have spent in his borrowed breeches.

What a green lad he was.

It was surely his greenness that made him lust over a woman who would have set a more experienced man to flight.

No matter how lovely. No matter how clever.

No matter whether she seemed to invite his touch.

His *innocent* touch, he reminded himself. She had merely needed his help. Curling his fingers in the bedsheets, he tried to make himself focus on something, anything else.

But the second of his desires, which involved ransacking Thornton's study under cover of darkness, was hardly less dangerous.

The book that had brought fifty pounds for poor Mrs. Croft...the French cookbook...was in fact the codebook upon which he had expended so many hours in the last months. And now he knew it had once belonged to Lord Thornton.

Did Thornton understand what he'd had? Were there documents to be deciphered in his possession...more letters in invisible ink, perhaps?

The trouble, Jeremy realized as he reflected on his dilemma, was that his desires weren't conflicting, but intertwined.

Lady Sterling had stolen the book from Thornton. Lieutenant Hopkins had happened upon it in his sister Laura's possession. And of course she would not have told the truth about where she had found it, for fear her secret identity would be revealed.

Could Scott have suspected the link?

No. No, certainly not. If he had, he would not have dallied for weeks while Jeremy struggled. He would have seized any opportunity to figure out the codebook. Though the general might have feared Lady Sterling was involved in espionage, not even he could have imagined her to be Hopkins's sister.

But now Jeremy knew.

Below him, in the study, might lie vital information that could help to ensure the safety and success of his fellow soldiers against Napoleon's armies.

Beside him lay a woman desperate to find a skeleton hidden in Thornton's cupboard, hoping that the threat of its disclosure would keep a man's basest behaviors in check.

Could giving in to one desire help him to satisfy the other?

He forced his hand to relax its grip on the sheet. *No.* There could be no *satisfaction* where Laura was concerned.

Even helping her would be a risk. But that, at least, was a risk he could afford to take. Together, they could stop Thornton from ruining any more lives.

He started, as if suddenly awakened. "Oh—sorry. Did I nod off?"

Her hair whispered across the pillow as she turned her head. To his dismay—no, *relief*—her body did not follow. "It's all right."

"It's not. You were telling me...telling me about the cook—"

"Mrs. Croft, yes."

"And a book. Did you say your brother was involved somehow?"

"Yes. Fitz sold the old thing to some bookseller. I had no notion a cookbook could be so valuable." Her quiet laugh fluttered up his spine like a feather-light touch. "I'm not really one for the domestic arts."

He made a noise somewhere between a chuckle and a grunt, and then eased onto his back. "Are you and your brother close?"

"We used to be, I suppose. When we were children. Then Mama died, and he was sent away to school, and I went to live with Aunt Mildred in Clapham. Between then and the reading of Papa's will, I hardly saw him."

"I did not know you had also lost your father. I'm sorry."

"You are kind. But will you think terribly of me if I say it was no great loss?" She squirmed beneath the awfulness of that confession. "When he drank, which was often, he said unspeakably cruel things to Mama and me, and lewd things to the maids and my governess. Governess*es*," she corrected with a sigh. "My aunt bought me a copy of *The Rights of Woman* and took me to lectures. I learned that my father's behavior was, sadly, far from unique but also that it did not have to be tolerated. Over the years, I began to imagine I could do something to stop men like him."

"And so you became Lady Sterling."

Their pillows sat close enough together that he felt her nod. "That was the same year Fitz joined the army." Finally, she turned over in bed and lay facing him, somehow in the process gathering most of the counterpane about herself. Though the room had grown cool with the dying of the fire, he did not begrudge her the blanket; he begrudged the blanket its closeness to her. "I hope it has not made him coarse."

"Coarse?" Jeremy echoed uncertainly. She could have no notion of what her brother had likely seen and done in Scott's service, just as Julia and Mama imagined that Jeremy did nothing more dangerous than shuffle papers in a pristine office in the Horse Guards, albeit at somewhat irregular hours.

"Forgive me, Captain Addison. I did not mean to imply that all soldiers… You are, have been, the very model of a gentleman. If my brother is not, I'm sure the blame lies with our father."

Jeremy did not know Fitzwilliam Hopkins well, but he knew that field agents played many parts, not all of them gentlemanlike. Knew, too, the weight of a father's legacy on his son. "I hope he has not behaved badly toward you?"

"Certainly he would never condescend to accompany his sister to the theater as you do." Jeremy could not decide whether the mocking note in her voice was meant for him or herself. "But on the whole, he treats me well enough. Still," she said, rolling onto her back, "I worry." He could too easily picture her gray eyes, clouded with concern, staring into the yawning blackness of the canopy above them. "When he brought me the money from the sale of the cookbook, he had a black eye and a split lip and looked as if he hadn't slept or eaten in a week. I could not help but think of how Papa looked sometimes, when he'd brawled over a hand of cards or something equally trivial."

In one sense, Laura had the right of it. Hopkins had been engaged in a deadly game of chance. During the days in which she had been waiting for him to return, her brother had been the prisoner of French ruffians in search of the codebook, which he had only just managed to pass on to an unsuspecting woman. He had been lucky to escape with his life.

"I should not like to have to pay Fitz a visit as Lady Sterling," she said.

Jeremy felt certain her brother would like such a visit even less.

"His commanding officer would not tolerate brawling, gaming, or drunkenness," he reassured her. It was not a lie; Scott frowned on all of those things, and Colonel Millrose was stricter yet.

But the whole truth was something an intelligence officer was rarely at liberty to divulge.

He could not, for instance, explain what the cookbook actually was, or that her brother's safety had been imperiled because of his involvement with it. He could not reveal his work as a code breaker. He could not even tell her what he suspected about Thornton—at least not yet; at present, he hardly knew whether his theory about the man deserved to be honored with the name of suspicion. Thornton was a lecher and thoughtlessly cruel to those who depended on his benevolence.

That did not make him a spy.

So many things Jeremy could not say to her, though he ached to do so. Then again, what would be the point in speaking of desires on which he could not act?

Hardly had the thought crossed his mind, when her fingers slid over his. In comparison to what she had done as Lady Sterling, it could scarcely be called an act of daring to let her hand cross the inches of bare linen that separated them. Yet he marveled at it, at the quiet intimacy of that innocent touch, at this silent yet extraordinary proof of her trust. A woman who had seen what she had would have been justified in never trusting any man, to say nothing of a near stranger.

"Thank you." Her words were barely a whisper, a breath of sound to match the brush of her hand.

For a moment, he could not think what he had done to earn her gratitude. That paltry reassurance about her brother? Or was it an expression of her faith in him? If she could see into his mind, know his thoughts, learn his secrets...

She deserved far more than he could give.

So he settled for what he could offer in return and hoped it would be enough. "Thornton's library here is full of books. Perhaps a closer examination will reveal something useful to Lady Sterling." *And the*

British army. "We can look tomorrow, after Mr. Phelps has another look at your ankle."

Her fingers curled, tangling his in a gentle squeeze. "Why not now?"

"Now? It must be after midnight." A feeble excuse under any circumstances, but particularly for a secret agent who often worked under cover of darkness. But, selfishly, he wanted nothing to disrupt the present moment.

"Too tired?" she teased, releasing his hand and pushing herself onto her elbows. If the laudanum had had any sedative effect, it had clearly worn off. "The longer we delay, the more time Thornton will have to hide anything that's truly interesting. And it's just downstairs—we can go and be back without anyone spotting us."

"Let me go, and report—"

"Not on your life. After what you described this afternoon, I need to see his collection for myself."

"Laura," he chided warningly.

"Really, Jeremy. What is it you imagine you're protecting me from?"

Me.

To think of examining those sculptures and paintings with her by his side—or worse, in his arms... He swallowed back the groan that rose to his lips, realizing that he was trying to protect himself most of all. "And if we're caught?"

"We'll say I couldn't sleep, which is true, and that I wished for something to read. Surely there must be something in that library that would pass for innocuous. And if not? Well, I am a married woman, after all."

He had to squeeze shut his eyes, despite the darkness all around them. "Indeed."

"So, what are we waiting for?"

With a sigh, he threw his legs over the side of the bed and sat up. "I'll fetch your gown."

"Oh, don't bother," she replied airily. "A dressing gown will do. More authentic to the part, don't you agree?"

He didn't bother to ask which part she fancied herself performing at present, didn't bother to argue at all. Instead, he fumbled his way into the dressing room, lit a candle, and returned bearing it and her borrowed dressing gown draped over one forearm.

Her face glowed with eagerness. "We're going to find something, I just know it. You'll have to carry me down the stairs, I'm afraid," she said as she took the heavy silk garment from him and draped it around her shoulders. "I can hobble across the floor, but the steps—"

"Need I remind you that hobbling across the floor nearly got you concussed?"

She made a dismissive noise and shook back the overlong sleeves to hold up her arms as she had last night, like a child demanding to be lifted. "Ready?"

Absent a second dressing gown, he was still clad only in breeches and shirt, not even stockings. "Don't you think I ought to dress, at least?"

Eyes sparkling mischievously, she looked him up and down—or perhaps that was only the flicker of candlelight in their pewter depths. "Not at all."

With more force than necessary, he thumped the candlestick onto the bedside table, tossed back the coverlet, and scooped her from the bed. *Ah, God.* It was torture when she wriggled to settle herself in his arms, her curls tickling the underside of his chin, and his biceps burning.

The sweetest torture imaginable.

At his first step, she protested. "The candle?"

"Can you carry it without setting me on fire, do you think?"

She snagged her lip between her teeth, poorly disguising a grin. "Most likely."

Against his better judgment, he let her snatch up the brass candlestick and light their way from the room. After all, if his judgment were sound, he would never have agreed to this midnight excursion in the first place.

Then again, would it have been any wiser to lie beside her in bed, holding her hand and dreaming impossible dreams?

* * * *

Lord Thornton's library was a spectacle unlike any Laura had ever seen; yet she had eyes only for Jeremy.

He had deposited her on a cushioned window seat and set about lighting more candles, his bare feet padding across the thick Turkish carpet in near silence. She could see the dusting of dark hair on his calves and on his forearms where he'd rolled back the billowing sleeves of his shirt. The thought that she'd invited—nay, insisted upon—such shocking dishabille ought to have made her blush. But only when he turned toward her again did she tear her gaze away, focusing instead on her fingers, tangled in the tie of her dressing gown.

She could have found fault with him, if she'd wished. Even with his perfect face, for she'd glimpsed the tiniest thread of a silvery scar above one eyebrow, and his smile was ever so slightly crooked. He was slender of build and not much above average height; whence came the strength to lift and carry her with such ease, she was not sure, though she had her suspicions. If she were ever fortunate enough to see him in nothing more than the fitted white breeches of his officer's uniform, she was wicked enough to believe those suspicions would be proved right.

And of course, his biggest fault was that he had not yet been entirely honest with her, about why he'd come after Lady Sterling or what he was meant to do with her now that he'd found her.

Not this, she felt certain, as he began to peruse the shelves on her behalf, not even knowing what he sought.

She took no particular pleasure in finding fault with men. Frequently, she wished they did not make it so easy to do. Her father, his perpetually drunken chums, every man from whom she'd stolen: Penhurst, Thornton, and the rest—any one of them would have been sufficient explanation for her determined spinsterhood.

But the truth was, she still nursed a flicker of hope in her breast—the foolish, foolish hope that she might one day meet a man who deserved her. A man of humor, grace, a modicum of intelligence. A man who believed in justice, and in Lady Sterling's cause.

And something about Lord Sterling—oh, but the gods did like a laugh now and again, didn't they?—had fanned a near-dying ember to full flame.

He reached for a book on a high shelf, and through the fine cambric of his shirt, she watched the muscles of his back bunch and stretch.

Or perhaps that heat at her core, curling into her limbs, setting her cheeks aflame...perhaps it was not hope. Perhaps it had another source entirely.

She set her attention to the room, scolding herself for forgetting why they'd come. The candlelight was insufficient to make out many details, but Thornton's taste was not subtle. She imagined the twisted delight such a man would take in ordering a girl like Dora to the library to fetch his tea, or suggesting poor Miss Godfrey search for a book for her pupils' lessons.

Laura was no prude. If Miss Godfrey sneaked down from the schoolroom of an afternoon to study the painting on the opposite wall, or the maids argued over whose turn it was to build up the library fire because they wished to gawk at the pair—or perhaps it was a trio?—of sculpted figures on the mantel, Laura saw no shame in it. But to have such sights thrust upon them, unknowing and unwilling, and then to have that experience followed by Thornton thrusting his—

"Are you chilly there by the window?"

Her thoughts, not the temperature, had made her shudder. "A little. But I'll be all right."

Jeremy resumed looking at the bookshelves, running his fingertips along a row of spines, here and there sliding a volume from the shelf, thumbing through its pages, and then returning it to its spot. "Remarkable."

From the way he spoke that single word, she almost wished he were looking at her, not the books. "What is?" she asked

"How...well, *unremarkable* it all is," he replied, looking up at the shelf before which he stood. "That is, it's an extraordinary collection, the work of generations. Which means, it's like looking for a needle in a haystack. Why, any one of these books might be—"

Valuable.

When he broke off his sentence before that expected word—stopped it, in fact, by snapping his jaw together with such force she heard the click of his teeth—she jerked her eyes to his profile.

What exactly was it he had thought to find?

Not something merely old. Even she, with an untutored eye and a cursory glance, had seen volumes that would have piqued the interest of an antiquarian.

"A good many of these books are common, and not exactly on the subjects one might expect of Thornton, looking around at all the rest." He waved an arm, taking in the room and its various contents in that sweeping gesture. "Take, for example, this one," he said, pulling a thin volume from the shelf in front of him and holding it out so that she could see the cover.

"*The Noble Game of Chess*," she read, squinting to make out the embossing in the dim light.

"Yes. Written over fifty years ago by a Syrian in Aleppo, and then translated from French. My father taught me, using this very book. I still have his copy." The ache of nostalgia in his voice made a lump rise in her own throat. "It's rather odd to me to think that Thornton's father might have done the same."

"Or that he's used that book to teach his own sons."

"Doubtful, and not only because Thornton doesn't strike me as a particularly paternal man. You see, Stamma's notation method has fallen out of favor," he explained, approaching her with the book held open to a random page.

Columns of numbers and letters greeted her eye. "It looks like a code."

Jeremy's smile was strange. "Yes, I suppose it does. He uses algebraic notation to lay out series of moves—"

She caught his boyish excitement and gestured toward a small game table a few feet away, its marquetry top designed in the pattern of a chessboard and the pieces sitting nearby. "Show me?"

He helped her rise and hobble a half-dozen steps to the nearer chair, then seated himself opposite. "Each number refers to a specific column on the board," he explained, showing her the page, itself divided into columns labeled White and Black. "One, two, three, and so on." He pointed as he spoke. "And each letter," he said, nodding toward the book, "indicates a piece. *A* for the queen's rook, *B* for her knight." He placed each piece in its appointed square, across the board. "Then starting over in the opposite direction for black."

"*P* for pawn?" she guessed.

"Exactly. And the crosses," he said, underlining a small symbol with his thumbnail, "show when a play puts the king into check. An elegant system that leaves little room for confusion."

There Laura could not quite agree, for knowing next to nothing of the game, every page seemed to her nothing more than a jumble of letters and numbers. Jeremy's ease in disentangling their meaning showed a side of him she had not previously suspected.

Now the board sat filled between them. "Shall we play?"

"I shall surely lose," she insisted with an embarrassed laugh.

He did not deny it. "This first game, almost certainly. But you have the sort of mind that could do well at chess. It requires looking ahead, anticipating the moves of one's opponent, knowing how to disguise one's own motives until it is too late for your opponent to recover."

Not a bad description of her work as Lady Sterling.

He knew her surprisingly well, and most surprising of all, he seemed to like what he knew.

He handed the open book to her. "Start here. Stamma shall be your aide de camp in this battle, while I must muddle through alone. Though, to be fair, I once had those pages committed to memory." He grinned at his own enthusiasm, and that lopsided smile made her heart flutter.

Dutifully, she followed each notation, thankful for his patience as she counted squares with her fingertip and murmured the letters and names of the pieces under her breath. Every turn required twice as long as it ought.

Several moves in, when she was about to lift her fingers from her queen, he shook his head. "That cannot be right," he said, curling gentle fingers around hers to return the piece to where it had been. Despite the chill of the room, his hand was warm. "Try again."

Thoroughly distracted, first by the sensation of his touch and then by its absence, she could hardly focus on the correct line in the chart. Finally, with a sigh of exasperation, she showed him the page. "If that is not the proper move, then I cannot make heads nor tails of it."

He reached for the book with easy confidence, and she held it out so that they could share it, maneuvering only slightly so that their fingertips would brush. "It does take some getting used to. Remember, you must count from left to ri—" He broke off with a frown and took the book entirely into his own grasp. "That's wrong. It should be *c*, not *e*. The queen's bishop, not the queen herself."

"Perhaps there's a blemish on the page," she suggested, peering, "and it only looks like an *e*."

His frown deepened. "I suppose that could be. We'd need more light to be sure." Suiting actions to words, he fetched a candlestick and set it on the table, and then held the book in his outstretched arm with the light between the page and his face.

Reluctant to be caught studying his features by that warm glow, she dropped her gaze to the chessboard instead. For just a moment, she imagined that what she saw were merely odd shadows, or perhaps the result of tired eyes, for it must now be very late indeed.

But no. As the candlelight flickered over the carved chess pieces, it highlighted certain details that had gone unnoticed in the dim room.

She pressed her fingers to her lips to stifle something between a gasp and a giggle. "Oh my."

Jeremy half turned toward the sound, his eyes still on the book. "Hmm?"

"What was it you said earlier? That you were surprised Lord Thornton would take an interest in something as ordinary as, er, chess?"

"How's that?" He glanced her way, still obviously thinking of the book. Then alarm flickered into his eyes at her expression, and he dropped his gaze to follow hers. "Oh. Dear God."

The chessmen were extraordinarily well-endowed little fellows, the knight with a bulging codpiece and the bishop with a veritable truncheon splitting his cassock. And every pawn was nothing more or less than a perfect replica of the male member in miniature.

When at last she dragged her eyes from the board, she discovered that shock had loosened Jeremy's grip on the book, and its pages were beginning to scorch in the candle's flame.

"Jeremy! The book!"

He jerked his wide eyes from the chessboard to *The Noble Game of Chess* and snapped the volume shut with such force that the candle sputtered and nearly went out. "Do forgive me, Miss Hopkins," he said stiffly, refusing to look down again. Marvelous color streaked across his perfect cheekbones. "Knowing Thornton's tastes, I ought to have made a more thorough investigation before we…"

"Nonsense," she said. "Neither of us should be surprised that Lord Thornton would have such a"—she circled one hand, searching for a fitting word—"*curiosity* in his possession. And *I* asked *you* to show me how the game was played, if you recall."

"Then you are not angry with me?"

"With you?" she scoffed. "If I let myself dwell for more than a moment on the thought of Lord Thornton looking on in satisfaction while some innocent parlor maid is made to dust and polish each of these pieces, I shall be furious indeed—with him."

He frowned and murmured in agreement, and she wondered whether there was another man in all her acquaintance who would have understood, to say nothing of shared, her righteous indignation.

"But in the absence of such thoughts," she went on in a lighter tone, "for a game between old marrieds such as ourselves, I confess I find the whole thing rather...amusing." She tilted her head to get a better look at a few of the pieces. "Even the queen doesn't seem to mind." The closest of the two female figures had her skirts hiked up almost to her waist and appeared to be pleasuring herself.

"Laura." The scold in Jeremy's voice was terrible, but a reluctant laugh tugged at the corners of his mouth.

Amusing, she had called it. *Arousing* would have been more honest. Not the chess pieces themselves, which were ridiculous, some adolescent boy's fantasy. But the soft, dim light. The memory of Jeremy's hand guiding hers, their heads bent together over the table. His solicitousness for her feelings. Those were the sorts of things that might make a woman's heart—and resistance—melt.

As could the anticipation of returning to their shared bed when he declared, "That's enough exploring for tonight."

He extinguished the candle, then rose to gather her into his arms. They ascended the servants' stairs in silence, their way lit by the single candle she'd carried down. She wanted to toss it aside and be free to lay her hand on his chest, to slide it over his shoulder and erase the last bit of space between them.

Oh, she did not want to *want* like this. To wonder like this.

Lady Sterling was quite unused to having her curiosity go unquenched.

Once in the blue bedchamber, he set her on the edge of the bed and took the candlestick from her, so that she could shed her dressing gown before lying down. Her nervous fingers fumbled with the tie. "I've been thinking..."

He placed the candlestick on the bedside table with a deliberate motion and said nothing. Tension radiated from him. She had felt it in his arms.

"I—I like you, Jeremy. I certainly didn't expect to, but I—I do."

Without turning, his head dipped in a mocking bow, the light of the candle highlighting every detail of his profile but casting his expression in shadow. "Am I now to thank you?"

"I shouldn't expect you to, no." She wound the end of one silk tie more tightly around her index finger. "But I did hope you might...kiss me."

A muscle ticked along his jaw. "Did you?"

"It would lend our performance as Lord and Lady Sterling a degree of authenticity."

"Even if no one sees?" One dark eyebrow rose in an incredulous arc.

"We...we could consider it further private rehearsal for our public roles."

"And will one kiss be sufficient rehearsal, do you think?" Slowly, he moved until he was facing her. He leaned forward, his hands resting on the mattress, one on either side of her hips. "Think carefully before you answer, because I cannot marry you, Laura." His gaze was remorseless, filled with something like anger. "You will never be Lady Sterling in earnest."

She wet her lips to speak and found them trembling. "You presume a great deal, my lord."

Instinctively, she had leaned away from him, which only seemed to encourage him to prowl closer. Close enough that she could see the truth: what she had mistaken for cruelty in the blue depths of his eyes was really pain. Pain, and a hunger she understood all too well.

"One kiss," she promised, closing the distance she had put between them. "No more."

"No more," he agreed and brought his mouth to hers.

Chapter 12

Twelve years had passed between Jeremy's first kiss and this one.

Twelve years also stood between his *last* kiss and the present moment. Twelve years since he'd inherited the title of Viscount Sterling and gone to the village pub, more to drown his sorrows than to celebrate, and Sally Miller, middle daughter of a local squire, had climbed into his lap and kissed him in front of half the townsfolk, and he'd realized that nothing would ever be the same again.

That afternoon, he'd discovered that a title he did not want and did not deserve nonetheless made him interesting to others. And eligible, in a way the son of the rector had never been. Knowing he could not afford to marry, Jeremy had gently set Sally aside and sworn off drink, kisses, and everything to which they might lead.

But twelve years, as it turned out, was a very long time. Long enough for such a vow to grow brittle, fragile. It turned to dust beneath the first brush of Laura's lips.

God, had anything ever been so soft and wonderful and warm? He was torn between wanting to devour their sweetness immediately and to savor it for an hour—for though she'd agreed to just one kiss, if he never lifted his mouth from hers, could not that one kiss go on forever?

Careful not to break the connection between them, he balanced his weight on one arm and slid the other hand beneath her head, tangling his fingers in her short, honey-gold curls and learning her gentle curves. The velvet plumpness of her lower lip. The peaks of the upper, as delightfully sharp as she. The advance and retreat of a dance for which he'd had no teacher and yet knew by heart.

If he was tentative, she was bold, wrapping her arms around his ribs and drawing him closer, welcoming his weight as he pressed her down into the mattress. He could feel her breasts rise and fall with her rapid breath, answering and echoing the drumming beat of his pulse.

Again and again, when the firm press of lips softened and shifted, he feared the end, thinking it could go on no longer. Then her lips parted beneath his, and he felt the wet heat of her breath, heard her greedy little murmur, and the kiss deepened. Open-mouthed and eager, she levered herself upward with one hand while the fingers of the other curled in his shirt, her nails lightly scoring the skin of his back. The first tentative touch of her tongue to his lips, a hint, a taste, and he was lost.

Not twelve years since his last kiss. Forever. And if he'd known such kisses existed in the world, he could never have survived the wait.

He opened to her, let her have her way, as she slipped her tongue inside his mouth, every stroke a lesson in pleasure and how to please. When she tilted her head, sealing their lips together, he took control of the kiss and showed her what he had learned. The erotic contrast of sharp teeth and slick tongue. The sensitive arc of the roof of the mouth. The trembling promise of a groan.

In his years in the army, he'd worked hard to develop a set of skills, numbers and letters, mathematics and languages, anything pertaining to the ancient art of cryptography.

Much as he might have wished it, however, those academic pursuits had not entirely erased his interest in other things. He'd spent a good deal too much time, alone in his monkish cell in the Underground, thinking of what it would be like to kiss a woman like Laura—

No. Not like Laura.

He had never been bold enough to conjure such a woman, even in his dreams.

One kiss. No more.

At the risk of breaking the kiss, and his promise, he shifted his lips from hers. One chance to know the velvet softness of her cheek, to explore the sensitive hollow beneath her ear, to feel the flutter of her pulse in her throat. To confirm that beneath her adamantine shell she hid a voluptuous, vulnerable core.

She hitched one leg over his hip and wrapped it around his waist to pull him closer yet, fitting their lightly clad bodies together as if they really were husband and wife, and he shuddered. She'd called him a gentleman, and a gentleman he would be, no matter how coarse his present thoughts.

Though *coarse* was hardly the right word to describe them: he could think of nothing but how she was soft as silk everywhere he touched, everywhere he wanted to touch, which rendered every inch of him rigid with need.

"I'm being poked." Her giggle hummed against his lips as he dragged them back up her throat to her mouth.

He stifled a groan, knowing he ought to apologize, though he wasn't sorry. He'd never been so hard. Though there was no hiding his state, he shifted a little, trying to oblige her. But that only seemed to make matters worse.

"Ow," she whispered, squirming beneath him. "What *is* that?"

"I, er..." *Oh, God.* Was there something wrong with him? Wasn't arousal a normal reaction to kisses? As quickly as he could make the taut muscles of his shoulders respond, he hoisted himself upright, taking all his weight onto his arms. "I'm sorry. I—" Heat rushed into his face.

She sat up too, her arms still wrapped around his body. "Not *that*, dearest husband." Her smile was sly, slightly naughty, not at all chagrined. "This." In a flash, she produced a thin book from behind his back and turned its cover toward the light. "Why did you tuck Lord Thornton's copy of *The Noble Game of Chess* into your breeches?"

Jeremy couldn't think of an answer. Every drop of blood seemed to have fled his brain, and he couldn't for the life of him remember what had possessed him to take the book from the library. When he finally did remember—because he believed the mistaken chess move might not be a simple misprint and wanted to study the pages at greater leisure—it wasn't an explanation he could offer to her.

And all the while, he was wondering how long *one kiss* might have lasted, how far they might have tested the limits of *no more*, if the spine of Philip Stamma's contribution to the game of kings hadn't jabbed Laura in the leg.

At the moment, he wished he'd let the damn book burn.

"Um. Well, you see..."

She tipped her head, the better to look him in the eye. "You did seem to be rather flustered by that naughty chessboard and in a hurry to get away. I suppose you must've accidentally—"

"Exactly," he agreed, snatching the book from her with one hand and running the other through his hair, as if by doing so he could set her appealingly tousled curls to rights. "Simple absentmindedness. I'll just take it back down now, shall I?" He tucked the volume under one arm and set about stuffing the hems of his shirt back into his breeches—when had they come loose? "You, um, you should retire for the night," he told her, nodding toward the bed and trying not to take pride in the fact that her breath was still a little ragged.

A frown flickered across her brow. "Are you…are you certain?"

"Yes," he lied. "I'm certain." One of them had to pretend. "Best if I—if you—well." She had lifted the sheets and was slowly sliding her bare legs into the bed. Oh, how he wanted to follow them, wanted nothing more than to revel in her kiss-swollen lips and her heavy-lidded eyes.

He picked up the candlestick. "I think I'll look around the library a bit more. Don't wait up."

She shuffled down in the bed and drew the covers up to her chin so that when she spoke, her voice was slightly muffled and he could no longer judge her tone. Disappointment? Mockery? "You'll take a chill."

God, he hoped so. A dip in an icy pond wouldn't go amiss, at the moment.

Except that even the thought of the cold, dark library made him want to stay and snuggle into the warm, downy bed with her.

"Your wifely concern is most touching."

Her smile peeked from beneath the linens, and some of the usual wry self-assurance returned to her expression. "You see? I told you that just one kiss would improve our performance as newlyweds."

He dipped his head. "I should never have doubted you."

"In future," she said, yawning as she settled into the pillow, "see that you don't."

"No, my lady." He stepped away from the bed, taking the candlelight with him. The shadows stretched between them. "I have learned my lesson."

He did not believe her passion had been an act. He knew his had not. Nevertheless, their fiery kiss was fresh proof that playing parts could be dangerous.

It was high time for him to remember his proper role: secret agent to the Crown.

* * * *

Lady Sterling had been kissed by half a dozen rakes, always with one part of her mind focused on evading their grasping hands, and the other part picturing the prize she intended to steal. She'd forgotten those kisses before they were over.

Laura herself was more of a novice in the art of kissing, having never had so much as a beau. Most of her experience was limited to listening to maids talk of bad breath and slobber, of tongues forced between lips and nearly down throats, and wondering how anyone could take pleasure in such an act.

Until tonight. Until that moment on the stairs, in Jeremy's arms, when she'd wanted...something. A closeness that wasn't merely practical, that definitely wasn't proper. Surely, in comparison to asking him to undress her and insisting he sleep in her bed, a simple kiss would be harmless?

Kisses, as it turned out, were not simple. They were wonderfully complex. A Shakespearean prologue that introduced the characters and established the tone and even revealed the plot—all without spoiling the play. Knowing how the story ended still left ample room to wonder how it got there, to wander the many side paths leading to that destination. Such a prologue merely whetted one's appetite for more.

And that, of course, was the problem. She had explicitly agreed to *no more*, and at the time, she had meant it. But kisses were quite pleasant after all when one liked the person doing the kissing. More than pleasant. Somewhere along the way, a kiss that had begun as gentle and tentative had transformed into something that did not quench fires but fanned them.

When had she grown cruel? Cruel to herself, for she still ached and wanted, even more than before. And cruel to him, for she felt certain he ached too, alone in the cold, dark library, where he'd so obviously fled rather than risk doing a dishonorable thing.

Not that kisses—or even more than kisses—were dishonorable in her view. What mattered was whether they were wanted by both parties.

Then she recalled the strange expression in his eyes. He'd been an eager participant in the kiss once things had got started, but she could not say that her suggestion of it had been precisely welcome. That glimpse of...something, rising from blue depths. Anger, she had thought at first. Frustration. Wariness. As if he'd bottled up some persistent pain until it was no longer recognizable as such—at least, not to those who did not wish to see it.

Hard on the heels of that enigmatic look had been his declaration that he would not marry her. Well, she neither wanted nor expected an offer of marriage. Not from him. Not from anyone.

It *had* smarted a bit, though, when he'd insisted that she would never be Lady Sterling in earnest, that hint that he did not think her worthy of sharing his title.

Upon reflection, however, she wondered whether his reservation stemmed from the same source as his pain. Not from her, but from something in his past, something inside himself. What might have happened to make an attractive, intelligent young gentleman decide never to...?

An ironic laugh rose her lips. Was not she an attractive, intelligent lady who had reached much the same decision? True, she had always considered the marital state as offering considerably more benefit to gentlemen than to ladies. Unless of course the lady was desperate, which she, thank God, was not.

Certainly not desperate enough to be thinking with any organ other than her brain. When had she ever let her desires dictate her behavior—other than a desire for vengeance, of course? Now, more than ever, she needed to be Lady Sterling, not Laura. She needed to put her investigative skills to use. Even if it meant spending more time than she liked thinking of Jeremy.

Right, then. Captain Addison had the same commanding officer as her brother. A coincidence? Unlikely. She'd always considered Fitz to be something of an idler. But Jeremy certainly did not strike her as such. Had she misjudged? Really, what sort of officers were allowed to hang about London, popping in for tea with their aunt or taking their sister to the theater? Or gallivanting off to Kent for a fortnight...?

No ordinary soldiers, that was certain. Would it be entirely too egotistical to think the British army really was after her?

Did they hope Lady Sterling would lead them to something important, something valuable?

Or had she done so already?

In the darkness, the memory of Jeremy's voice came to her: *You were telling me about...a book. Did you say your brother was involved somehow?*

She screwed shut her eyes and tried to remember everything Fitz had said and done the day he'd called unexpectedly on Aunt Mildred, who had been from home, and spotted an old book lying on the table by the window—the one she'd taken from Lord Thornton, with Mrs. Croft's help. He'd lifted the green cover, trying to pass off his nosiness as idle curiosity. Had he reacted somehow to what he'd seen when the title page was laid bare? Had he thumbed through the pages? Made a noise in his throat? Or was she embellishing the memory?

She couldn't be certain. She could remember her own surprise at his interest; Fitz had never been much of one for books. Even greater had been her astonishment at his subsequent offer to see what could be got for it, after she'd lied about both its provenance and its purpose. She had assumed he'd intended to perform a kindness for their aunt, nothing more. But what if his motives had been...well, not *selfish*, exactly? Not altruistic, either.

Jeremy's interest in books struck her as more in keeping with his character, though she hardly knew him well enough to make any such claim. But he had a scholar's pallor, and he remembered not just the plots of plays, but scenes and lines and actors. Fitz might have squired his sister to every performance at Covent Garden for a season and still been immune to such knowledge.

Of course, what was truly striking was Jeremy's interest in the story of one particular book, and in Lord Thornton's prior possession of it. Jeremy might have been sent to follow her, but he did not regret the fact that she'd led him here.

She recalled the way he had scanned the shelves downstairs, the principles guiding his search still unclear to her. Once she had told him about the cookbook, he clearly expected there would be something more in Thornton's library—but more of what? What did the earl have that Jeremy—and the British army—wanted? Her fingertips crept down to test the small tender place behind her knee left by *The Noble Game of Chess*. Why had he secreted the little book out of the study? Had he found what he sought?

Had she?

Slowly, she drew her fingers up the inside of her leg. The ache at the joining of her thighs had quieted to an occasional throb of heightened awareness. Like the chess queen, she had only to lift the hem of her shift to silence that second pulse—for the time being, anyway. With her first finger, she stirred the sensitive hairs through the thin cotton; the lightest brush, and still it made her breath quicken.

Whether it was wrong to touch herself was not a question she ever entertained. It harmed no one and cleared her head for more important things. But would it be wrong to touch herself and think of Jeremy? Disrespectful, somehow, to imagine his blunt-tipped fingers in place of her own, raising her shift and parting her crisp curls?

If he came back at just that moment and caught her, glimpsed her flushed cheeks by the light of his candle, heard the telltale slickness and saw the busy rhythm of her hand beneath the linens—*oh*—he would blush too, at first, and look away. She could almost picture him, there by the door. But then... then—*ooh*—the man who had kissed her with such hunger would surely step closer, his eyes dark with understanding and, yes, desire. Would he be content to watch or would he set aside the candlestick and join her in the bed? Would he touch himself? Touch her—?

"*Aaaah.*" Her climax shuddered from her, unmuffled and unrepentant.

The door to the bedchamber remained closed.

After a few moments, as her breath and pulse returned to their normal, steady pace, her tangled thoughts began to smooth and order themselves, like ruffled waters after a storm.

She had been moved by Jeremy's affection for his sister and his grief over the loss of his father. She had been intrigued by the idea that he knew her brother, knew her, knew things about her, like her fear of the rain, that she doubted even Fitz understood.

She should never have let herself lose sight of the fact that this man was interested not in Laura Hopkins, but in Lady Sterling.

Well, he had found her. Accompanied her to Thornton Hall. And now, thanks to her injured ankle and a spur-of-the-moment decision to claim he was her husband, she required his help. But if he found something in the study that brought the earl down, it would be worth it.

Needing Jeremy was only a temporary arrangement.

And wanting him, she thought as she tugged her shift back down to her knees where it belonged, *was a problem that could be easily and efficiently addressed.*

Chapter 13

"Were you ill, milady?"

In the dressing table mirror, Laura saw Dinah's reflection tilt her head to the side and watch with uneasy fascination as Laura dampened her fingers and twisted sections of her hair, each time leaving behind a springy curl. The early morning sunlight had given Laura's golden locks a reddish hue.

"Pardon?"

"Whyever did you cut off all your lovely hair?"

"Because it's eminently practical," Laura said, smiling as she tucked the last curl into place. For one thing, it was much easier to disguise beneath a wig. "And fashionable."

But most of all, because my papa forbad me to do it.

"If you say so, milady," agreed Dinah doubtfully. Her hands not needed for the arrangement of Lady Sterling's hair, she was busying herself with tidying the few items in the dressing room. She plucked up a gentleman's shirt to shake it out, and several sheets of paper fluttered to the floor. "Oh, dear."

Laura turned and held out her hand for them, and the maid obliged without obviously trying to pry into their contents. When Laura glanced down, she discovered that Dinah would have seen very little, even if she had studied them for an hour. The small pages, folded together, were covered with the bold strokes of a masculine hand, columns of letters and numbers that appeared to have been copied from *The Noble Game of Chess*, with a few emendations.

W.				B.		
p	~~e~~e	4		p	e	5
g	f	3		~~d~~b	c	6
f	c	~~7~~?		f	c	5

And so it went, down the rest of the page and onto the next.

Though she could make neither heads nor tails of the changes, she was so absorbed in the effort, she did not realize they were no longer alone until Dinah dropped into a deep curtsy. "Good morning, milord."

"I'll assist my wife from here," Jeremy told her in a gruff voice. "You may go."

Dinah scampered past, then hesitated on the threshold of the open doorway between the dressing room and the bedchamber. "Shall I—shall I bring the breakfast tray, milady?"

"Thank you, Dinah." She darted a glance toward Jeremy. "In a quarter of an hour?"

At his brusque nod, the girl was gone, leaving Laura at liberty to study Jeremy's glower. As his discarded linen and the folded notes had made plain, he must have returned at some point after she had fallen asleep, though she was certain he had not returned to their bed. He was fully dressed now, and in his own clothes, which had been sponged and pressed by Thornton's valet. She would have said he looked perfectly respectable, if not for the smudges of shadow beneath his eyes, which somehow made his scowl fiercer still, and the unshaven state of his jaw, which made him look like a ruffian.

A very handsome ruffian.

"I did not think you would snoop," he said, snatching the notes from her fingers.

"Those papers weren't exactly hidden. Dinah found them when she picked up the shirt you wore last night," Laura said, and went back to fidgeting with her hair for something to do with her hands. "I don't know what you imagine you have to be angry with me about. It's not as if anyone can read the things. It's like they're written in some kind of—"

Her speech slowed as she neared the end of the sentence, and though the word *code* never passed her lips, all the pieces of the puzzle fell into place behind it. The cookbook. Captain Addison of the British army. A game of chess.

"You're a spy," she breathed, more to herself than him as she spun about on the dressing table stool to face him.

He opened his mouth to deny it, then crumpled the papers in his hand and sagged against the door frame. "Apparently not a very good one."

"Because I figured it out?" She shook her head. "You mustn't expect to be able to keep such things from your wife."

"Laura." Again that half-pleading, half-scolding note. He crossed his arms over his chest and squared his shoulders, as if steeling himself for whatever she might say next.

She thought she'd cured herself of last night's unwelcome attraction to him. But she had to admit there was something unexpectedly appealing about a handsome man with an unshaven jaw leaning in a doorway.

Gripping the edge of the dressing table, she got to her feet and took a hobbling step toward him. "You might as well tell me the rest while you help me into the other room."

He didn't immediately move to pick her up and carry her, for which she was at first grateful. She didn't trust herself to be able to hold those inconvenient feelings at bay while wrapped in his arms and cradled against his chest.

But as it turned out, curling an arm around his taut waist and leaning heavily against his side was equally likely to stir up unwanted sensations.

"Bed?" he asked, and it might as well have been last night all over again, so powerful was the physical memory of him pressing her into the mattress with that kiss.

"Sofa," she answered with a determined shake of her head, only partly to disguise a shiver of longing. "I'm not an invalid."

"As you wish." Their thighs brushed on the first slow, careful step. "My dear."

The last two words were tacked on, a sort of teasing afterthought. So why was she so glad to hear him speak them?

They were a reminder that all of this—the words, the solicitousness, even the kiss—were pieces of a performance. A performance with a specific, and important, goal: to keep Lord Thornton from preying on his housemaids and his children's governess. Laura's first sight of Jeremy this morning, his tousled hair and the inky scruff shadowing the sharp angle of his jaw, had almost made her forget.

"So...?" she prompted, hoping that what he had to tell her would be sufficient to distract her from the twinges in her ankle, and elsewhere, as they progressed across the floor. "You're a spy."

"That's not a word to be bandied about lightly," he cautioned her, his voice low. "Not, in fact, a word I would choose to use at all. I'm a code breaker. Or fancied I was."

"And Lord Thornton?"

"I'm not sure." A long pause. "But I've seen enough to be suspicious."

"Of?"

He pressed his lips together, as if deciding whether to say more. "This is dangerous stuff, not some youthful indiscretion or a stolen pocket watch to be lorded over him." When she only looked at him expectantly, a reluctant sigh shuddered from his lungs. "I believe he may be engaged in treason."

"Treason?" Despite what Jeremy had said, that seemed like precisely the kind of information Lady Sterling could use.

"Laura." His voice had lost that thread of humor, as if he knew what she'd been thinking. "I'm sure even the maidservants at Thornton Hall would prefer their master not be found guilty of aiding the French. Because if he is, he'll be swinging from the end of a rope."

"But he's an earl."

"That can change," he said as he tossed the crumpled papers on the side table and then helped her to sit down. "For this, he can be stripped of his title, made to face his crimes as a commoner. *If* I'm right." Slipping one hand beneath her calf, he matter-of-factly lifted her foot, while with the other he arranged the pillow on the footstool just so. As if, after only two days, caring for her had become a matter of course. As if, last night, *care* had not given way to something more carnal. "But I cannot—cannot quite—"

"Is this all to do with the misprint in the chess book?" she asked, picking up his notes and smoothing them against her outstretched leg.

"More than one, at least as I remember Stamma's instructions. I spent most of the night playing out chess moves—in my head," he hastened to add as he sank into the nearby chair. "And I don't think they're misprints." He nodded toward the papers she held. "But the pattern eludes me. I've tried four languages and every algebraic twist I can think of, and still I can't sort out the meaning of the changes."

Once more Laura studied the columns of letters and numbers he had written, the cross-outs and question marks. *Four languages? Algebra?* She had misjudged Jeremy in more ways than she could count. "I always thought coded messages were brief and to the point—a letter, a note on a scrap of paper. It seems an awful lot of trouble to print and bind a whole book, and then—and then just tuck it away on a library shelf? How does that help the French or—or anyone?"

"Both the code and the method of conveyance depend on what sort of information needs to be encrypted," he explained. "But I suspect what Thornton has in his possession is the cypher, the key that allows a code to be broken."

She weighed that information against what she already knew. "And the cookbook?"

"The same principles apply." He tipped his head back against the chair to stare at the ceiling. "I've been cudgeling my brains for weeks over that one, though I'm no closer to understanding how it works. And now," he sighed, "there's another."

Thank God for her sore ankle, or she might have given in to the sudden urge to go to him and stroke gentle fingers over his temples and whisper words of reassurance to ease his fatigue. The way a wife might.

He had obviously set aside last night's intimacies, and she would be well-advised to do the same.

She busied her hands with refolding the notes instead. "And Fitz is…he knew, then, what he'd found? Or rather, what *I* had found?"

His head moved against the chair's high back in a sort of nod. "I'd just decoded a message about the theft of a priceless codebook disguised as a French cookbook. He and several other field agents were on the lookout for it."

"Surely he suspected I wasn't telling the truth about where I'd got it?"

A shrug. "He might have thought someone was trying to erase their connection to it, or using your aunt as an innocent go-between to pass it off." At last he lifted his head from the chair and trained his gaze on her, clear and intense despite his fatigue. "Any man who cared for you would want to get it far away as swiftly as possible. The story about taking it to the bookshops was quick thinking on his part."

"A bargain at fifty pounds," she said with a wry smile, torn between offering to repay her brother and asking him why, since he'd made up the sum, he hadn't given her more. Mrs. Croft might've had a small fortune. "And I thought it wouldn't fetch fifty shillings."

"Why shouldn't a rare old book fetch a fair price?"

"The bindings were old, I'll grant. But the value of a cookbook is in its use, and that one obviously was no favorite." A puzzled frown notched the space between his brows. "The pages were pristine," she explained.

"The pages?" His frown deepened. "But—"

A tap at the door presaged Dinah's entry with the breakfast tray. Jeremy leaped to his feet to help her with it. "Thank you, milord," she said, wide-eyed.

"I spoke gruffly to you earlier, and I had no cause. I'm sorry."

That apology rendered the maid speechless. Laura could well imagine she did not often hear the like in Thornton Hall. "I was just trying to explain something to Lord Sterling," Laura said, pulling the girl's startled gaze to herself. "Tell me, does the cook here rely much on a cookbook?"

"A book o' receipts, like, you mean? Oh, aye. Her ladyship's most partic'lar."

"Does the cook have a favorite?"

"Aye, milady." She glanced uncertainly toward Jeremy, who was pouring himself a cup of coffee, and seemed to debate where her duty lay: tending to the breakfast tray for his lordship or answering her ladyship's odd questions. "One or two."

"And what do the pages of those books look like?"

Dinah's expression was now nearly as puzzled as Jeremy's. "Look like, milady? How do you mean?"

"The paper itself. Is it clean?"

"Oh, gracious no. Why, some of the pages are so spattered with grease you could use 'em for windows. An' flour, an' meal, an' bits o' this an' that stuck here an' there. You must know how it is, milady, or you wouldn't have asked."

"I do."

Jeremy approached and handed the cup and saucer to her. "I thought you said you weren't skilled in the domestic arts," he said in an undertone.

She accepted the cup and took a sip before replying in an equally low voice. "But I like to eat. And over the years, Lady Sterling has befriended a number of cooks."

"Tell me," he said, turning back toward the tray and toward Dinah, "does the cook ever prepare dishes in the French style?"

"I couldn't say, milord. I don't wait at table, an' we wouldn't have such in the servants' hall. Was there somethin' in particular you fancied, sir?"

"No. I was only thinking…no matter," he said, with a little shake of his head, as if to cast off his distraction. "Thank you, and thank the cook, for the tray. We'll manage from here."

"Aye, milord," Dinah replied with a curtsy and was gone.

Absently, Jeremy poured a second cup of coffee, stirred it vigorously though he had not added either milk or sugar, and then wandered back to his chair. As Laura eyed the remaining contents of the tray, stacks of buttered toast and a plate of coddled eggs with the steam still rising from it, her stomach rumbled. Jeremy seemed not to hear.

"Of course," he cried a moment later, and set aside the cup of coffee, untasted.

"'Of course' what?"

His only answer was to leap to his feet and begin to pace before the fire as he had on the evening of their arrival, though now the hearth was empty and he was wearing his boots, polished to a mirror shine. The length of the mantel could be measured in three long-legged strides and a turn. She watched him repeat the process in each direction: one, two, three, turn. Today's breeches were considerably more well-fitting than last night's.

Finally, on his fourth pass, he did not pause and turn back, but instead skirted the breakfast table and came to sit beside her on the sofa. "Don't you see?" he demanded, and in the morning light, his eyes were dazzling. "A real cookbook would look considerably more like the ones Dinah described."

"Yes," she agreed. "That's precisely why I doubted it was of much val—"

"It's a copy," he spoke across her, unable to contain his enthusiasm. "With some slight changes to the original. The quantity of an ingredient, for instance. Just like—"

With one fingertip, she unfolded the notes lying in her lap. "The moves in *The Noble Game of Chess.*"

"Precisely. And if the genuine article is as common as Stamma's guide, I will be able to find the real cookbook, compare them, sort out the differences, and perhaps with a more complete picture, I'll—"

"You'll know the cypher." He nodded eagerly. "Last night," she ventured after a moment, "you were surprised by the number of ordinary books in Thornton's study. Do you suppose—?"

"That the Latin primer and his copy of Euclid are similarly error-prone? Quite possible, I'd say." His hand shot out—for his notes, she thought at first. Then his fingers closed around hers. "There could be a dozen more."

"A dozen? How would Thornton, or anyone, determine which cypher to use when a coded message arrives?"

"They'll likely have a code for that too. A single word would be enough. Who would bat an eye at a letter that began by mentioning having enjoyed a favorite dish?"

My, but his hand was warm where it rested against her thigh. "Or playing a game of chess."

"They cannot all be as memorable as ours," he said and winked.

Her heart leaped, like a roe starting at danger. It was entirely too easy to want him when he looked at her that way; worse, when she herself was flushed with success. She had ferreted out another of his secrets, rather like a code breaker herself.

Her conscience prickled warningly at that notion, though she tried to ignore it. She had not let that beast trouble her for some time, at least where men were concerned.

He revealed who and what he is, whispered a quiet voice inside, *because he trusts you.*

Ruthlessly, she probed her heart, her mind, hoping to rouse the part of herself that earlier had found Jeremy naïve, a means to an end. But she found only softness toward him, in the place where a plate of armor ought to be.

Well, it was really no surprise that she would feel something like desire for a man who was handsome and gentle—

And brilliant, piped up that annoying voice.

Laura glanced down at the notes. *Very well.* Jeremy was handsome, gentle, *and* brilliant. Wanting such a man was understandable. Needing him was, at present, unavoidable.

More than that? Impossible.

As if he also recognized the impossibility, Jeremy squeezed her fingers once, released them, and stood. "I've got to get back to London. I'll make some excuse about the house party and—"

"What about Miss Godfrey, Dora, and the others?" Laura asked quietly, to disguise a rush of panic at this sudden change of plans, at their inevitable separation.

"They'll be safest when Thornton is gone for good."

"But—" she protested automatically, though it was a premise with which she could not argue.

Jeremy smiled knowingly at her and plucked his notes from her fingertips. "This time, my dear, I think *Lord* Sterling must be the one to set the trap for the villain."

My dear. He was teasing, yet her heart warmed to those words. When he set about filling a plate from the breakfast tray and then handed it to her, as if thinking of her needs first was the most ordinary thing in the world to him, she felt the last reserves of steel in her spine, the ones she relied upon when things were toughest, begin to melt.

She reached for the plate, but he did not immediately release it. "I've forgotten Mr. Phelps," he said, his brows knit together over this fresh puzzle. "He's sure to say you shouldn't travel with that ankle."

"I had wondered if perhaps you intended to leave me here."

Annoyance twitched across his features at the suggestion. "You're the one I was sent to find. Besides, I'll need your help in concocting an excuse for our abrupt departure."

It was hardly a declaration, but still her spirits lifted at the suggestion that he needed her too. "Have you seen *Repent at Leisure*? No?" *Probably for the best.* "Leave it to me, then. But I think before Mr. Phelps arrives, you should shave."

"The part calls for boyish charm, eh?" he asked, scrubbing one hand over his jaw.

The gesture made her own fingers tingle. "Not exactly." In fact, his present roguish appearance was more suited to the role he was about, unwittingly, to play.

But she needed to concentrate, and she was struggling to keep herself from imagining how his lips would feel against her skin now, that hint of roughness.

Oh, she was helpless. Hopeless.

How utterly foolish of her to have asked him for just one kiss.

Chapter 14

Jeremy was wiping the last traces of shaving soap from his jaw when a knock at the door heralded the arrival of Lady Thornton and Mr. Phelps. As he hurried to knot his cravat, he listened to them greet Laura in the soft, concerned tones generally reserved for the very ill. He could picture her wan smile of reply as well as the exasperated roll of her eyes that hid behind it, though the countess and the physician would never notice the deception. She was an excellent actress, just as she'd said, more than capable of charming when and whom she wished.

Perhaps he'd been wrong to offer her honesty, when it was impossible to know what he would receive it in return.

The fight against Thornton had forged a connection between them; Jeremy had been ready to help punish the despicable man even before Laura had revealed his connection to the cookbook. It was tempting to tell himself that their shared mission was reason enough to trust her with information he would never have revealed under ordinary circumstances.

But he knew that wasn't the sole explanation. Despite his best intentions, last night's kiss had changed everything between them. Despite what he had told her, he wanted more. He was beginning to enjoy thinking of her as Lady Sterling.

And that was nearly as dangerous as talk of codes, spies, and treason.

In the next room, voices had risen above a murmur. Lady Thornton was making noises of concern, and Mr. Phelps, sounds of protest. A sudden rush of nerves assailed Jeremy, as if he really were an actor waiting in the wings for his cue. He'd felt much the same on that day in General Scott's home, realizing how ill-prepared he was for the part his commanding officer expected him to play.

Whether his performance earned rave reviews or rotten fruit depended a great deal on what happened next.

He slipped on his coat, tugged the sleeves into place, and stepped into the bedchamber. "Is there some problem, ma'am?" Though he'd intended to address those words to his supposed wife, Lady Thornton was the first to turn and look. Laura stared resolutely ahead, a mulish expression on her face.

Mr. Phelps, who had been crouched beside the sofa where Laura sat, rose and shook his head. "Perhaps you will have better luck, my lord."

"Luck with what?" Jeremy asked, stepping closer to the trio.

Laura twisted her head and fixed him with a glare. "With me," she snapped.

"Her ladyship refuses an examination, my lord," Phelps explained, rather hesitantly. "She says that—"

"I see no need for him to poke and prod," said Laura. "Whether the ankle is healed or not, you will refuse to take me home."

While shaving, he had given some thought to what Laura's plan might be. Her aunt and Julia shared similar tastes for farce and comedy, so he thought he could guess what sort of school *Repent at Leisure* represented, though the particular play was unfamiliar.

He had not considered that he was to be the villain of the piece.

"My husband," Lady Thornton explained to the physician, "expects a number of gentlemen to arrive shortly for cards and shooting—"

"And other sport, I'm sure," Laura interjected, sending another gray-eyed glare in his direction, before turning back to Phelps. "He has invited Lord Sterling to be one of the party. Meanwhile, I am to sit here quietly, all alone, and make no complaint, for—my lord and master says—it was my own stupidity that brought us to this pass to begin with and a sore ankle is the least of what I deserve."

"Now, now, Lady Sterling," Mr. Phelps murmured in a voice of practiced consolation, "have you any left of that tonic I prescribed?"

"He took it," she cried and pointed at Jeremy with a shaking finger. It was true, of course; he'd slipped the little vial into his pocket after she'd hit her head. "By coming after me when I ran away, he ensured that everyone would believe him the devoted husband. But the truth is, he wants me to suffer."

Even knowing she but played a part, he had to stop himself from fumbling to return the bottle to her. She was, as she'd said from the first, the better actor. Still, he must rise to the occasion. If she wanted a villain, she would have one.

Ignoring her pained expression, he stepped closer, stopping a little more than an arm's length from the back of the sofa and setting his feet apart in a dominant stance. "Would you compete with me over who suffers more in this marriage, ma'am? I assure you, I like my odds."

Laura covered her mouth with her handkerchief and blinked at him, as if momentarily dumbfounded by his reply, and he feared he had drastically mistaken the role he was to play. Then he realized that while she was indeed surprised by the energy with which he had taken up the part, mostly she was trying to hide a smile.

Lady Thornton twisted her fingers before her in a show of worry, and again he had the sense the countess was in her element, relishing the drama while pretending to care. "Oh, dear. Of course, my husband did tell me there was some…misunderstanding between you and Lady Sterling earlier, but I thought, after yesterday, all that was past. That story about your marvelous proposal—"

"All a ruse, ma'am," Laura said, her voice and her eyes cool as she gave him a last dismissive glance before turning toward Lady Thornton. "He acted the lover, but it was my dowry he desired, and he followed me into Kent to ensure our marriage was consummated so that nothing could come between him and my money."

Even the physician looked shocked by her bold words, and Lady Thornton developed a sudden fascination with the pattern of the hearthrug. "Oh, my," she breathed and fanned herself with a handkerchief. Jeremy wondered whether she might not go so far as to pretend to faint. Was there anyone in Thornton Hall not playing a part?

He lifted his chin and looked straight at Laura, trying not to let himself imagine how close he'd come last night to doing with her what the others now believed him to have done. How close he'd come to making her his. "I think you mean *my* money, dearest wife."

Laura made a noise in her throat reminiscent of an angry cat, which he answered with a world-weary laugh. Then her lip trembled, most convincingly. "I want to go home."

Unwittingly, he took a half step closer to her, some words of reassurance ready on his tongue. Phelps, who seemed to regard the movement more in the nature of a threat to his patient, came around the corner of the sofa to stand between them, one hand raised.

Jeremy mustered another laugh. "Very well, my dear. We will leave the moment Thornton's carriage can be made ready to take us. I'll go down and explain the situation to him myself," he said, moving toward the door. "You'd best let the good doctor have a look at that ankle, though, for I won't hear one complaint about it on our journey. And," he added, opening the door, "once you are installed at Everham, my lady, do not expect ever to leave. No, not so much as a visit to the milliner. I know your tricks now. You will not get away from me so easily again."

Once in the corridor, with the door closed behind him, he paused to collect himself. Had he said the right things? Done the right things? Then he reminded himself of the urgency of his mission. He had to get back to London as quickly as possible, no matter what.

He did not descend via the servants' stair, but took the more public route, striding along the corridor to the grand staircase at the center of the house. He found the library, empty of their host. Grateful for the solitude, he stepped to the desk, took up the nearest sheet of blank paper, dipped a pen in the salacious inkwell, and set out to write a note of explanation.

The first drop of ink revealed the page had not been blank. Blackness seeped into the fibers of the paper, filling in around the lines made by the colorless liquid with which the letter had been written. Letters, fragments of words, took shape:

Dea
The
a ba
E

Jeremy's heart began to thud, loudly enough that he almost missed the approach of footsteps. Quickly, he blew on the page to dry the blot of ink, then folded the letter and stuffed it in his breast pocket alongside the notes from *The Noble Game of Chess.*

By the time the earl reached the threshold, Jeremy was striding toward him. "There you are, Thornton. I thought I'd find you here. I'm sorry to say that my shrew of a wife demands to leave this very moment, and I must ask you to make good on your offer of the loan of your traveling coach."

Thornton arched one brow. "What did I say about teaching her to know her master, Sterling? You young pups will be henpecked to death if you refuse to heed the voice of experience."

"Believe me, sir, I have taken your words to heart," Jeremy insisted. "I intend to take her back to town until Everham can be transformed into a suitable prison. She'll learn her lesson, I think, with no company and no entertainments."

"No company? Barring the occasional conjugal visit, I assume?" Thornton asked, leering.

"If the work of the past two nights proves insufficient," Jeremy agreed with a bitter sort of laugh and shrugged. "One must have an heir."

Thornton joined in the laughter, clapping Jeremy's shoulder. "I would tell you to send her and stay yourself, but...

"Lady Sterling is not to be trusted," Jeremy finished for him.

"Ah, well. You are welcome to return with the coach, if you wish, and join me and my friends. After a journey like that, you will be sorely in need of rational company."

Jeremy knew full well the sort of company in which he would have found himself had he stayed, and *rational* was the last word he would have used to describe it. "A generous offer, Thornton." He paused, as if weighing the matter. "I would not wish to delay your servants. But I suppose I might leave her under the supervision of some trusted friends. Yes, I think I shall come back to Thornton Hall, as quickly as I can make arrangements."

Arrangements for sufficient men and arms to arrest a traitor.

"Very good, Sterling," Thornton said, giving his shoulder a squeeze before releasing him. The papers in his pocket crinkled beneath the press of the other man's thumb, but the earl evidently did not notice, or if he did, the sound did not raise his curiosity. "I'll order the coach brought round."

"I'm in your debt, sir." Jeremy bowed and walked from the room at a leisurely pace.

Had he given Phelps enough time to tend to Laura's ankle? Given Lady Thornton enough time to fuss and exclaim and generally alert the household to the latest gossip about their guests, as Laura must have hoped when invoking that play? At the far end of the corridor, he thought he saw Dinah scurry through the door to the servants' stair, perhaps on her way to pack their meager belongings. After a count of ten, he followed her.

The stairwell was nearly as shadowy as it had been last night, and he thought of how he'd carried Laura up and down these steep, well-worn steps, little imagining—

No. In the privacy of his thoughts, he surely did not have to lie. He had been imagining what it would be like to kiss Laura the very first time he'd put his arms around her.

Well, perhaps not the first time, at Vauxhall, when she had run pell-mell into him in the dark. Then, he'd fancied he was only doing a good deed, helping some poor young woman who'd got herself into the hands of the wrong man.

Had she ended up in the arms of the right one?

General Scott would surely say yes. Jeremy still had his doubts.

Footsteps echoed in the stairwell, and he pressed himself against the wall to allow the servant coming down to pass unimpeded. But as luck would have it, the light tread belonged to Miss Godfrey, who was descending from the schoolroom.

"Oh!" Her hand flew to her chest when she spied him. "Lord Sterling. What a fright you gave me. I didn't expect to see you on the servants' stair."

"It is the quickest route to the blue room, as you most helpfully pointed out on the night of our arrival. And I'm glad we've met here," he went on, lowering his voice even further, "for there's something Lady Sterling would wish you to know. We're leaving for London as soon as the coach can be got ready."

"Leaving?" Her fingers curled convulsively, wrinkling her fichu. "But what of Lord Thornton—? And his guests—?"

"We have a plan, never fear. I hope to be back before the other... gentlemen arrive, and once I return, you will be perfectly safe. He will not be at liberty to harm you or anyone else. But between now and then, look sharp." He offered her an encouraging smile. "Keep that hat pin to hand."

Miss Godfrey did not look reassured, but she nodded. "I will, my lord."

He bowed and let her pass, then made his way to the landing and out onto the corridor. All was quiet when he stopped beside the door to the blue room. After a moment's hesitation, he opened it.

Lady Thornton and Mr. Phelps had gone. Laura still sat sideways on the sofa, both legs stretched across the cushions, her skirts carefully arranged so that her injured ankle did not show, her reticule nestled in her lap. Her eyes appeared to be closed, and she was dabbing at the end of her pink nose with her handkerchief. *Crying.* Was her pain so great, then? Had he entered into his part with too much enthusiasm and upset her in earnest?

The click of the door latch alerted her to his presence. Her eyes popped open, red and watery, but she crumpled the handkerchief in the palm of one hand and pressed a finger to her lips, then pointed to the dressing room. Through the open doorway he could hear various rummaging noises, accompanied by a whistled tune.

"Dinah," Laura mouthed, then motioned him closer.

"Are you all right?" His face, he knew, must make his question as plain as the movement of his lips.

She favored him with a watery smile and revealed a silver vinaigrette in her hand, half hidden by the handkerchief. "Lady Thornton insisted on giving me her smelling salts. I think"—amusement twitched about her lips, even as her eyes continued to stream tears—"I think I've singed the hairs in my nose."

Relief rushed from his lungs in the form of a silent laugh.

"I can't seem to find your bonnet, Lady Sterling," Dinah called from the other room.

Laura waggled her fingers, shooing him toward the door. "Make an entrance, Lord Sterling" was her silent demand.

He nodded and stepped back, silently opening the door and then shutting it firmly. "Well, madam. The carriage has been ordered. You may dispense with the tears—they'll earn you no sympathy from me."

Dinah appeared in the doorway and gave him a bold stare before dipping into the shallowest of curtsies. "Milord."

"Are the bags ready?"

"Aye, milord. All set, 'cepting her ladyship's bonnet."

"It was ruined on the journey." Laura sniffled. "I left it and my gloves behind in that dreary little pub."

That answer earned him another glare from the maid, as if she suspected he were somehow responsible for the loss. "Well, then. That's that." Her voice softened as she focused once more on Laura. "Be there anythin' else, milady?"

Laura blew her nose and then shook her head. "No, Dinah," she said in a quiet, ragged voice. "Thank you for your many kindnesses. I shall not forget them."

"Of course, milady." She gathered up their bags, one in each hand, and walked toward the door, casting a chary glance his way as she passed.

"I've spoken to Thornton," Jeremy said to Laura, pretending to ignore the maid. "He's invited me to return, once I've delivered you home, and I intend to. Why should I not enjoy...?" He spoke louder than necessary until he felt certain Dinah was out of earshot. "Well." He lowered his voice to its normal tone and stepped closer to Laura, crouching down beside the sofa. "That was an adventure. We've certainly given them lots to talk about after we're gone."

"Distraction is the watchword," she reminded him. "I hated to give you such a despicable part to play. I did not think it in your nature. But you acquitted yourself well." The slightest uncertainty in her voice made him wonder whether he had played the part a little too convincingly.

"I think you mean, I acquitted myself terribly. I have heard actors claim that the villain's role is always the most enjoyable to perform, but—" He gave a shiver of distaste. "I don't think Dinah will ever forgive me, particularly not if she learns of the things I said to you earlier."

Laura's lips twisted with a wry smile of satisfaction. "Which I have no doubt she will, at the rate word seems to travel around Thornton Hall." Then her expression shifted again, and the hint of approval left her eyes.

"She thought you handsome and charming from the first. When you apologized to her this morning, you gave her a spark of hope that some gentlemen were different from those she's had the misfortune to know." She dropped her gaze and fiddled with the vinaigrette. "Skepticism and wariness will serve her better."

"Men aren't to be trusted, you mean?"

She drew a pleat in the damp handkerchief, between her first and second fingers. "I think you already know the answer. Sometimes we women have little choice but to trust, of course. But it's not easy to know which men deserve that honor...and which ones may be simply acting a part. Better to assume the worst." Before he could form a reply, knowing she was not wrong and reluctant to defend himself or anyone else, she shook off her grimness and offered him a weak smile. "She'll likely come around again where you're concerned, though, when you clap Thornton in irons and save her sister from an ignoble fate."

"Is that all I must do?" He slapped his hands against his thighs with considerably more heartiness than he felt and pushed himself to standing. "Well, I'd best get to it, then. You are ready?"

She nodded and swung her legs over the side of the sofa, curling the fingers of one hand around the drawstring of her reticule and reaching up with the other for him to help her rise. "Mr. Phelps bound the ankle again, so it feels stronger. I think I can walk, so long as you are willing to go slow."

He understood how highly she valued her independence. But he also understood the importance of haste. "Would it not be more in keeping for the dastardly Lord Sterling to sling you over his shoulder and toss you into the coach?" he teased.

"You may be right," she conceded with a laugh. "But I'll settle for being carried down in the regular way. One last time."

One last time. One final excuse to gather her in his arms and hold her close, to behave as if she really were his wife. He bowed over her outstretched hand. "It would be my pleasure, Lady Sterling."

Chapter 15

Not until the earl's traveling coach lumbered away from Thornton Hall did Laura allow herself to breathe easily.

"Were you worried?"

Jeremy did not pull his gaze from the window as he spoke. He was seated across from her and surely could neither have felt nor heard her sigh of relief. His perceptiveness, the way he seemed to read her feelings and anticipate her reactions, ought to have been disquieting, yet she caught herself exhaling again, easing into the comfort of his presence.

After two days of autumnal weather, the warmth of summer had returned to tease them. She unbuttoned her pelisse as she spoke. "Weren't you?"

The corner of his mouth curled in something that wasn't quite a smile. "I still am." He reached into his breast pocket, withdrew some papers, and held them out to her: the notes from earlier, which she recognized, and what looked to be the start of a letter. "I thought I would have to leave a note for Thornton, explaining our departure. I found this, instead. I don't know if it was wise to take it, but I needed some way to test my theory about the cyphers."

"An unfinished letter?" She turned the sheet of foolscap this way and that in the light.

"Not unfinished. It's the second letter I've seen in Thornton's possession that seemed to be written in some form of invisible ink. When I put the pen to what I thought was a blank sheet of paper, the words began to appear. Once I get access to the proper tools, I'll be able to reveal the rest. What's written on that page," he said, nodding toward it, "may show me how the cypher is to be used."

She heard a note of hesitation in his voice. "But?"

"If Thornton notices it's missing, figures out I've taken it, well..." He leaned back, tossed the papers onto the seat beside him, and rubbed the back of his neck with one hand.

"He'll be too occupied with preparations for his guests to spare a thought for his correspondence," she said, not knowing whether it was true but wanting to reassure him.

"Let's hope."

With nervous fingers, she plucked at the ribbon of her reticule, her own uncertainty bubbling inside her chest. "I understand, of course, that what Lord Thornton may be involved in could affect the safety and security of far more than his household staff. Nevertheless, I fear what might befall Dora in the next few days," she confessed in a rush. "Or Miss Godfrey. I didn't even have a chance to speak with her before we departed. I've been so busy trying to distract everyone around us, I think I—I let myself be a little distracted too."

Leaning forward, elbows on his knees, he reached for her hands. "I saw her on the servants' stair and explained the situation as best I could. Advised her to keep her weapon at the ready," he added with a crooked smile.

It was dazzling, that smile. And his eyes in the morning light, on the first sunny day since they'd left London. She blinked half a dozen times, rather than be caught staring.

His smile turned slightly baffled. "What is it?"

"I was just thinking that, on the night we arrived, I told you I was the better actor. Now, I...I'm not so sure."

"Well, as it turns out, we're both professional liars and secret keepers." He brushed his thumb over her knuckles. "But I'd still give you the nod, purely in terms of experience. I do my best work behind the scenes, seated at a desk, with a stack of books."

Experience. Yes, she had a great deal of experience in playing parts and finding out things that others wished to keep hidden and using those secrets—or threatening to use them—to achieve her own ends.

But she hadn't any experience she could use at the present moment, no experience in trusting and caring and letting someone see past the shield of charm and cleverness she'd been wielding for years.

"How's your ankle, by the way?" He jerked his chin toward her injury. "What did Phelps say?"

"Considerably less painful. Still, I'm not to put any weight on it, and should keep it elevated when possible." She glanced around the interior of the carriage. The bench seat wasn't long enough for her to sit as she had on the sofa in the blue room. On the floor of the carriage sat a small wicker basket with a lid. "I suppose I could use Mrs. Tenney's hamper for a footstool?"

"Higher would be better, yes?" When she nodded, he released her hands, shrugged out of his greatcoat, and folded it into a cushion, heedless of the wrinkles. "Here," he said, positioning the makeshift pillow on his knee and patting it to indicate she might rest her leg there.

It was at once generous and intimate, and she bit her lower lip to keep a sudden flood of emotions—tears or laughter, she couldn't decide which—at bay. How could such a small, silly gesture send her off-kilter? "I couldn't possibly," she insisted when she trusted herself to speak. For one thing, her foot was bare except for the bandage, as she had not wanted to trouble Dinah for help with her stocking after the doctor's examination; for another, the thought of sitting across from a man in such a posture was shocking, even to her.

He didn't argue, but neither did he move his folded coat. The coach jostled over a rut, and the unpredictable movement made her ankle throb. "Well," she said, after a moment, "I suppose it would be all right for a little while." She hitched up her skirts a few inches and straightened the leg; he curled one hand beneath her calf and set her foot gently into place, then carefully arranged her skirts to drape over her ankle and his knee. Her pink toes peeked from beneath the hem.

"Better? I thought as much."

"Where did you learn how to…?" *How to treat a lady,* she'd almost said. But it wasn't that, not really. Gentlemen were rarely called upon to do the sorts of things for ladies that he had done over the past three days.

Except, perhaps, for kissing her senseless.

He tilted his dark head to one side and lifted his brows expectantly. "I can't answer until you finish your question. Or rather, I'm at least clever enough to know better than to try."

"I was wondering where you learned about codes and cyphers and how to break them. But I suppose the answer is obvious: in the army."

He riffled through the papers he'd laid aside, then picked up one of the pages of notes Dinah had found that morning. "The army took what I knew and refined it into something…well, *useful,* I suppose one might say. But I learned all the building blocks from my father. Latin, Greek, French, philosophy, mathematics." A smile played about his lips. "Chess."

"He must have been a very educated man."

"He was a clergyman. At one time—" The curve of his mouth deepened, though it lost some of its humor. "At one time I intended to follow in his footsteps."

It was not difficult to imagine. There was a gentleness about him, an earnestness, a desire to help. He would have been well-suited to a life of peace and quiet.

Instead, he'd become a soldier. And not entirely by choice.

She thought back to the last ride in this carriage, his conversation with Lord Thornton about debts and dowries, and Jeremy's insistence that he would not marry her. She was accustomed to thinking of men as being free to do what they wanted, with little to stand in their way.

But clearly that wasn't always the case.

What could she say in response to such a revelation? "Dora Pratt and Emily Godfrey will be glad you turned your hand to code breaking."

He had been studying his notes, or rather staring at them. His thoughts seemed to be far away. But when she spoke, he lifted his gaze and fixed her with those extraordinary eyes. "And you, Laura? Are you glad?"

He might have resumed calling her "Miss Hopkins." No one else could hear them now. It would have felt strange and impersonal, true, but she would have accepted it as inevitable.

"I—I'm sure you're very good at what you do," she managed to stammer. "The deduction about the chess book seemed quite brilliant, and—"

He tossed the paper aside but did not watch it flutter down to join the rest. "I think you know that's not what I meant."

"I—yes." She swallowed, suddenly nervous, unable—unwilling—to break his gaze. "I'm glad you're here. Glad *I'm* here—well, not glad about my ankle or about Thornton, of course, but…glad to be with you. More than glad, actually."

Good heavens, when had she become a rambler? Sitting here, with her foot cradled practically in his lap and his eyes blazing down at her like the summer sky, the *needing him* and the *wanting him* were tangling together inside her. Worse, on the very journey back to London, back to their ordinary, separate lives, she was losing the will to distinguish between wanting him and needing him. Losing the will to keep denying to herself that she felt something more for him, besides.

"So am I."

The sound of his quiet confession was lost to the creak and rattle of the coach. But she watched his lips form the words, certain of what he'd said even as she wondered what he meant. Last night, she had felt ample evidence that he wanted her. But did he need her?

And what about the *something more*?

"I'm glad I was sent to find you, and that I was able to play the parts you demanded of me with reasonable success. A little improvisation is good for the soul. Keeps the mind limber too. The attic had got rather cluttered," he said, tapping one temple. "Why, I might never have sorted out that cookbook if not for you. When you said that bit about the pages being too clean for a real cookbook, everything finally fell into place. I could've kissed you—"

He had shaken off his momentary solemnity in favor of a light and merry tone. Nevertheless, when he sucked in a sharp breath after those final words, she wondered whether he wished he could take them back.

She tilted her head. "Why didn't you, then?"

"Dinah would have been scandalized," he said, after clearing his throat.

"At seeing a pair of newlyweds share a kiss? I doubt it. She strikes me as a young woman with some knowledge of the world. But if that was your excuse," she said, winding the reticule's ribbon around her first finger, "what's stopping you now?"

Jeremy dragged his gaze to the window, passing slowly over Laura on the way, watching the ribbon loosen and unfurl. "Last night, we agreed... It would be wrong..."

"You have a religious objection, I suppose."

A muscle twitched along his jaw, not anger, but some emotion, barely suppressed. "Not as such, no."

"From what I understand, it's quite usual for couples who've had a spat—even a manufactured one—to kiss and make up." He turned toward her again and opened his mouth to speak, but she held up one finger to stay him and talked on. "You must not worry about my reputation. You have already made clear that you will not marry me, and I think I understand your reasons. But you should also believe me when I say I do not want—that is, I'm not eager to give up my independence. Or my work." She turned her peremptory gesture into a dismissive wave of her hand. "Where would I find a husband who would willingly allow me to go on being Lady Sterling?"

His lips parted, but for a long moment, he said nothing, and when he spoke at last, she had the distinct impression they were not the words he had at first intended to utter.

"*Wrong* was perhaps too strong. Say, *unwise*, then." He turned back toward the window. "Because I fear I won't be able to stop at a kiss."

She drew a deep breath, expecting that scolding inner voice to warn her away from this precipice. But before it could speak, she said simply, "Then don't."

The breath she had taken in seemed to shudder from him. He tossed his hat aside and leaned forward in one motion, as if afraid to hesitate.

One strong hand curled around the back of her neck, pulling her into a kiss that picked up where last night's had left off: hot and open-mouthed and demanding.

She reached out and grabbed the lapels of his coat, both to steady herself and to drag him closer still. His greatcoat slid onto the floor in a heap as they fumbled to rearrange themselves within the narrow confines of the carriage.

When he joined her on the forward-facing seat, he wrapped one arm around her shoulders, while she draped her legs over his knees, her injured ankle sticking out in mid-air, the toes of that foot not quite touching the window.

"This would've been easier last night," she said, thinking of the blue bedroom's expanse of clean linens and plush featherbed.

"Too easy," he countered. "We might have been tempted to go too far."

Too far. The meaning of those words was clear. She should have been prepared for him to be sensible, even in this, but she could not deny her disappointment.

He read her reaction with unsettling ease. "If you were to end up with child, Laura, it would not be just your reputation but also my honor and an innocent's future at stake. I won't take that risk."

"All right," she agreed. "From what I've heard, there's more than one way for us to enjoy one another's company."

She felt his smile against her cheek as he dragged his lips from her mouth to her ear. "Several, I daresay. But I should warn you. I don't have much—any—practical experience in these matters." As he spoke, he swept one broad, warm palm up her leg, over her skirts, his fingers splayed as if he could not quite believe his good fortune and feared that touching her would break the spell.

She would have been far more astonished if he had claimed to be a rake. "You don't kiss like a man with no experience." She stifled a gasp when his lips found the sensitive place below her ear.

His answering chuckle vibrated against her skin. "Well, I believe that when a man truly wants to know something, he must throw himself wholeheartedly into his studies." Then he traveled down her throat on a string of kisses. "And I've always been a quick learner."

Once, she would have said the same of herself. But she was nonetheless amazed to discover that kisses could be playful and passionate all at once, that the mere promise of pleasure was almost enough to tip her over into ecstasy.

His hand skated over her hip and came to rest against her ribs, below her right breast. She wanted to urge him to keep going, but her mouth was occupied just then by another kiss, gentler, a reminder that they had hours together yet before reality intruded. She could afford to be distracted now.

The fingers of his other hand slipped through her curls, following the contours of her skull, sending sparks of sensation across her scalp. Without a bonnet, there would be no disguising her tousled hair, and anyone who saw it would easily guess what—or who—had put it in that state. Never, never had she cared less for her appearance. She murmured her encouragement against his mouth.

"You like that? Tell me what pleases you."

"You seem already to have guessed." His fingers tangled in her hair, his lips against her skin, moving ever lower as he planted a string of nibbling kisses along her throat.

"I strive to be an excellent student," he murmured, between kisses. He'd nudged aside the collar of her pelisse and found a spot at the joining of her neck and shoulder that made her breath come faster. "But I should like to hear you say what you want, all the same."

She couldn't decide which she liked more, his determination to give her exactly what she desired, or the possibility that he enjoyed hearing shocking things from her lips. Perhaps a bit of both.

With her left hand, she toyed with the dark, silky hair that brushed his collar, while she laid her right hand over his left where it curved against her side, intertwining her fingers with his. "I confess I don't have much practical experience either." At least, none that involved another person. "But I know I like your kisses. On my lips, my throat, my—"

She tried to urge his left hand higher, but he resisted. "Tell me," he insisted, even as his mouth moved lower.

"Sometimes, I—" It felt wicked, somehow, wickedly good to make this confession. "Sometimes, I touch my breasts. They're s-s-sensitive," she hissed as his tongue traced the line of her collarbone. "I toy with my nipples, and—"

His thumb swept against the curve at the underside of her breast, part torture, part reward. "And?"

"P-pinch them."

"And you wish me to do that?"

"Yes," she agreed eagerly, arching to his mouth. "And kiss them." How could she crave a sensation she'd never experienced? "P-please."

This time, when she tried to guide his hand, he let her, settling his palm over that gentle swell. As heat seeped through her gown, her nipple peaked, chafing impatiently against the cotton of her shift. He rubbed gently across her breast with the flat of his hand, then more firmly, and finally circled her nipple with his thumb just as his mouth reached the edge of her bodice. "Tell me, Laura. Where else do you touch yourself?"

"B-between my legs." Heat flamed into her cheeks, but she did not regret her honesty when he plucked her nipple between thumb and forefinger again and again, coaxing it to an aching peak.

"Until you gain release?"

"Yes." She could feel his hot breath against her breast, through the thin muslin of her gown, as his lips closed around her nipple. Slight though the fabric barrier might be, she wanted to tear off her dress, be bare to his mouth, his tongue.

"Show me."

Oh, God. His voice alone might make her shatter. She had no desire to disobey.

Like the naughty chess queen, she gathered her skirts and petticoats in one hand and hiked them up almost to her waist, hesitating only when his clever fingers managed to tug her bodice low enough to free one breast. She felt rather than heard his growl of pleasure and triumph as he brushed the edges of her rosy-brown areola with gentle kisses before drawing her nipple into his mouth.

Her hips bucked as he began to suck, the unexpected power offering a pleasure she had never known, the sensation echoed in the greedy pulse of her sex, as if a silken cord connected those two parts of her body.

As she had last night, she ran her fingertips through the crisp golden-brown hair that guarded her mound, unwilling—nay, unable—to deny herself. He raised his head from her breast and ran his hand back down her side, coming to rest near her knee, pushing her legs ever so slightly apart. No hiding that most secret part of herself from his gaze. While he watched, she slicked her fingers between her folds and began to circle her nub.

"Laura," he whispered reverently, and she could feel his breath against her bare skin. "So beautiful. Everywhere." Her fingers began to move faster. "Do you never tease yourself? Draw out the sensation?"

"Yes, sometimes. But right now, I—I—"

"Shhh." He raised his mouth to hers in a gentling kiss, and then looked into her eyes, his own dark as sapphires. "May I?"

She nodded and would have withdrawn her hand, but his was there before she had the chance, tracing the delicate bones of her fingers, sliding over them into her slick folds, learning everything she could teach. And oh, he was a quick study. Gentle, curious, sure, taking the lead when she grew weak with need, teasing her when she would have hurried to the crisis point, circling the entrance to her body until she began to plead with incoherent sobs, and finally bringing her to a release that made her see stars.

Slowly he called her back to earth with soft but hungry kisses, smoothing her skirts once more down her legs before settling a possessive hand over her hip.

She had not anticipated how the pleasure would be different when shared, that another's touch could find places, sensations she had not discovered on her own. It would ruin her, the knowledge that wanting him and needing him were one and the same.

Worse still was the discovery that she wanted to be ruined.

"Jeremy," she whispered against his lips, his name both a question and an answer. "Can I see you? Touch you?"

His soft laugh stirred the curls on her forehead. "You must know by now, I can deny you nothing."

She levered herself more upright and managed to kneel beside him on the padded bench seat, her injured ankle all but forgotten as she raked her gaze up and down his body. His coat, though not in the first stare of fashion, was too tight-fitting to be easily removed within the space of the carriage. The many buttons of his double-breasted waistcoat and the knot of his cravat were similarly intimidating. She wanted to be able to touch and see the arms and chest and back that had carried her about so effortlessly for the past two days.

"Gentlemen's clothes are not conducive to trysts," she declared, in a tone of voice just shy of a pout.

He answered her with a sly smile. "Consider that part of the pleasure may be in the unwrapping." Lifting her hand from his shoulder, where she had been gripping him for balance, he planted a soft kiss on her palm and then brought that hand to his chest.

Her hand slid easily beneath the silk of his waistcoat, coming to rest over his heart. Through the thin cambric of his shirt, she traced the hard wall of muscle. "Can you—?" she began, her mouth suddenly dry, "Can you retie your neckcloth without aid of a looking glass?"

"I'll manage."

Her hurrying fingers at first made the knot of his cravat tighter, and she hissed in frustration at her ineptitude. His only answer was to gather up her fingers in both hands and kiss them, one by one, before setting them once more to their task, his eyes never leaving her face. After that piece of magic, the strip of cambric seemed almost to untie and unwind itself. Tossing it aside, she unbuttoned the single small button and laid open his collar to reveal that delightful notch at the base of his throat and a wedge of skin dusted with dark hair.

She'd seen as much last night, of course, but now she was at liberty to touch, to acquaint herself with all the textures of him, soft and smooth and silky and—

"I wish I hadn't asked you to shave," she said, running the backs of her knuckles over his cheek and jaw.

He reached up and trailed his first finger down her throat and along the neckline of her gown. "You're as delicate as a rose petal, my dear. My whiskers would've left a mark everywhere I kissed you."

Her breath caught. "Yes."

And then she kissed him, afraid she had said too much already, afraid of saying more. Now that she was in the dominant position, slightly above him, he gripped her waist beneath her pelisse with both hands and held her steady, freeing her to set the tempo of their kisses, freeing her to plunder his mouth and discover what pleased him.

Inside his shirt, her fingers roamed across his chest, and when her nails scratched lightly through the fur there, she felt another growl rumble through him and swallowed it with eager delight. He let go with one hand only as long as it took to rip his shirt free of his breeches so that she might run her hands underneath it, over his whole abdomen, tracing the contours of muscle and bone, eliciting shivers of delight. When one fingertip slipped inside the band of his breeches, he gasped, and his hips jerked.

"Did you not just counsel me against impatience?" she teased, drawing back to study the bulge tenting his breeches just below where her hand rested. "Tsk, tsk. More troublesome buttons to undo."

"I'll help you." His breath was ragged as one hand dropped to his fall and made quick work of it.

His manhood sprang from its prison of linen and wool, dark with need, surrounded by a nest of black curling hair. "Oh," she breathed, leaning forward, fascinated and slightly awed by the sight of it. "Now I understand."

"What?" he managed to ask, sounding dazed.

"Thornton's chess set. You're quite the, um, kingly figure." She tilted her head, curious as to how one would go about putting something of that size inside—

Pink streaked across his cheekbones, although she did not think embarrassment was the cause. "Another time, you may shower me with extravagant compliments. But for now, touch me, please, before I disgrace myself—"

At once eager and uncertain, she ran a fingertip along his length, discovering the extraordinary combination of velvet over steel. "You and I have very different notions of disgrace."

"Wrap your hand around my cock." Without hesitation, she did as he asked, almost scorched by the heat of him. "Yes, that's right. Tighter. Now move your hand up and down." As it had during their game of chess, his hand covered hers to guide her movement. "Oh, God," he grunted. "Feels so good." His hand fell away as she caught the rhythm, learning the speed and pressure that pleased him most, every sensation intensified by the steady jostling of the carriage.

His legs stretched out, taut, the toes of his boots pressing against the base of the seat opposite. Recognizing the rictus of climax, her body answered; instinctively, she squeezed her thighs together to strengthen the pulse throbbing at her core.

"I'm going to—"

"Yes."

He came in spurts that surprised and delighted her, and when his body sagged, utterly spent, eyes closed, she leaned forward and brushed her lips across his, trying to seal the moment in her memory.

Another time, he'd said. But that had been lust speaking, the wanton pleasures of their last hours together, on one of the last golden days before autumn settled in and winter followed hard behind.

And a few moments later, as he rummaged in his pocket for his handkerchief and efficiently wiped away the evidence of their encounter, she knew he understood it too. After peering out the window, and announcing that they were nearing a village, he began methodically to set his clothes to rights, tucking in his shirt hems, buttoning up his breeches, and making an effort at tying his neckcloth before turning to her with a lopsided smile.

"I don't suppose this is one of the dozens of things you're unexpectedly good at?"

She was still kneeling beside him, leaning into his solidness and strength. "I'll try."

While she fussed over the knot, he tried to smooth her disordered curls. "It was marvelous, Laura. Beyond my wildest imaginings," he said after a moment. "But was it unwise?"

"What a question," she said, arranging the last folds and then laying her palm in the center of his chest, firm and steadying.

Thankfully, before she could be expected to say more, the carriage rolled to a stop in Dartford, where they were to rest the horses. On the village green, they enjoyed a picnic lunch from Mrs. Tenney's hamper and spoke deliberately of other things. Afterward, Jeremy took a walk to stretch his legs and returned with a pretty bonnet and pair of kid gloves she doubted he could afford and which she knew she should not accept, though she did.

When they resumed their journey, he invited her to rest her head against his chest. Wrapped in his arms, she dozed, waking to discover that the sun would soon set.

Of course it had been unwise. All of it.

But she refused to waste a moment on regret.

Chapter 16

"We're nearly to London," Jeremy whispered against her hair, reluctant to wake her but knowing he had no choice.

God, yes, it had been a mistake to go along with her ridiculous game of pretend, to kiss her and touch her, to hold her while she slept.

And he would do any of it, all of it, again in a heartbeat.

But London loomed on the horizon, which meant he wouldn't have a chance. He was about to become Captain Addison again, would soon be absorbed in his usual duties. He would concoct some excuse to tell Mama and Julia about where he'd been and why, which they would believe, and would concoct another excuse for General Scott, which he would not.

And Laura would go on doing the dangerous work she had to do. He would listen when Julia read of Lady Sterling's exploits in the papers and would try not to worry.

He would fail.

Well, it wouldn't be the first time.

Laura stirred and straightened, buttoned up her pelisse, then made a project of fluffing her hair before she put on the new bonnet and gloves, retreating into respectability.

He reached into his pocket for the stockings he had taken off her the night before, and held them out to her. Foolishly, he'd kept them with him—had hoped to keep them always. "So you won't have to go barefoot."

"Thank you." She extended her leg, and he hurriedly drew the stocking over her injured ankle, daring to travel no higher than the turn of her calf. The spare stocking he draped over her lap. All the while, she looked out the window, as if in search of some familiar landmark. "Where are you taking me?"

"General Zebadiah Scott's house."

She whipped about to stare at him; mercifully, her eyes were in shadow, so he could not make out her expression. "That's Fitz's commanding officer. Yours too, I gather."

Knowing how quick she was, knowing no reply was needed, he said nothing.

"It was he who sent you in search of Lady Sterling, wasn't it?" Laura went on after a moment. "In search of a clearer understanding of my intentions, I believe you said. Why does he want such a thing?"

He hesitated for a moment. But what was the use in keeping this secret, given what she knew? "He intends to ask you to turn spy."

She looked thoughtful. "For the Crown? Or for him?"

"One in the same."

"Are they?" She turned back toward the window. "So, you're handing me over to him tonight." Her voice was flat, emotionless. "After we—"

"He's in Brighton, on holiday." Jeremy spoke across her, hoping the explanation would reassure her, though it probably ought not. Miles were rarely an impediment to General Scott. "You may recall that Lord Sterling does not actually have a grand house in town. I did not want Thornton's coachman knowing where you live." He glanced out the opposite window. "And I did not think my mother's humble cottage would suit the characters we've been playing."

She felt around her for her reticule and stuffed the unneeded stocking into it, revealing nothing of what she felt. "Will the general's servants give us cover, do you think?"

"Let us hope."

When they arrived in Audley Street, lights blazed in the general's study, the windows of which faced the street, and for a moment, Jeremy felt a pang of anxiety. Had he led Laura straight into a trap, just as she had feared?

He waited impatiently for the groomsman to unfold the steps, then hurried down them to lift Laura out, while the groomsman gathered up their bags. "Give a knock, my good fellow," he ordered the man, nodding toward the front door. "I hadn't time to alert the household to our arrival."

The groomsman did as he had been bid, as Jeremy helped Laura hobble up the wide stone steps. After an interminable wait, the door swung open to reveal a footman on the other side. "Look sharp," the groomsman said, handing off the bags. "Here be yer lord and lady."

Jeremy's heart stuttered when the footman goggled and shook his head in disbelief and denial. Three days of subterfuge about to be undone.

Then a voice spoke behind the footman. "Take those bags inside." Once the footman had gone, the butler stepped into the doorway. "My lord," he said to Jeremy and bowed. "My lady. How good it is to have you home."

To disguise Scott's missing horses and carriage, Thornton's coach and coachmen were dismissed to the nearest livery stable with the excuse that his lordship's groom had been given leave to visit his sick mother. Feeling Laura begin to sag beside him, Jeremy swept her up and over the threshold into the house, and the butler shut the door behind him.

"Captain Addison, is it not?"

"Yes, er—?"

"Highsmith, sir. You know that General Scott is from home?"

"I do. And I'm most grateful to you for playing along with our little charade. I've been... Well, this is—"

"Laura Hopkins," she told him, without hesitation. "Lieutenant Fitzwilliam Hopkins's sister. And if it isn't too much trouble, I daresay Captain Addison would like to put me down."

"Of course, ma'am," Highsmith said and showed them into Scott's study.

"I sprained my ankle while traveling, you see," Laura explained as Jeremy settled her in one of the leather chairs by the fire and dragged over an embroidered footstool. "The general had sent Captain Addison into the country on some other mission, but when he found me, he dropped everything to escort me back to London."

"I couldn't leave the sister of a fellow officer in distress."

Highsmith looked from one to the other of them, clearly not sure what to make of their story or why they were telling it to him. Jeremy recognized a degree of skepticism in his otherwise impassive face. "Will Miss Hopkins require a room for tonight?" he asked.

Jeremy noted his own omission from the question; of course General Scott's butler must know full well that Jeremy had somewhere else to lay his head.

"No," she said, before he could answer. "If you will call for a hackney, I will return to my aunt in Clapham."

"Very good, ma'am. In the meantime, I'll send in tea."

"He doesn't believe us," Laura said to Jeremy when Highsmith was out of earshot. "We gave a more convincing performance in Kent."

He quirked his lips in what he hoped would approximate a smile. In truth, he was weary of parts. Neither aristocratic coolness nor brotherly concern could do justice to his present feelings for Laura. "You were fast asleep when I concocted this scheme, and I had nothing from the last season's worst plays to guide me."

"And the best plays aren't much use to people who have found themselves in the sorts of improbable situations we have over the last few days," she conceded. Pain or weariness or both had dulled the lively sparkle in her eyes. "Your ankle is troubling you." He reached again into his pocket, this time withdrawing the little glass vial of Phelps's tonic, and knelt to offer it to her. "Once you are home, take a drop or two before you retire."

She took it from him without either arguing or agreeing. "I could do with a night of dreamless sleep," she said as she slipped the bottle into her reticule. It clinked softly against Penhurst's stolen watch.

"I should get to work." He patted his breast pocket, where his notes and Thornton's letter once more hid. "I don't foresee getting much sleep for the next few nights, dreamless or otherwise."

"You will tell me," she said, reaching for his hand, "what comes of it all?"

"If I'm right, news of what Thornton has done will appear in all the papers. But yes," he conceded, squeezing her fingers, "I will find a way to let you know what I safely can."

"And General Scott?" Her eyes searched his face. For all her fatigue, they had lost none of their sharpness. "What will you tell him?"

"That with respect to Lady Sterling, my mission was unsuccessful." Unable to hold her gaze, he chafed his thumb over her knuckles, watching the supple kid leather shift over those delicate ridges, wishing he hadn't bought the damned gloves. He wanted nothing between them. "If that is what you wish me to say."

"You would risk displeasing your commanding officer? To protect me?"

Jeremy darted a glance around the room, taking in the dark coziness of it, remembering how it had felt to stand before Scott's impossibly neat desk and receive those unwelcome orders. Finally, he raised his eyes to her. "Have I not already shown my willingness to take risks where you are concerned?"

"You have," she conceded, a mischievous smile playing about her lips. "With certain notable exceptions."

"Laura." He was tempted, even now, to throw that last caution to the wind, to scandalize Scott's servants and make her his forever, right there on the hearthrug. To tell her why he'd kept to himself all these years. To ruin her—ruin everything.

Her throat bobbed. "At least kiss me goodbye, Jeremy," she said, tilting her face to him.

He couldn't deny her such a simple request, or rather, he couldn't deny himself. His kiss would have to say what he should not. When their lips met, he understood with sudden clarity that strange old expression of having one's heart in one's mouth. It was fear, yes, but hope and hunger too, everything he wished to give her and could not.

She dragged her mouth across his cheek, baring her throat to him. The bristles of a day's growth of beard scratched her tender skin, just as he'd warned her in the carriage.

"Be careful," he urged, though God knew he would gladly have buried himself in her softness.

A bitter laugh vibrated against his lips. "Too late."

The sound of footsteps in the entry hall brought him to his senses. He broke the kiss, released her hand, and stood. "I must go, my dear."

She nodded. "I know."

Outside the door, he met the butler himself carrying the tea tray. Much of the staff had been given time off in the general's absence, he supposed. "Duty calls," he told Highsmith, who nodded his understanding. "You will see that Miss Hopkins gets safely home?"

"Of course, Captain. I'll send Searle to assist her."

It was on the tip of his tongue to ask Highsmith to say nothing of the matter to Scott when he returned. But he had no business making such a request of an honest and faithful servant. "Thank you," he said instead. Opening the front door for himself, he stepped out into the night.

* * * *

On the carriage ride to Clapham, Laura realized that the pain in her ankle had been driven out of her mind entirely by a new ache. *Odd, that.*

She had always assumed heartbreak was a figurative condition.

For years now, she had devoted herself to the protection of others. She had never considered—never allowed herself to dwell on the possibility that she was in truth trying to protect herself. The more she saw of men's depravity, the more determined she had been not to make herself vulnerable. Not to let herself be hurt.

"Too late," she whispered again into the darkness, as the streets of London hurried past, indifferent to her pain.

She had every intention to go on as she had begun, helping the mistreated, seeking justice. Lady Sterling would ever be an ally to those in a world seemingly made up of foes.

But now she knew she wanted something else, too, something more. She wanted a future with the one man who placed no limits on who she was or who she might become.

Except, of course, to say that she would never be Lady Sterling in earnest.

In one way, she understood his reluctance. She herself had spent so many years thinking of what she would lose if she ever married: her independence, her freedom, the better part of her fortune. She had not let herself dream of what she might gain: true support, true companionship, true love. But she had caught a glimpse of all of those things with Jeremy. What kept him from imagining a future with her? Something, or someone, had chased him into the shadows, where he had learned to dwell but forgotten how to live. If she could ever persuade him to be totally honest with her about what it was that troubled him, could he still look her in the eye and try to tell her that they wouldn't suit? That he wasn't happier and more successful when she was beside him? That they weren't better off together than they had ever been apart?

He was too logical and sensible to ignore the truth for long, if only she could figure out a way to help him see it.

He would realize that Lord Sterling didn't have to go on working alone.

Three days later, with no word of Lord Trenton's fate or anything else, Laura walked to the breakfast table with only a slight limp and addressed herself to Lady Sterling's neglected correspondence. Nothing like a pile of desperate, tear-stained pleas to put one in a proper frame of mind about men.

Only a handful letters awaited her. The first was a scathing critique of the damage she had done to the nation's "fine, upstanding gentlemen," accompanied by a collection of newspaper clippings; Laura tossed the lot into the fire.

The second was from the housekeeper of a clergyman, who had, in her own words, "caught the master messing the scullery maid about." Laura considered how such a man might be shamed into better behavior. Surely a clergyman would not want his parishioners, or the bishop, to know what he had done. She wrote out a reply to that effect, directed to the housekeeper, with a postscript indicating that she was to write again if he dared to dismiss the girl or if either of them wished assistance in finding a new post. Before sealing the letter, she enclosed one of her cards, hinting that it might conveniently be left lying about for her employer to find.

The sight of the words *Lady Sterling, thief-taker* had humbled more than a few.

When she broke the seal on a third letter, she was still gleefully picturing the vicar's face when he spied the card propped on his mantelpiece. Several moments passed before she realized she was holding another shakily written missive from Emily Godfrey.

My dear Lady—

*He knows. While cleaning the blue room in preparation for
his guests, one of the housemaids found a calling card. Unable
to read and thinking it might be something of importance, she
showed it to her ladyship, who told her husband, who is most
seriously displeased. He spoke with every female domestic,
trying to determine who had contacted you. I am, regrettably, a
poor liar. He immediately wrote to delay his friends' arrival and
returned to London in search of you and your husband. My dear
lady, please take care.*
   E.G.

Laura refused to allow her own hand to tremble. Thornton relished women's fear, and she did not mean to give him the satisfaction.

She pushed to her feet, returned to her bedchamber, and dug her now-shabby reticule from its hiding place behind her dressing table mirror. With a shake she spilled the contents on her bed. Penhurst's watch bounced on the coverlet, colliding with the tiny glass vial of Phelps's tonic and a few coins. Another shake dislodged the lone stocking and a crumpled handkerchief.

The card she had tucked in Penhurst's fob pocket, the card Jeremy had returned to her, was nowhere to be seen. It must have fallen onto the floor with Miss Godfrey's letter and gone unnoticed.

With measured movements, she restored those items to their hiding place. In a clean reticule, she placed Miss Godfrey's second letter, a fresh handkerchief, and a few other items. Then she put on her pelisse and bonnet, gathered up her gloves, and stumped down to the kitchen, where she found Betty with Aunt Mildred's other servants: Mrs. Whyte, who served as cook and housekeeper, and her son Daniel, a good-looking lad of twelve who did odd jobs about the house and dreamed of growing tall enough to be a footman at one of the elegant houses on Grosvenor Square.

Betty, who had been seated at the table chopping vegetables, leaped to her feet. "Good gracious, Miss Hopkins, what is it?" Laura knew from having stood before the looking glass to tie the ribbons of her bonnet that the strain of Miss Godfrey's letter showed on her face. "Did you have bad news from Mrs. Hayes?"

"No. That is, it is not news from or of my aunt, but it can hardly be described as good." She looked among the three anxious, wide-eyed faces, as she spoke. "I must go out. While I am gone, do not leave the house. If someone comes to the door, do not answer it. Say nothing of me or my aunt to anyone, not even to someone you trust." Here she gave a pointed look at Betty, thinking of Penhurst's servant. "And do not," she added, turning to Daniel, "try to be brave. There is something I must do, but you must promise not to interfere."

Mrs. Whyte and her son looked at one another before nodding solemnly. Betty was nearly in tears as she followed Laura to the door. "Is it to do with—?"

"It is," Laura acknowledged before the name could be spoken. "Someone is looking for her. For me. And as you may guess, he is not the sort of man to scruple at doing harm."

"N-n-not Captain Addison?" It was the first time the girl had mentioned her encounter with Jeremy.

"No. In fact, he may be in more danger than I." Which was precisely why she needed to find him. To warn him. "Now, bring me one of Aunt Mildred's walking sticks. And remember." She laid a finger to her lips in a call for secrecy. Betty nodded her understanding.

Within the hour, Laura was in a hackney rattling across the Thames. On Audley Street, she ordered the driver to wait while she ascended the steps of General Scott's home, one painstaking tread at a time, and rapped at the door with the head of Aunt Mildred's ebony walking stick.

Mr. Highsmith himself opened the door. "Miss Hopkins. I am pleased to see you so well recovered from your injuries."

She nodded her acknowledgment. "May I come in?"

"General and Mrs. Scott are still from home."

"I assumed as much. It is you with whom I wish to speak."

Surprise flitted into the man's dark eyes, though nothing else about his expression betrayed any emotion whatsoever. He bowed, admitted her into the hall, and then directed her toward the study with a wave of his arm. She shook her head, refusing to go farther. "How may I assist you, ma'am?"

"I wish you to direct me to Captain Addison, please."

"I'm afraid I cannot."

"Cannot or will not?" She laid her free hand atop the one already holding the walking stick.

"It amounts to much the same thing, Miss Hopkins."

"But the other night, you seemed to know him." She fought against the rising note of desperation in her voice. It might be misunderstood.

"I recognized Captain Addison as one of the officers who serves under General Scott's command, yes. But as a rule, I know very little about the general's work. He is scrupulous about maintaining a separation between this house and the Horse Guards. And even if he were not, it would nevertheless ill become a man in my position to speak of his employer's affairs."

She was painfully aware of the irony: she, who had just exhorted her aunt's servants to say nothing to anyone, desperately needed the general's butler to tattle.

"Certainly not," she agreed. Ordinarily, charm would have been her weapon of choice to disarm the man, but she could not muster it. She felt deflated, defeated. Then, in the depths of her cluttered thoughts, something rattled loose. An inconsistency in Highsmith's words. "If General Scott is so careful not to bring his work home with him, how did you happen to recognize Captain Addison?"

"Well..." Highsmith pressed his lips together, clearly unused to being questioned. "The day before he left for Brighton, the general ordered Captain Addison to call here. Most unusual." Yet the butler had been quick to go along with Jeremy's story the other night, she noted, almost as if he was more used to spies showing up on the general's doorstep than he let on. "I was the one who showed him in."

"Ordered to call?" she echoed. "And how was the general's order delivered?"

Highsmith stiffened, almost imperceptibly. "I do not know."

"No messages left from this house?"

"Only to the general's tobacconist." He named a shop in a part of town near Whitehall, on a less than reputable street, one she knew to be replete with gaming hells and pleasure clubs. Fitz had once mentioned strolling down it—little suspecting that Lady Sterling would be familiar with the area.

Fitz had mentioned it...

It could of course be nothing more than a coincidence. Perhaps the general, who was so meticulous about the organization of his study, was similarly particular about who blended his tobacco.

But she doubted it.

"Thank you, Mr. Highsmith." A shallow curtsy was the best she could manage. "I will not take up any more of your time. If you could just"—she fished into her reticule and withdrew a calling card—"see that General Scott gets that when he returns."

The redoubtable butler took the card, glanced at it, then read it. His eyes bulged, moving from her to the card and back again. "Of course." He bowed. "My lady."

Chapter 17

Elbows on the table, Jeremy dropped his head into his hands and grabbed two fistfuls of his hair, hoping that the prickle of pain along his scalp might improve his focus.

Not that he had been exactly comfortable before that. The Underground—working and living quarters for some of the top domestic intelligence officers in Scott's service, hidden beneath a tobacconist's shop in an unprepossessing area of town—was always cold and damp. The furniture in the windowless workroom consisted entirely of straight-backed wooden chairs and slab tables. His bed, not that he'd seen much of it, was a sagging rope cot in a cell hardly large enough to contain it.

No one, including Jeremy, complained. The work was the important thing, and he had at his disposal all the materials he needed to complete it: pens and paper, books in a dozen languages, a magnifying glass that could distinguish a fleck of ink from a fly speck. Someone had quickly found him a copy of *The French Pastry-Cook*, as battered as a beloved cookbook should be, according to Dinah's description. In two days, he had managed to generate a substantial list of subtle changes from the original to Thornton's version and begun to work out how they might function as a cypher, though they hadn't yet any text to decode. The letter he'd stolen from Thornton's desktop either wasn't otherwise encrypted or used some other key.

Thankfully, his mind had been too occupied to think of other things… or people. And when he allowed himself to collapse on his bed for an hour or two, he made certain he was too tired to dream. His plan was working swimmingly until he turned to analyzing *The Noble Game of Chess*.

The character by character, line by line, page by page comparison of an unaltered book with the notes he had taken on Thornton's copy was tedious work. He could not afford to let his thoughts wander. Yet on every page lay the memory of a chessboard, a touch, a kiss. It was impossible not to see Laura's twinkling eyes and hear her mischievous laugh every time he came across the notations for king or queen. Impossible not to wonder how she fared and whether she was thinking of him too.

Unclenching his fists, he tried to pass off the gesture as brushing his hair out of his eyes. He'd let it grow overlong. It was a wonder Colonel Millrose hadn't chided him. Mama surely would, when she saw him.

Laura had seemed to like it, though. She'd toyed with it, albeit absently, every time he had carried her and she had passed an arm around his neck. If he closed his eyes, he could almost feel her fingers…

"Captain Addison?"

Mrs. Drummond, who managed the domestic affairs of the Underground and occasionally acted as salesclerk in the tobacco shop upstairs, had to speak three times before he jerked his thoughts back to the present time and place and scrambled to his feet, slipping his arms back into his coat as he rose.

"Forgive me, ma'am." She was a pretty widow, hardly older than he. Half the officers in the Underground fancied her. Her perpetual black gowns, reserved demeanor, and icy-blue eyes kept them at a proper distance, however.

He bowed his apology, then looked up to find her studying him, a curious lift to one penciled brow. Colonel Millrose had ordered her to don a wig, fearful her extraordinarily fair hair might draw too much attention, but so far as Jeremy could tell, the present dull brown hairpiece offered little real disguise.

"There's a young lady above," she said. "Asking for you."

"For me?" His heart thumped erratically and sweat dampened his palms. "I don't—who?"

Her head tilted, matching the eyebrow for skepticism. She said nothing.

"I'll just—" Quickly he marked his place and began to pile up books. Code and map work were never left unguarded, even here. "I'll be right there."

By the time he had safely locked away the papers on which he had been scratching out notes, she was already at the bottom of the stairs, and he hurried along the corridor to follow her. Halfway up the steep, narrow steps, he paused as she opened the door into the shop and sunlight spilled into the stairwell, making spots dance before his eyes. Was it morning, then? He'd lost track. Passing a hand through his hair again, he tried to remember when he'd last changed his shirt or had a shave. Finally, he stepped into the tobacco shop, drawing a deep breath of the warm, spicy air, uncertain who he was about to see and hardly daring to hope.

The shop's only customer stood admiring a display of enameled snuffboxes, her head tipped forward so that all he could see was the top of her bonnet. The top of a familiar bonnet. One on which he'd spent his last ready coin.

He parted his lips to speak, then hesitated. He couldn't call her *Laura*. Best not to go on indulging that familiarity. But he doubted she would thank him to be associated with the names of *Sterling* or *Hopkins* either. Not publicly. Not here. He settled for clearing his throat.

When she lifted her face, she gave a most convincing performance of being dragged unwillingly from considering an important purchase. Annoyance. Hesitation. Surprise.

Then her expression cleared, and she favored him with the slightest smile. "Ah. Good morning. Thank you, ma'am," she called over her shoulder to Mrs. Drummond, who, in the absence of other customers, was making notations in a ledger. In a lower voice, Laura said to him, "May we talk?"

"Yes, of course." He lifted the hinged section of the countertop that formed a pass-through between the clerk's side and the customers' and stepped to her. "How did you—?"

"Not now." Her whisper was sharp. Peering beneath the brim of her bonnet, he glimpsed a flicker of worry in her gray eyes. "Thornton knows."

Lord Thornton might have learned many things, all of them dangerous. Before Jeremy could ask for more particulars, however, the bell above the door jangled, signaling the arrival of a customer. Two gentlemen, reeking of smoke and brandy, walked—or, more accurately, staggered—into the shop, evidently turned loose from one of the gambling dens down the street. "Where's Billy?" one of them demanded.

"Mr. Millrose is below stairs," Mrs. Drummond informed them.

"Well, better fetch him. I promised my friend here two ounces of that prime cut he sold to me last week. But damn me if I can remember what it was called."

"Of course, sir," was her mild reply. "I won't be a moment."

In her absence, the two men leaned their backs against the counter and began speculating as to whether someone named Kilburn was likely to make it home with his purse or without the pox. Laura fidgeted impatiently with her reticule—not the one she had carried into Kent and apparently no longer containing Penhurst's stolen watch. Her fingers now traced a different shape, long and thin. A hat pin, unless Jeremy missed his guess. The two gentlemen had much to be grateful for, more than they knew, when the door behind the counter opened again to reveal Mr. Millrose.

Colonel William Millrose, that was, trusted aide to General Scott, commander of the Underground, and as far as the rest of the street was concerned, purveyor of fine tobacco and snuff. When General Scott had created this secret den to guard his intelligence officers and their work from suspicion, he had insisted that it continue to function as a shop to further the ruse, with the result that Colonel Millrose and some of the Underground's other denizens, most recently Mrs. Drummond, had been forced to become quite knowledgeable about tobacco products.

A friendly smile split the man's dark brown face as he approached the two men. "You caught me at my breakfast, sirs," he said with a hearty laugh. Jeremy very much doubted it was the truth. "How can I assist you?"

While they conducted their business, Laura returned to her perusal of the snuffboxes. Jeremy could see nothing of her profile beyond the brim of her bonnet and found himself wishing he had opted for the little frippery of a hat the milliner had shown him instead.

After several minutes of back and forth, in which Millrose was required to gather several different jars from the tall shelves that lined the shop's walls and the two gentlemen sniffed, debated, and almost fell into an argument, the transaction was at last completed and the harsh jangle of the bell above the door signaled their departure.

Hardly had the door latched when Jeremy said, "Knows what?"

"Not here," Colonel Millrose declared before she could speak. With an eye to the wide windows facing the street, he lifted the section of counter and jerked his chin toward the door to the Underground. "Miss Hopkins," he said with a nod as she passed him.

Jeremy hardly knew which of them was more startled by the colonel's use of her name: Laura or himself.

At the bottom of the staircase, Laura hesitated and, not knowing what else to do, Jeremy gestured to the workroom. In another moment, Colonel Millrose had accompanied them inside.

"The number of women who have lately found their way here alarms me," he said, leaning against the door after he closed it and crossing his arms over his chest.

Jeremy knew he referred not only to Mrs. Drummond, who had been placed in the Underground for her protection, but also the incident over the summer involving Major Stanhope and Lady Kingston. Stanhope, a favorite of General Scott, could expect to be forgiven for the breech of protocol. Jeremy doubted he would be so fortunate.

Yet Colonel Millrose had been the one to usher her inside the belly of the beast. "How is it you know Miss Hopkins?" Jeremy asked. Laura, who had been openly staring around the room, turned her gaze on Millrose, as if equally curious about the answer.

"You're Fitzwilliam Hopkins's only sibling. The elder by eleven months. You live with your aunt in Clapham and take an active interest in various philanthropic endeavors. I make it my business to know my men's...points of vulnerability, shall we say?" And before you ask, Addison," he said, turning toward Jeremy with a stern look, "I know about yours, too."

All of them? Jeremy wondered, but did not dare to ask.

He shifted his attention back to Laura. "What I don't know is why you're here."

"Hopkins didn't discover the codebook," Jeremy explained. "She did. She took it for a mere cookbook, of course, and her brother never told her otherwise. I realized the connection in Kent, when she...that is to say, when we..."

"You were also in Kent?" Colonel Millrose turned sharply toward Laura, as his eyebrows began an ominous creep up his forehead. She nodded. "May I ask why?"

"She—" Jeremy began, then bit off whatever story he'd been about to tell. He dropped his gaze to the floor.

"Because the governess to Lord Thornton's children wrote and asked for my assistance. You see, sir, I am also known as Lady Sterling, and—

"*The* Lady Sterling?" Jeremy looked up in time to see Millrose goggle. "The one they write about in the papers?"

"The same. Evidently your General Scott has taken an interest in my work and sent Captain Addison to discover my identity."

Why was she telling Millrose this? Not that secrets weren't safe with the colonel. But it felt as if she had made some determination, some decision about her future, to which Jeremy was not privy.

Not, of course, that he had any right to expect to be consulted. Had he not already, foolishly, foreclosed the possibility of a future together?

"Captain Addison and I soon discovered that we shared an interest in seeing Lord Thornton brought to justice, albeit for different crimes. We decided that, under the circumstances, it would be most beneficial if we... assisted one another."

Jeremy let himself hesitate only for a moment before blurting out, "Thornton believes—or, believed—that we are married. Lord and Lady Sterling."

The eyebrows rose higher, though not precisely in disbelief. "Lord and Lady Sterling," Millrose repeated, looking between them.

"It was, er, General Scott's suggestion, sir."

At that, Laura's pewter gaze bored into Jeremy, all astonishment, but Millrose's face relaxed. A puff of wry laughter swelled his chest and lifted his shoulders. "Of course it was."

"Does Thornton know," Jeremy asked Laura, "what I took from his study?"

"I'm not sure." She leaned her walking stick against a chair and produced a folded letter from the reticule that dangled from her wrist. "Miss Godfrey says only that he has discovered we were not telling the truth about our—rather, *my* identity—and followed us to town in a fury."

"How did he discover this?" Jeremy demanded, while Millrose held out a hand for the letter.

After quickly perusing the contents, the colonel looked up. "What's this about a card?"

"Oh, God," Jeremy said, realizing instantly what must have happened. "That calling card I took from Penhurst. Did it fall on the floor with the letter, under the bed? I never saw it—"

Laura dismissed his self-recrimination with a flutter of fingers, then fished once more in the little silk purse and handed the colonel a fresh calling card. "Girls and women in domestic service contact Lady Sterling when their employer feels himself entitled to...more than their labor, shall we say? I steal something of value from him, something that will help to ensure both that the young woman's material needs—and often those of her child—will be met, and also that the gentleman is not tempted to commit such follies in future. I leave a card like that"—she nodded toward it—"to remind him I know something he would rather no one did."

Millrose flicked a corner of the stiffened paper with his thumb. "You traffic in secrets."

"Yes." Laura's lips curved in something that wasn't a smile. "Rather like a spy."

"Rather," agreed Millrose, once more looking between them. "It's not clear from this letter whether Thornton knows what secrets of his you uncovered. We may still have that advantage. Nevertheless," he went on, folding the letter and returning it to Laura, but keeping her card, "he won't have much trouble tracking down Addison—or should I say, Lord Sterling? A viscount can't hide as easily as some might like."

He wasn't wrong. Thornton was well-connected. A few questions to the right people, and he would know far too much: the names of those who held Jeremy's debts, the precise location of a certain cottage in Fulham. "My mother and sister, sir," he said, stepping toward Millrose. "They could already be in danger. I have to go to them."

"Only if you take your wife with you."

Jeremy opened his mouth to protest, but before he had spoken a word, Laura was sputtering. "No, no. I must return to my aunt's house. I've left her servants absolutely defenseless."

"Write them a note of explanation." Millrose pointed her to pen and paper. "I'll send it along with a pair of men to keep an eye on things," he promised. "But we know where Thornton is most likely to go. When he shows up at Addison's house, we'll be ready for him."

"You can send half the British army to Fulham if you like," Jeremy said, "but I'm not waiting here to learn whether my mother and sister are safe."

"By all means, go to them," Millrose agreed, moving away from the door. "But I want the two of you"—he pointed with the tip of the card, first to Laura and then to him—"to stay together."

"Why?" Laura asked.

Jeremy thought he knew, and he wanted to damn Millrose for it. "To bait the trap."

A better trap than Millrose knew. Jeremy could guess exactly what Mama and Julia, neither of whom had ever understood his refusal to marry, would say when he entered Briar Cottage with Laura on his arm and explained that the two of them had been pretending to be wed.

Millrose tipped his head. "Partly, yes. But also because it will be easier to protect you if you're together. If Thornton were to separate you, he might try to use the threat of harm to one to draw the other out."

Jeremy wanted to deny that such an attempt would work. But it would be a lie, and Millrose would know it. *I make it my business to know my men's points of vulnerability*, he had said.

Where Laura was concerned, Jeremy had made himself vulnerable indeed.

A hint of color rose to her cheeks. "I strove not to leave anyone in the earl's household with the impression that I care overmuch for Captain Addison."

Millrose shrugged. "Yet, when you got that letter, you rushed here to warn him."

In the midst of the frustration and fear warring inside Jeremy rose a flicker of possibility. The colonel was right. Laura had come searching for him this time. And, being inordinately clever, she had found him.

Could he be clever enough to keep from losing her again?

Laura stood and handed the note she'd written to Millrose. "I've also written down the name and address of my wigmaker—for the lady upstairs. If she's in need of a disguise, as seems to be the case, she deserves a better one."

Amusement twitched at the corner of Millrose's mouth. "Thank you, Lady Sterling."

"Right, then. Let's go," Jeremy said, stepping to her side. When she laid her fingers on his arm, he had to tamp down a surge of selfish regret that she no longer needed him to gather her into his arms. "We need to get to Fulham before Thornton does."

Chapter 18

Laura collapsed onto the seat of what appeared to be an ordinary hackney, although she suspected it wasn't. Her injured ankle, which had been hardly noticeable at the start of the day, was beginning to ache again after all the hurrying up and down stairs and along corridors and into carriages.

Jeremy climbed in a moment later, holding out her aunt's walking stick. "You nearly forgot this."

She wrapped her fingers around the knob. "Thank you."

He sat down beside her but said nothing more as the carriage rolled into motion. The view sliding past the windows was largely unfamiliar to her as streets tightly packed with houses gradually gave way to more open spaces. At its fringes, London could have passed for a country village.

"Did you grow up in Fulham?" she asked.

"No, I was raised in Oxfordshire. When I—when General Scott brought me to London, I wanted a place for my mother and sister that would be near to me, but still remind them of home," he said, as if their destination required some explanation. "Of course, I think Julia would have preferred somewhere livelier."

He was not looking at her but out the window, and the midday light behind him, although not brilliant, still cast his profile in sharp relief. Not for the first time, she was struck by something familiar about that profile, the perfect angles of his cheekbones and nose. "Julia," she echoed, thoughtful.

"My sister, yes."

"The one who enjoys the theater." He had spoken of her many times at Thornton Hall, but Laura could recall hearing him speak her name only once before. "I wonder…does she also, perhaps, enjoy the entertainments at Vauxhall?"

He snapped around to face her. She had no doubt he knew why she had asked. "On occasion, yes," he admitted after a moment.

"My God. It was *you*. That night." She shivered, her scalp tingling at the recollection of Penhurst's remorseless grasp, the rest of her tingling at the memory of Jeremy's hold on her arm and her relief at his unexpected decision to release her. "Had you been sent there to find me?"

"No. That encounter was merely a—" One corner of his mouth lifted. "Merely a coincidence, I was going to say. It wasn't until the next morning that General Scott told me that he wanted Lady Sterling found and I was the agent he had selected for the task. Because the coincidence of our names amused him, he said, and I thought to myself—" His gaze grew distant, his expression more wry. "I didn't believe in coincidences. But when I spoke with Penhurst not an hour later, I realized you and I had already met."

"Coincidence or no, you must have cursed your luck. You had me, and you let me go."

His eyes searched hers, and in their blue depths she glimpsed a strange welter of emotions. "I did, didn't I? Foolish. Are you angry with me for not telling you sooner?"

She thought perhaps that she ought to be. But she wasn't.

For a week, she had been baffled by her own willingness to trust a stranger, only now to discover that she had known him all along. Known the sort of man he was, at least. In the darkness of Vauxhall's unlit alleys, where for all he knew he had nabbed a whore and a thief, he had not sided with Penhurst and all those who assumed such a woman deserved whatever she got. Jeremy had set her free. And when they had met again in Kent, some part of her—a sentimental, dramatic sort of woman would have been tempted to call it her heart—had recognized him and had known she was safe in his arms.

Maybe her choice of an alias hadn't been a coincidence but something stronger. Maybe it had been fate.

"I could pretend to be angry with you, if you'd like," she teased.

He smiled and held up one hand, palm outward, as if pleading for clemency. "On no account. I am still scarred by your performance at Thornton Hall."

"I did try to make it up to you," she reminded him with a sly, sidelong glance.

His reaction did not disappoint. He called her *Laura*, in that voice that could not make up its mind whether to be scandalized or scolding, tempered with the hint of a smile and streaks of color across his chiseled cheekbones.

Relenting for the moment, she turned the conversation. "Do you also live at Briar Cottage?"

"I have a room there. I visit when I can. Lately, I've spent far more time in the Underground—that's what the men call the quarters beneath the tobacco shop."

"Fitting, certainly. A proper hideout for a den of spies."

"Intelligence officers," he corrected mildly. "Mama and Julia know very little about the nature of my work."

Laura pressed a fingertip to her lips. "Your secret is safe with me."

His breath caught, as if he started to speak then thought better of what he meant to say. The slightest frown darted between his brows. "And yours with me."

But what if the most important secret she was keeping wasn't her alias? What if it was the depth of her feelings for him?

He had already turned back to the window to gauge their progress through the narrow streets.

"Your devotion to your mother and sister is charming," she said, watching him.

"I have little else to give them."

She wanted not to challenge his words but to reassure him. To tell him it was enough. She would be elated by such a gift, if it were offered.

At last the coach slowed and he scoured their surroundings, leaning first one way and then the other, before opening the door and stepping out. With her less practiced eyes, she could see nothing out of the ordinary. Not a soul was in sight. The lane itself was unremarkable, the houses varying from ramshackle to quaint. Roses and ivy wound their way up the brick walls of Briar Cottage, like something from a storybook.

She accepted Jeremy's arm, leaning more on him than on her walking stick as they approached the house. A face peeped from behind a curtain and disappeared.

"Have you some play in mind, a particular script for us to follow?" He glanced down at her when they reached the doorstep, where she had paused to inhale the sweet scent of flowers.

"I think I'm done with the theater for the time being. Acting out parts, anyway."

Again, the sensation that he was tempted to speak but restrained himself. Before she could urge him, the door opened.

"Jeremy! Why didn't you tell us you were coming?" The face that had been at the window belonged presumably to Julia, whose brown hair, not quite as dark as her brother's, framed a round, smiling face. Laura guessed her to be about seventeen. "And who is this?"

"If you'll let us inside, she'll likely tell you." Julia took a step backward to give them room. Jeremy released Laura's arm to let her cross the threshold, then doffed his hat and still had to duck beneath the lintel. "Is Mama in the sitting room?"

Julia shook her head. "The garden."

"Ask her to come inside, will you, please?" Laura did not miss the glance he sent over his shoulder into the empty street before closing and locking the door behind them.

When Julia stepped away to do as he'd asked, Laura said in a low voice, "Colonel Millrose will send the promised protection, I'm sure."

"He already has. If you could easily spot them, they would not be doing their job. But I still do not wish to be caught off guard when Thornton arrives."

The house was a perfect square, with a staircase running up the center. To the right sat a room behind closed doors, while to the left a window-filled room ran the length of the house, combining the functions of dining room and sitting room, cluttered with furnishings for its varied tasks. Charming though the house was, its modest size could not help but recall to her mind what Jeremy had told Lord Thornton about his financial woes.

She followed Jeremy into the room on the left and had hardly sat down in the chair he indicated before he brought her a small stool. "I can tell your ankle is still troubling you."

She gave him a grateful smile. "I've been bustling about a bit more than I planned today."

In another moment, though, she was standing again as Julia entered the room with a woman, presumably her mother, who was simultaneously unknotting her apron with one hand and smoothing her hair with the other and hurrying to give Jeremy a kiss when she spotted Laura.

"Oh! Julia didn't say we had a guest." Her cheeks flushed with that same color that so often brightened her son's, and indeed it was easy to see where Jeremy had got his sculpted features and good looks, though Mrs. Addison was fair-haired. She was a beautiful woman, and if Laura hadn't known that she must be fifty or very near it, she would never have guessed.

"I said there was a surprise," Julia retorted. "My brother hardly qualifies as that—though it would behoove him to give us some notice next time, particularly if he intends to stay for luncheon."

"I may stay rather longer than that, just to torment my dear little sister," he said, giving her a playful grin. One would never have known, to look at him, how much he hid behind that smile. "Now," he went on, "may I introduce Miss Laura Hopkins, who is the sister of a fellow officer. It seems that we—"

"*I,*" Laura corrected, speaking across him, "have landed your brother in a spot of trouble. I hope you will forgive the intrusion, Mrs. Addison, Miss Addison." She dipped into a curtsy, but fatigue made her ankle buckle. Though she managed to disguise it, and to muffle the gasp that rose to her lips, Jeremy was once more at her side—a little too quickly to pass off as mere politeness, if the speculative glance exchanged between mother and daughter was anything to judge by.

"Any friend of my son's is of course welcome," said Mrs. Addison as he helped Laura back into her chair.

Laura smoothed her skirts over her knees. "I wonder if you will feel the same about his wife?"

Mrs. Addison sat abruptly down in the chair closest to the fireplace. Julia's eyes flared, and she stifled a gasp—or perhaps a giggle—behind her hand before sitting down near her mother.

Jeremy, who was standing beside Laura's chair, gave her a stern glance before explaining. "What Miss Hopkins means is… Well, we—*I* was sent on a mission by my commanding officer. To find someone. I happened upon Miss Hopkins in distress." Laura waggled her toes where they rested on the footstool and promptly regretted the gesture. "And, well, with one thing and another, it became clear that if we pretended to be a married couple, we would both be benefited." Julia smothered another noise, definitely a giggle this time. "We explained that we were newlyweds, and misfortune had fallen upon us—"

"We said I had run away from you. Because I feared as Lord Sterling's wife, I would be tainted by association with the woman who calls herself 'Lady Sterling,'" she said by way of clarification to Julia and Mrs. Addison.

"The one from the papers?" asked his mother.

His sister nodded eagerly. "I've been teasing him about her for ages. I think it's why he's not married yet."

Jeremy sent her a warning look. "It is *not.* Now, if I may?" Though his sister did not look terribly chastened, he continued. "The gentleman took us in and got medical attention for Miss Hopkins. But in general, he has a very bad reputation. He mistreats his servants. He's…well, he's something of a rake, I suppose you could say." That description visibly piqued Julia's interest, which earned her another chiding glance. "And he is in possession of information the British army and the Crown feel strongly he should not have."

"Which must be why you were sent after him." Pride beamed from his mother's face, and Jeremy did not try to disabuse her of her conclusion. "That sounds like an important responsibility, my dear. I'm very proud of you—though it doesn't exactly sound safe."

"It isn't," Laura agreed. "Which is why we're here."

"The gentleman, Lord Thornton, has discovered the trick we played on him to gain his sympathies and get access to his house. I do not know whether he suspects all that we learned about his misdeeds. But I'm sure he fears it, and he would readily harm another, especially to save his own neck. He has come to London looking for us." He gestured between Laura and himself.

"Well," Mrs. Addison said, with a dismissive wave, "he isn't likely to look here."

"Actually," he spoke in a soothing voice as he approached his mother, "he is. I feel quite sure he will have no great difficulty discovering that Lord Sterling is deeply in debt, was forced to take the king's shilling and join the army because of it, and can do no better than rent a cottage in Fulham for his mother and sister."

"Jeremy."

Laura understood then where he had acquired the talent for speaking her name and freighting it with half a dozen meanings all at once. She heard exasperation, worry, and love mingled in his mother's voice.

"This isn't the time to discuss it, Mama," he said.

"But why," asked Julia, and though her eyes were not the same brilliant blue as her brother's, they shared some of the same cleverness, "if he's so dangerous, did you lure him to us?"

"It wasn't a matter of luring—he would have found Briar Cottage inevitably, don't you see? My commanding officer said that the safest thing would be for all of us to be together, so that a guard could be established for our protection."

Julia hurried to the window and nudged back the curtain to peer out, as she had on their arrival. "I don't see anyone."

"You won't," Laura told her. "At least, not according to your brother."

Julia's lips twisted with something like disappointment, and she scoured the lane left and right again before letting the curtain fall and returning to her seat. "How long will we be stuck here?"

"Did you have plans?" Jeremy retorted, with unaccustomed sharpness. Regret immediately softened his posture. "I'm sorry. It's just that I—I'm worried too. It's one thing for a soldier to be in danger, and quite another to put you in harm's way."

"I think your commanding officer must know you well," Mrs. Addison said. "It sounds as if this Lord Thornton would not scruple to use a threat to us to lure you out into the open. Your commander knew you would want to protect the women you care about, all of them"—and here she sent a pointed glance at Laura—"from danger."

For just a moment, Laura thought that Jeremy, who had begun pacing back and forth in his familiar fashion, might have missed that look.

Then he stopped. "Mama. You understand that Miss Addison and I are not actually—

"But you could be—"

"No, we—"

"I did not set out to snag a husband, ma'am," Laura interjected. "And to his credit, Captain Addison was quite clear from the first that he was not able to marry me, even if our game of pretend led to rumors and suspicions. It would have been folly on my part to have formed any expectations. Or any, ah…" Here, Laura had the greater folly to look up at Jeremy, to meet those eyes that had a way of seeing right through whatever part she had chosen to act. "Attachments," she finished lamely.

His breath left him audibly, though whether a sigh of relief or of despair, she couldn't decide. "You can't mean—" he insisted. "You don't know—"

"Julia," said Mrs. Addison, "why don't you take Miss Hopkins upstairs? I'm sure she would like to…" She made an aimless circle with one hand, as if searching for a word, an excuse, to get Laura out of the room.

"Freshen up?" Julia suggested helpfully.

"Yes. Exactly. Freshen up before luncheon."

Jeremy looked agitated, as if he could not make up his mind whether he wanted to hear what his mother had to say, and Laura parted her lips to refuse to leave, ready to stay and support his spirits as he had supported her body. But before she could speak, he gestured toward the door with his chin, urging her to follow his sister.

Wrapping her fingers around the knob of her walking stick and drawing a determined breath, Laura rose and left the room.

Thankfully, the stairs were not steep, though that also meant that the ceilings on the upper floor were low. Jeremy surely could not have stood upright. The cottage had only two rooms upstairs, one on either side of the house, tucked under the eaves. Laura was both eager to sit down again and rest her ankle, and sorry to see Julia direct her to the room on the right, rather than the one above the sitting room, where it might have been possible to overhear some of the conversation between Mrs. Addison and her son.

"This is my room," Julia explained. "If you'll be spending the night, and it seems you may, then you can sleep here, and I will go with my mother across the landing."

"You are too kind. I am sorry to put you to any trouble."

"It's no trouble," she insisted, as she began to gather two small piles of nightclothes, one to take to her mother's room and the other for Laura, as it was obvious she had not brought a bag other than her reticule. "There are fresh linens and a comb on the washstand, and books on the bedside table, if you wish something with which to amuse yourself."

As Jeremy's sister worked, Laura did her best to make herself comfortable on the cushioned bench at the end of the bed, stretching out her injured limb along the seat, at Julia's urging, and arranging one of the low bolsters at her back. "I understand from your brother than you like the theater."

"I do indeed." Julia placed a folded shift on one pile. "Above all things. If it weren't so scandalous, I would like to become an actress." She tilted her head and looked thoughtful. "Why is it scandalous, do you suppose?"

Laura said nothing. The theater had a long history of disrupting boundaries between the various ranks of society, hierarchies that those most benefited by them were adamant about keeping in place. The assumption that actresses were but a half step from prostitutes, selling the spectacle of their bodies, was merely one part of it. All of it, as far as Laura was concerned, was ridiculous. If the theater provided respectable entertainment for ladies, why should it not also provide a respectable living for them?

But it was hardly her place to speak of such things to Jeremy's younger sister.

"Really," Julia went on, "when one considers how every moment of a woman's life is a performance for someone's benefit, I fail to see why acting on a stage should be regarded more severely than acting interested in a gentleman's opinions in a ballroom or acting pious at church."

Laura could not hide her smile. She liked Julia very much. "Well said, Miss Addison. I agree. Women are expected to play roles that offer them no advantage, and far too often without any remuneration at all."

"Wouldn't it be lovely not to have to think at all about money matters?" Julia said with a sigh. "We could do as we pleased then. I could be an actress and not have to consider my reputation and the opinions of future suitors. And my brother could—well." She turned away to rummage through a drawer, giving the distinct impression she had almost said too much. "I suppose he could do a great many things."

"Such as leave the army? Or marry?"

Julia glanced over her shoulder, her expression a mixture of sheepishness and surprise at Laura's forthrightness. "I'm sorry he and Mama have chosen today for another of their conversations about the matter. They've surely discussed it fifty times already, always to no avail. He has such an overblown sense of duty, to my way of thinking of it. Determined to pay off debts that aren't even his. I really thought Mama had given up trying to talk sense into him, but I suppose when you arrived…" She sighed again as she turned back to the drawer. "He has never even mentioned a lady's name, either to Mama or to me. Did not want to get our hopes up, I suppose. That's why I first started teasing him about the Lady Sterling in the papers. And then I began to assume that his interests must lie…elsewhere."

Laura was surprised to hear a young woman speak of such matters so frankly.

"Have I shocked you, Miss Hopkins? Mama says it's what comes of reading novels and going to plays. I suppose she isn't wrong, but I—I just want my brother to be happy." A pause, as she stood and gathered a small bundle into her arms. "Is your brother equally obstinate, Miss Hopkins?"

"Comparatively speaking, I think mine is far worse. Your brother has been excessively kind and thoughtful."

"That's easy enough to explain." She stifled another giggle as she moved to the door to carry her things to her mother's chamber. "He likes you—and I, for one, am very glad to see it. Though I suppose the more important question is, do you like him?"

Laura's first instinct was to deny it, though it would be a lie.

Deception is protection. It had been her guiding philosophy for so long, she had refused to see the danger in it. It was one thing to fib to keep her aunt from worrying overmuch, or to play a part to lure men like Penhurst and Thornton into giving up information that could destroy them.

But when it came to her feelings for Jeremy, she was ready to be done deceiving herself. She wanted more than a pretend marriage with him, more than a few stolen hours in a rattling coach.

Having posed the question, Julia had not waited for an answer. When the door opened briefly as she slipped out of the room, the soft murmur of voices rose up the stairwell, though their words could not be heard. Would Jeremy's mother have any better luck this time convincing him that he could afford to seize happiness?

Despite what Julia had insisted, Laura sensed that Jeremy's hesitation toward marriage had to do with much more than money. What secret was he still keeping?

Or what secret had been kept from him?

Chapter 19

Jeremy lowered himself into the chair his sister had vacated. "I'm not sure this is the best time for a tête-à-tête, Mama."

"I only hope it's not too late," she replied, more acerbically than was her nature. "Jeremy, my dear, anyone can see from her expression that Miss Hopkins is smitten with you—"

Was it true? "I wouldn't say—"

"And you," she went on, ignoring him, "obviously care for her. Have you really known each other only a few days?"

He paused before answering. To confess to his mother that he'd given his heart away to a woman he'd known for less than a week was a humiliation he would prefer to be spared. "I saw her first last Christmastide. Lieutenant Hopkins, her brother, brought her to an officers' dance."

"But it was on this latest…mission, I think you called it, where you came to know her well?" she pressed.

"Yes. That is, no. I shouldn't claim to know her well. Our supposed relationship was only—"

"Make-believe," she finished for him, then paused to muse on the implications for a moment. "And you are sure you did not raise her hopes? For all her bravado, I do not think it was only pretend to her."

"What makes you say that?" Damn him, but he could not keep the hopeful note from his voice.

"Women know things, my dear." She reached for his hand and patted it. "Not everything, of course. I wish I knew what troubled you so. Why you persist in claiming that a few debts should keep you from marrying and settling down—keep you from happiness."

"It's more than a few debts, Mama." He had tried his best, over the years, to hide the extent of the trouble from his mother and sister. Perhaps it was time to speak plainly. "The lease on Everham doesn't begin to pay the mortgage. Every building on the estate is in need of repair. The farmland is worn out—sometimes I think Mr. Gilly rents it out of the goodness of his heart, for it certainly cannot do much more than repay his investment in seed and labor. An officer's pay is not so princely as to be able to dig us out of that hole."

Mama did not show surprise, but she was silent for a moment, as if considering how such a problem might best be surmounted. "You are handsome, personable. A viscount. You might marry a woman of some fortune," she suggested, not for the first time.

"Yes. Wealthy merchants supply daughters and dowries enough to meet even the most penurious nobleman's needs," he said, repeating Laura's sardonic observation on the way to Thornton Hall.

Mama nodded, though her expression was wary, clearly sensing that his apparent agreement was to be regarded with skepticism. "It does not sound much like recipe for a love and happiness, I suppose."

"And that is not even to speak of the other debts," he went on, ignoring her attempt to venture into increasingly dangerous territory. "Debts incurred in the name of Sterling."

"Debts of honor, debts to shopkeepers," she scoffed. "You are under no obligation to make good on another man's, a stranger's, promises."

"And starve the families of other men who had no way of knowing the sort of man the late Lord Sterling was?" he objected. "If the title had come to Papa instead, would he have behaved any differently than I have?"

By the way she pressed her lips together, he could guess the answer was no.

"But your papa would also want you to be happy," she pointed out. "He would not want you to try to go through the world alone." Jeremy nodded, not entirely sure she was right. "Having only just met her, I will not presume to say that Miss Hopkins is the lady most likely to ensure your happiness. But I think you also know that the man who taught you about honor would not like to see you dishonor a young lady by playing with her affections or endangering her reputation."

Unable to sit still beneath her reproachful look, he pushed to his feet and walked to the window. A dog trotted happily past the house, no sign of its master. No sign, in fact, of another human soul. He hoped he had told Laura the truth about the unseen watchmen, at least.

"It's because of Papa that I cannot offer for her," he said at last.

Behind him, Mama made a small noise, not exactly of surprise. "Whatever do you mean?"

"Before he died, he took me aside and told me…" He turned away from the window but did not meet her gaze, though he suspected she knew what he was about to say. "I am not his son."

"Oh. I…see." With nervous movements, she smoothed her skirts around her, watching her own fingers press the fabric against her legs. "I wondered if he hadn't done as much." For a moment, he thought she was bracing herself against harsh words from him, judgment. Then she lifted her chin and looked at him. How could he have doubted her strength? "And is it because Richard Addison's blood does not run in your veins, that you feel this, this…guilt over the title you inherited? Do you imagine someone else would have borne the burden better?"

"I might have done," he admitted, "when I was seventeen and knew less of the world. Now, however, I wonder whether it came to me because I deserve the burden more." In two steps, he was at her side and dropped onto one knee by her chair. "I'm sorry, Mama. So dreadfully sorry at having been the cause, however innocently, of sorrow and pain."

Sudden creases surrounded her eyes, and her head moved slowly side to side in confusion and disbelief. "Sorrow and pain? He loved you with a father's heart—God willing, someday you will understand how a parent can grieve and fear and still love." With cool fingertips, she traced the contour of his cheek, so similar to her own. "He was proud of the boy you were, and he would have been proud of the man you've become—glad to have had a hand in shaping the man you are."

"But *you*, Mama—what of your grief? To think that every time you look on me, you must recall—" He turned away from her gentle touch. "No. It's *his* blood I won't pass on to a child. And as for Laura—she has risked her life and reputation to avenge young women mistreated and abandoned as you were. How could I ever propose that she tie herself to the son of a—?"

"Jeremy?" She sounded both stern and baffled. "What did your papa tell you?"

He pushed to his feet. "Surely, you will not wish to relive—"

"I think I must."

The memory was with him always, as clear and sharp as if the conversation had taken place yesterday and not more than a dozen years ago. He could still feel the brilliant sunshine of a midsummer afternoon, unable to warm the chill, somber house in which a death sentence had been pronounced. He had wanted to pace but couldn't, confined within the space of his parents' bedchamber in the little stone rectory, Papa sitting up in bed, his face already gaunt, but his voice steady, speaking with the same unwavering certainty with which he spoke from the pulpit.

"Very well. He told me that when you were the age Julia is now, living in Philadelphia with your family, a British soldier—" He turned away, unable to face her. "You must believe, Mama, I would have done anything rather than don a uniform that must be repellant to you, but what better choice did I have? The law, the Church—every other avenue would have taken years I did not have before they yielded sufficient income for me to keep a roof over your head."

When she spoke, his mother's voice was quiet but even. "What exactly is it that this British soldier was to have done?"

He had to swallow twice before he could speak the words. "Had his way with you."

"Had his way with me," she repeated, as if the language was strange in her mouth. "Forced himself upon me, you mean. Your father told you this."

They were not questions, but Jeremy nodded nonetheless.

"Are you telling me that all this time," she went on, her voice growing ever sharper, though still quiet, "you have imagined yourself to be the product of—of violence and hatred? Not...passion? Not love?"

He turned slowly toward her, feeling as if his blood had congealed. "Mama?"

"And your father was not...confused?" She had the stiff, uncertain movements of a person in shock.

"No," he assured her. The illness that had claimed his father had been devastating in its progress, at last taking even his mind. "This was a month, at least, before the end."

"Oh, God." Her breath shuddered from her. "Can he truly have believed...?" She pressed trembling fingers to her lips, muffling a sob. "I suppose my father must have told him—and he would never have asked—and it would not have occurred to me to say—oh."

The broken sentences stuttered from her, driven by a sort of hysteria. He could not piece them together, quite, but he understood enough to ask, "What *did* happen, all those years ago?"

For several moments, she only stared into the empty hearth. When she spoke again, her voice was calmer, but distant, as if lost in the past. "We were living in Philadelphia—that part is true—when the war started. Your grandpapa was a physician, and a Loyalist, and after the Battle of Germantown, three of the injured British soldiers were quartered at our house. My sisters and I were instructed to tend to them. One of them, the sergeant of a platoon, required constant watch. For a time, we did not think he would survive. But he was young, about your age now, and healthy in the main, and he did recover, though it took some months. And over those same months, we—" Her color rose, as if she had just remembered who was listening to her tale. "We fell in love. When he was pronounced well enough to return to England, he told me of his plan to leave the service and come back for me. We would marry, he said..."

"But he never returned?"

At last she looked up at him, where he leaned against the mantel. "He did, actually—though not for more than a year. And by that time, I was already married. Unbeknownst to either of us at the time of his shipping out, I was with child—*you.*"

Jeremy gave a sharp nod of understanding and strode back toward the window.

"Upon discovery," she continued, "my papa was unhappy, of course. *Furious* might be a better description. He decided the whole family would go to England, the better to keep my terrible secret—as he saw it. While on the voyage, he struck up a friendship with a Mr. Addison, who had just been granted a living in Oxfordshire and was on his way to accept it. He was in the market for a wife and, though he was twice my age, began to pay court to me, as the most eligible young lady aboard the vessel. Shortly before we landed, he spoke to my father. Papa must have owned up to my condition—it could not have been kept hidden for much longer, anyway. I suppose he might have felt it would be more palatable to a gentleman to imagine I was blameless in the affair."

How frightened she must have been, trading a familiar world for an unfamiliar one, a dream of love for a practical, necessary union, arranged by a father desperate to cover what he thought of as a stain on her honor.

"Dear, dear Richard," she murmured, her eyes sparkling with tears. "He never asked me for details, never pressed. Never reproached me. He loved you," she said, tipping her face to Jeremy, "never doubt it, but I suppose the past weighed on him. He would have thought you entitled to know, and I'm sure he believed he was telling you the truth. Oh, I wish I'd known. All these years..."

"And did you...?" he began, still struggling to make sense of what she'd revealed, knowing that the question he most wanted answered was one he had no business asking. He paused near the corner shelf by the window, filled with china ornaments. With one fingertip, he traced the flawless porcelain face of a shepherdess, a remnant of their long-ago life in the rectory, in what had seemed to him a simpler time. "Did you love him?"

"Your papa?" Her nod was careful, though not hesitant. "I grew to, over time. He was too good, too gentle, not to inspire affection. Not in the way of my first love, of course. But my grief at his passing was genuine, you may believe."

Jeremy knew it was true; he had witnessed their devotion to one another. He came closer, perched on the edge of the chair facing hers. "And the soldier? May I know his name?"

Her nod was more eager this time. "He is Arthur Remington."

"He is still alive?"

"Very much so." She smiled, though not at Jeremy. "After my mourning ended, I took the liberty of making some enquiries after him, and much to my surprise, discovered he was living here, in London. We have…renewed our friendship." Pink suffused her cheeks, and he could easily guess from her blush that more than friendship was involved. Perhaps this explained why she had seemed more youthful and vibrant of late. Even in daylight, her blond hair showed no signs of gray, and her complexion was as unlined as a girl's. "He is planning to pay a call tomorrow morning, in fact."

Jeremy glanced toward the window, not yet sure he was ready to face the man. "Does Julia know?"

"Not our history, of course. But she knows him. They get on well." Again, that secret smile. "He has a way about him—some might call it charm, I suppose, though I always think the word has a suggestion of falseness about it, and he is unfailingly forthright. He's very clever, too. With all due respect to your papa, I suspect you inherited some of your gifts from Arthur. I think—I hope you will grow to like him."

Jeremy managed a single nod of acknowledgment. "Is he still in the army?"

"No, although he did return a few years ago to serve in a civilian capacity, as a personal aide to—oh, what was the gentleman's name?" She tapped a finger to her lips. "Major Laurens, I believe."

"The Duke of Raynham?" That name, Jeremy recognized. Until giving up his officer's commission in favor of the responsibilities of his dukedom half a dozen years ago, Raynham had been one of General Scott's best field agents.

Which must mean that this Remington fellow also had Scott's approval.

"Yes," she agreed, "that's right. The very same. And before that, he handled the affairs of the Marquess of Ashborough—the one who's said to be so very bad," she added in a whisper that conveyed more excitement and interest than shock, "although Arthur will have none of it. Besides, the marchioness keeps her husband well in check now, he says. She is Irish, you know."

"And a famous writer," he added, not hiding his surprise. "Your Mr. Remington certainly moves in exalted circles." It was not intended entirely as a compliment. Jeremy had always been a little suspicious of men who ingratiated themselves with wealth and power, never more so than after spending a few days in the company of Thornton.

"As might you, if you could accept that you are a viscount," she reminded him. Then she softened and offered him another gentle smile. "Of course, 'Captain Addison' is also very well and good."

Jeremy tipped his head against the chair's back and studied the ceiling, his mind buzzing with his mother's revelations. A decade of telling himself that he must never think of love and marriage and children, because the blood of a blackguard ran through his veins and deserved neither present nor future honors. Everything he'd thought he knew about who and what he was, upended by a few moments' conversation.

Now he would have to decide what to do with the information. Determine afresh just who he meant to become.

His mother rose, dropped a kiss on his cheek, and turned toward the stairs. "I'll leave you to yourself for a bit. You have been very good to worry about your mama all these years, but you must occasionally think of yourself, and what you want. I would not wish to be the only Mrs. Addison in your life. Unless," she glanced over her shoulder, and mischief twinkled in her eyes, "you would prefer a Lady Sterling?"

Chapter 20

When Mrs. Addison appeared at luncheon with red-rimmed eyes, and Jeremy did not appear at all, Laura could guess that the conversation had been a difficult one. How difficult was impossible to determine, as Mrs. Addison retired to her bedroom after eating—"a touch of the headache, nothing to worry about"—and Jeremy remained hidden.

"He often does this," Julia explained, glancing up from her needlework to nod toward the closed door across the entryway from the sitting room. "He has half of Papa's library in there, and Mary will have taken him a tray."

"I wasn't worried," Laura defended herself, returning her attention to the book in her lap—only to discover that she had been holding it upside down.

Briar Cottage felt like a bubble, in which she was alternately cushioned and trapped. The desire to know what was happening outside its doors, even outside the sitting room, kept both her mind and her gaze wandering all afternoon.

Eventually, Mrs. Addison came downstairs to write a letter. Jeremy emerged shortly thereafter, looking slightly rumpled—Laura was almost certain he had been sleeping, and her fingers twitched with longing to smooth his hair—but on the whole, acting himself. A sense of normalcy pervaded the household, despite the threat outside.

Only Laura dropped her book when the wind rattled the leaves on the tree outside the window, or jumped out of her skin when Mary, the servant, announced that dinner was ready. Jeremy spoke low to her as he escorted her to the table. "Thornton isn't going to barge in on us. You're safe here. I promise."

The evening passed in much the same fashion as the afternoon, everyone occupied by polite conversation or some cozy domestic task, the lamps lit and curtains drawn as dusk slid into darkness. Eventually Mrs. Addison announced that she was ready for bed, and a moment later, Julia leaped to her feet to follow her. Laura could not quite decide whether her hurried movements were the result of a prompting look from her mother, or whether she had imagined the exchange. Laura laid aside her unread book and moved as if to rise.

"What might I do to tempt you to stay?" Jeremy's voice was low, seductive.

Laura sank back into her chair, though the same restless tension that had agitated her limbs all day made it impossible to relax. "I hardly need to be tempted. If you wish it, I will certainly stay."

He was slumped in the chair by the fire, which had been crackling merrily an hour before but was now smoldering. His booted legs were stretched out before him, crossed at the ankles, the very picture of ease.

But when he finally looked up from his study of the patterned wool carpet, the intensity of his gaze nearly robbed her of breath. "You are in an obliging temper. I wonder whether I oughtn't to have wished for something more than your company?"

"Such as?" Her voice was barely a whisper above the clatter of her pulse.

Instead of answering, he hoisted himself from the chair, strode to a corner shelf filled with knickknacks, and came away with a pretty inlaid box. "Will you play?" He opened the box's hinged lid to display a set of chess pieces. Ordinary pieces, this time, fashioned of ivory, the detailed carvings softened by years of use.

"I still know nothing of the game," she warned him as he cleared a space on the little table beside her chair and began to remove the pieces from the box. "Even with Stamma's assistance, I was lost."

"I will teach you, this time." Once it was empty, he opened the box wide, and the fancywork on its exterior was revealed to be the board itself. She watched his long fingers make quick work of arranging the pieces on their proper squares. Finally, he drew one of the other chairs closer to the table and perched on the edge of its seat, so that their knees almost brushed.

She had expected the game would be a pretext for conversation, but for a quarter of an hour, he said nothing but what was relevant to the movement of pieces, when to capture and when to surrender. He had set the black pieces before her, to acquaint her with defensive strategies, he said, though at the moment it was he who seemed to be behind a shield.

While shaking his head, he nudged her queen-side knight from its square with one of his bishops, and then picked up her displaced piece, pausing to study it beneath the lamplight rather than simply adding it to the growing pile of black pieces at the far side of the board. The horse's flaring nostrils and blank eyes leaped into relief, then passed into shadow.

"I have been operating under a misapprehension," he said.

"About the game?"

"About myself." He curled his fingers around the piece so that it disappeared into his palm. "I planned an elaborate defense against an opponent who never even existed." The hand clutching the knight dropped to his leg. "And now that I am free to make a different set of moves, I—I find myself a little lost. I thought I knew who I was, but…it seems I was wrong."

Instinctively, she reached for him, curling both hands around his fist where it rested against his thigh. "I wasn't. I knew from our first meeting that you are a gentle, caring, clever man. I've always been…independent-minded, my aunt calls it." The corners of his mouth rose at that description, though his gaze was still focused on the chessboard. "I chided myself for trusting you, a perfect stranger. But I wasn't wrong to do it. I wasn't wrong about you."

She spoke with confidence. Of course, she did wonder what his mother must have told him earlier that day. Whatever it was, it certainly seemed to have changed his outlook on the future. But she did not need to hear it herself to know that he was unchanged in fundamentals. She knew exactly the sort of man he was, the sort of man he had always been, the sort of man she had never dreamed she would find.

"Thank you." He brought his other hand over to surround hers. "Though I suppose it won't matter overmuch. I'm still poor as a church mouse. And you're still…independent-minded? Was that the term?" His smile deepened even as it grew more self-deprecating.

She snagged her lip between her teeth. "I realize that sort of independence is a luxury few women can afford."

"Afford," he echoed. A scoffing sound huffed from his chest. "I don't suppose you're going to tell me you're dreadfully rich?"

"Well, I wouldn't use the word *dreadfully*. Although I am my aunt Mildred's sole… Anyway, as you say, it won't matter overmuch, since most of the money is tied up in my dowry, and you've already told me I'll never be Lady Sterling in earnest."

"Laura." That voice again, that wonderful, scolding, scandalized voice, the vowels of her named shaped by a hint of laughter. "You said you didn't want to marry."

"No. If you recall, I said that I did not think I would ever find a man willing to let me go on being Lady Sterling—which is to say, I did not think I should ever find any man willing to let me be...myself."

"As changeable as a spring wind, in other words."

"Yes," she conceded. No point in denying what he already knew to be true.

He released her hands only to lift his palm to her cheek and draw her closer. "My very favorite season," he whispered against her mouth before kissing her.

She brought her hands to his chest, then slid them upward to curl around his neck. The chess piece made a soft *thump* as it slipped from his fingers and fell to the floor. When his other hand reached for her, she leaned forward, closer and closer, until it was the most natural thing in the world for her to tumble into his lap.

"I'm quite sure this is still madness," he told her, as he trailed his lips to her ear.

"Why? In the brief history of our fake marriage, we've already conquered the main challenges: richer, poorer, sickness, health," she said, ticking them off with her fingers. "I'd say we're off to a grand start."

"A real marriage might involve a few more complications."

"And also," she countered, toying with the buttons of his waistcoat, "a few more benefits."

"Why, Lady Sterling. Are you suggesting what I think you're suggesting?"

"Indeed I am."

"I think we'd better make this official first."

"Oh." She couldn't quite disguise the disappointment in her voice. "You're right, of course. Better to wait until we're actually mar—"

"After all we've been through, even I am not prepared to be such a stickler as that," he said, after stopping her words with a kiss. "I'll settle for your answer to this: will you marry me, Laura? Because you've stolen my heart, just like you stole my title. You've turned my orderly, logical, bookish world upside down, and I wouldn't have it any other way. It might be madness to say it, but I've fallen in love with you, and nothing would make me happier than to spend the rest of my life wondering what's next."

Tears stung her eyes and the back of her throat. "Jeremy. That's ever so much better than anything I've heard in a play. Yes. Yes, I'll marry you," she cried, raining kisses on his brow, his cheeks, his lips. "I tried to make myself stop wanting you, stop needing you. But I couldn't—and now I know why. Because I've fallen in love with you, too."

"Sounds like the makings for a scandalous marriage," he said.

She recognized the teasing reference to the play she had first suggested as a model for their performance in Kent—the story of two people trying, and failing, to disguise their true feelings for one another. "I predict a successful run and rave reviews from even the most persnickety critics."

"In the meantime, could I interest you in the prequel? It's called *A Scandalous Engagement*." He nuzzled a soft kiss into the hollow behind her ear. "All the action takes place in the downstairs bedroom of an unassuming little cottage on the outskirts of London."

"Intriguing. Tell me more."

She felt the muscles in his shoulders and legs tauten as he gathered her closer, then got to his feet with her cradled in his arms. "I'd rather show you."

* * * *

Jeremy nudged the door of his bedroom open with his hip. The only light inside was that of the moon, slipping in like quicksilver through a narrow gap between the draperies. As he bent to lay her on the bed, his muscles quivered, strain and worry giving way to desire.

Quickly he shucked off his coat and boots before joining her. "You're sure, Laura?" he whispered, leaning over her. After years of self-abnegation, self-recrimination, the thought of a future with her was still so new, so fragile, like the first delicate shoots of a plant he'd kept dormant for most of his life, now unfurling cautiously toward the sun.

"Sure about what?" Her tone was teasing. "That I love you? That I want to marry you? That I want you to make love to me tonight?" In the hint of light from the window her eyes glittered as she nodded. "Yes. Yes. Yes." She wrapped her arms around his neck and reached up to kiss him.

Her lips were hot and sweet—he'd almost persuaded himself he'd dreamed it before, their soft eagerness, the little noises she made, the way the mere touch of her tongue to his sent a bolt of lust straight through his core.

He kissed her back, harder, struggling to restrain his hunger, a starving man who'd suddenly found himself at a banquet. Denying his desires had become second nature. But he could not, would not deny what he felt for her. "I want you, Laura. I need you."

"Yes," she hissed again in the darkness, fumbling with the buttons of his waistcoat. "I need you too."

"Let me." He straightened to strip off waistcoat and shirt, tossing aside the tangled garments as her palms swept over his chest and back, then began to tug at his breeches, devouring him with her touch. "Easy, love," he whispered, catching her roving fingers. "This is already bound to go too fast."

"Then we'll do it again," she said, slipping free of his grasp.

His breath hissed from between his teeth as she brushed his erection in her haste to undo his fall, the pleasure so acute it was almost pain. "Let's get you undressed first," he said, stepping just out of her reach.

With a flounce of impatience, she stood and turned her back to him. "Hurry."

The darkness was a hindrance, but as the fastenings of her gown gave way, memory supplied an image of her flawless skin. He pressed his lips to the top of her shoulder, kissing his way down as he unlaced her corset and peeled away layers of muslin and linen. He pictured her rosy-tipped breasts as he cupped them, and her tremor of pleasure as he dragged his thumbs over her nipples made him harder yet.

Momentarily releasing her with one hand, he pushed her clothes over her slender hips, listening to them rustle to the floor before sending his breeches to join them. Then he wrapped his arms around her, snugging their bodies together, the heat of his cock a brand against the comparative coolness of her bottom.

When a needy moan shuddered from her, he put his lips to her ear. "Your ankle—does it hurt to stand like this?" Her curls danced across his cheek as she shook her head. "Good. Then set your legs apart," he said, dragging his palm over her belly to the top of her thigh.

She readily complied, inviting him into her warmth, into her wetness. He closed his eyes, the better to sharpen the memory of her golden-brown curls and slick pink folds, the memory of how she had touched herself and shown him how to pleasure her.

As his fingers explored, she arched helplessly against him, snaking one of her arms behind her, around him, to draw them closer together still. "Please. I want you inside me. I want to be yours."

"You are mine," he reminded her, accompanying that gentle scold with a pinch to one nipple. "And I know you can feel how much I want you." With the middle finger of his other hand, he teased her nub. "But come for me first."

"Yes. So good," she sobbed as he ruthlessly built her pleasure.

"I had an excellent teacher."

Her whole body shook as the crisis approached, then she went rigid with ecstasy before sagging in his arms. With practiced ease, he once more laid her on the bed, then kicked his feet free of his breeches and set one knee to the mattress beside her.

Whatever he'd fantasized as a randy adolescent, whatever he'd believed he was denying himself in all the years since, it had never come close to this, the sight of his Laura, soon to be his wife, the contours of her face just visible in the moonlight, drowsy and needy, reaching for him.

"What are you thinking about?" she whispered.

"There's a moment—I suppose every code breaker has experienced it—when something that was a mystery just a moment before suddenly breaks open, and all the secrets are revealed." He traced her lips with his fingertips, then reached up to brush a stray curl from her brow. "A beautiful, terrifying moment—just like this one."

He felt, rather than saw, her bemused frown. "Terrifying?"

"I don't want to hurt you. I don't want to disappoint you. But I'm afraid, in my eagerness and my ignorance, I'll do both."

The wrinkle in her brow smoothed itself out. "Oh, my love. The only way you could disappoint me, or hurt me, is if you tried to tell me you don't need me the way I need you." Her arms came up to encircle his shoulders, urging him closer. "Please."

He slid over her body, let her hardened nipples graze his chest, as her legs parted wider to make room for his hips. "Guide me," he murmured, and her cool fingers closed around his throbbing cock as she slicked him through her wet folds, set him at her entrance, and lifted her hips in invitation.

As slowly as he could bear to move, he nudged forward into her molten core, thrusting shallowly as her body adjusted to the invasion. After a moment, the tension ebbed from her, and he sank deeper, all the way to the hilt. "Oh," she breathed, wriggling her hips experimentally. "That feels nice."

Nice? Even he, who was fluent in a half-dozen languages, hadn't words for the sensation of being fully inside her, surrounded by her. The discovery that something could be so perfect and so primal all at once. "I need to—" His hips thrust forward instinctively before he could even complete the thought.

"Yes," she hissed, rising to meet him. "I want all of you. Don't you dare hold back."

He wasn't sure he could have, and he certainly didn't need to be urged twice. He surrendered himself to the moment, to the urge to claim her, fearing the act itself would be over far too soon and yet relishing the knowledge that they had a lifetime together to build on the love between them. A deep groan of satisfaction rumbled through his chest when he felt her shudder beneath him, the pulse of her orgasm setting off his own.

Afterward, he would have rolled off her, but she clutched him to her. "I hope I was worth waiting for." The words were muffled against his shoulder, but he still heard an unaccustomed note of hesitancy in her voice.

He lifted himself on one elbow so he could press his lips against her forehead. "My love, it was worth everything to find my one and only Lady Sterling."

Then he stretched out beside her, smiling when she burrowed against him in sleepy satisfaction. Their bodies entwined, he let himself drowse—at least until he recovered the energy to show her how much he loved her all over again.

Chapter 21

When Laura awoke, the room was gray with the light of early morning peering in around the edges of the draperies. With a careful stretch, so as not to wake Jeremy, she turned so she could examine what darkness had earlier hid from her eyes: a small, simply furnished room, with the bed tucked in one corner so as to make as much space as possible for a desk, a chair, and bookcases filled from top to bottom. She smiled to herself, unable to imagine a more perfect encapsulation of the man himself.

If she had set out to design a man to suit her, Jeremy Addison would not have been that man. Fate—in the person of General Scott, who had sent Jeremy into her life on such a curious whim—had had other ideas. She still scoffed at the notion that a woman needed a man to complete her or fulfill her. Sometime in the last few days, however, she had discovered that needing a person, the right person, was not a sign of weakness, but of strength.

She had been whole before she had met Jeremy. But she was stronger with him at her side.

As if aware of his place in her thoughts, he stirred a little, though he did not wake. Snugging closer, she laid her head against his chest purely for the pleasure of listening to his heartbeat. Would every morning begin thus?

Would every night pass like the one before?

She supposed in the course of a lifetime together, they would spend a great many nights and mornings in less enjoyable fashion, facing life's ups and downs. But she was nonetheless intrigued by the possibility that future mornings and nights could be even better. That the first night's occasional twinge of discomfort or momentary awkwardness would give way to bodies and hearts that knew one another with a degree of intimacy possible only over time.

She was just on the point of waking him to test how far one night had advanced their shared knowledge when someone knocked at the door.

Not the door to the bedroom, but the door of the cottage. Though the sound was muffled, it was unmistakable.

"Jeremy," she whispered, suddenly uncertain. "Jeremy, darling, someone's here."

He was instantly awake and alert at the sound of her voice, never more a soldier than in that moment, as he sat up, indifferent to his nakedness, and scanned the room for some unseen threat.

"There was a knock at the front door," she explained, gathering the sheet around her. "I suppose it must be one of Colonel Millrose's guards, for who else could—?"

He held up a finger, calling for silence, straining to hear if the knock came again.

It did not.

Climbing over her, he paused for a kiss. "You're probably right, but I'll just check. Don't move." After he tugged on his breeches, he slipped from the room, leaving the door open just a crack.

Though the order to stay put was almost certainly about protecting her, she was tempted to obey on the possibility he intended to pleasure her when he returned. But since it was morning, and his mother and sister could be awake at any moment, she rose too.

Snatching up the first item of clothing she laid her hand on, his discarded shirt, she pulled it over her head and crept over to peer around the door. The entryway was still in shadow, but she watched him draw back the bolt and lift the latch. "Is someone there?" he asked as he began to open the door. "Why, Miss Godfrey! How did you come to be here?"

Laura bit back a gasp when she heard the governess's voice. "I'm so sorry, my lord."

And then a deeper, masculine voice. "Let us in, and she won't get hurt."

Emily Godfrey stepped into Briar Cottage with the Earl of Thornton no more than half a step behind her, his pistol at her back.

It took every bit of strength for Laura to restrain herself from running to Jeremy's side. Instinctively, she knew she had a far better chance of helping him if she could manage to catch Thornton by surprise.

"Ah," said Jeremy in a remarkably pleasant voice, as if he'd expected their arrival. "How chivalrous, Thornton. Taking a woman hostage to get past the guard."

"I knew the damn fools wouldn't shoot her. A fatal weakness."

"One I suppose the French do not share?"

Thornton's answering laugh was humorless. "I thought you might've caught on, when you saw the letter that ignorant chit drenched in coffee. But just to be clear, I've no love for the Frogs, either—just their money. And for that, I need what you stole. The letter, the cookbook, all of it."

"Or you'll shoot Miss Godfrey, I suppose."

"Miss Godfrey must help me leave, just the way she helped me in. But I'd gladly shoot that thieving whore who was pretending to be your wife. Where is she?" he demanded, shoving Miss Godfrey into Jeremy, knocking him off balance, and scanning the rooms to either side, the pistol following the arc of his gaze.

She wasn't sure whether he'd seen her or just the open door. Either way, he took a step in her direction, then stopped and looked up the steps.

From the top of the stairwell, Julia shrieked, "Jeremy, there's a man with a gun!"

"Hide!" Laura shouted to her, as Jeremy took advantage of Thornton's momentary distraction to push Miss Godfrey back out the door with an order to run.

As a door slammed above them, Thornton swung around to point the pistol at Jeremy. "I know you think you've got proof I've committed treason. But the charge won't stand. I've got friends at the very top, Captain Addison." He spat out the rank, as if it were beneath him even to speak it.

Jeremy's eyes flashed. "As it happens, my lord, so do I."

His movements were a blur. Laura heard the pistol rattle to the floor almost before she saw the blow that had sent it there. Fists began to fly, Thornton's first punch colliding with Jeremy's jaw, and Jeremy's answer landing with a solid *thunk* in Thornton's gut, driving the air from his lungs.

Jeremy was faster, stronger—seeing his bare arms and chest, she no longer questioned how he'd been able to carry her so effortlessly. But Thornton was heavier, and more desperate. Using his weight, he drove Jeremy to the ground and scrambled to recover his gun, which had skittered beneath the chair on which she'd been sitting last night, just out of the earl's reach.

She didn't give herself time to think. She opened the door, picked up the first thing at hand she could use to defend him, and crossed the floor as quickly and quietly as her ankle would allow. Raising her aunt's ebony walking stick high, she brought it down on the back of Thornton's skull—once, twice. The earl slumped forward with a groan and lay still.

"Are you all right?" Jeremy asked, scrambling to his feet and hurrying to her.

She couldn't seem to stop shaking, even with his arms wrapped tightly around her. "Is he d-d-dead?"

"A hard-headed devil like that? I doubt it. But when he wakes up, he'll wish you'd grabbed your hatpin instead."

And then she was shivering and laughing and crying all at once. Soldiers, some in uniform and some not, were coming in through the front door, eyes and guns trained on Thornton, apologizing to Jeremy. And Julia was thundering down the steps. "Jeremy, Miss Hopkins's bed hasn't been slept in! I can't think where she—oh."

Jeremy turned toward his sister, revealing Laura in his embrace.

"Well," Julia said, glancing at Laura, then at the stretch of bare leg beneath the hems of her brother's shirt, and finally at her brother. "She seems to be all right."

"I am," Laura agreed, the words muffled by Jeremy's chest.

While Julia retreated up the stairs again, he steered Laura out of the way so that a pair of soldiers could carry Thornton out, one at his head and the other at his heels and neither of them especially inclined to be gentle.

As they were passing through the door, two more people came in: Miss Godfrey, accompanied by a spry older gentleman with pewter hair and bright eyes.

"Oh, Arthur," Mrs. Addison called down the stairs, "I take it you didn't get my note. And who is this?" She greeted the newcomers pleasantly, as if having an intruder break into her home at dawn under cover of a hostage and be dragged out by soldiers was a perfectly ordinary occurrence.

Jeremy released Laura and took a step away. Now she could see the grazed skin near his chin, the mark left by Thornton's fist, and the shivering began all over again.

The older gentleman shrugged out of his drab greatcoat and laid it around her shoulders. The hems dragged on the floor. "This young lady is Emily Godfrey, who was just telling me her story," he said. "Dragged here from Kent by that Thornton fellow, who caught her writing a letter and figured she could lead him right to—"

"Me," Jeremy said, a noticeable edge to his voice.

"Ah, so you're Lord Sterling," the man said and held out his hand.

To Laura's shock, Jeremy did not immediately take it. "And you're Mr. Remington."

They were clearly sizing one another up, though to what end Laura couldn't imagine. She began to wonder whether more fisticuffs weren't about to break out. After what seemed an eternity, Jeremy nodded brusquely and shook the man's hand. "I'm glad to know you, sir."

Something suspiciously like tears gleamed in Mr. Remington's blue eyes. "And I you, lad." He turned toward Laura. "This must be—"

"His wife," said Miss Godfrey, then slapped her hand over her mouth, obviously having not intended to speak.

Mrs. Addison took her by the arm. "Why don't you come with me, Miss Godfrey, and I'll have Mary make us a pot of tea," she said, leading her through the sitting room to the table.

"This is Miss Laura Hopkins," Jeremy said. The flags of color on his cheeks were nearly as red as his jaw. "Soon to be Lady Sterling."

Mr. Remington bowed. "Pleased to make your acquaintance, ma'am." Then he turned back toward Jeremy, leaning in and speaking low. "Seems to me that you'd best make it sooner than soon. Perhaps today."

"Today?" Laura cried. "How could we possibly—?"

"A special license," he replied, as if one could simply be plucked from the nearest tree.

"I understand from my mother that Mr. Remington is well connected and counts the Duke of Raynham among his friends," Jeremy explained.

Mr. Remington dipped his head in acknowledgment. "I do indeed. Though in matters involving the possibility for scandal"—his face split in a knowing grin—"it's Lord Ashborough's help you'll want." Laura sucked in a breath; though his heyday was some years in the past, everyone had heard of the notorious Lord Ash. "He's here in town for some falderal with Lady Ashborough's latest book, and I suspect he'll be glad of a distraction. We'll have things sorted before the sun's an hour higher in the sky."

"A generous offer, I'm sure," Laura said, glancing sideways at Jeremy. "But I was hoping for at least enough time to get a dress."

"Best not to delay when it comes to such things as this," Mr. Remington opined, rising up on the balls of his feet to peer into the other room, where Mrs. Addison sat. "You will not want to regret it later."

Jeremy's expression was strange as he watched the man watch his mother. "I wonder, sir, why you haven't availed yourself of Lord Ashborough's matrimonial assistance?"

Mr. Remington turned back and met Jeremy's look. A flicker of surprise passed over his face. "That's a capital idea, lad. Do you suppose we can get the bishop to let us have two for the price of one?" he asked with a wink. When Jeremy did not smile in return, Mr. Remington sobered. Then he clapped a hand on Jeremy's bare shoulder and shook it. "With your blessing, I'll speak with her right now," he said and sauntered toward Mrs. Addison.

Laura's bafflement must have shown on her face, for when he was gone, Jeremy reached over and tugged the man's greatcoat more snuggly around her. "He's my—my father, Laura."

"Oh." Suddenly, she understood the nature of yesterday's conversation with his mother.

Some of the familiar pain rose in Jeremy's eyes. "Does it matter?"

"To me? Not in the slightest. But does it matter to you?"

The answer seemed to require a moment of reflection. "It did," he said at last. "A great deal. For many years, I thought him a scoundrel. But it seems I was wrong." He glanced toward the other room. "And now my mother has another chance at happiness."

Her hand came up to cover his where it still curled in the coat's lapel. "As do you. I love you, Jeremy Addison."

Just as he leaned forward to answer her with a kiss, Julia appeared at her elbow, draping a woolen blanket around Jeremy's shoulders. "If you love her in return, dear brother, you'll let her sit down."

"My God, yes. I'm sorry, dearest."

She had to protest when he made motions to carry her into the sitting room. "I'm fine, honestly. My ankle hardly hurts at all." She glanced warily toward the walking stick, still lying on the floor between the rooms, half expecting it to be bloodstained, though in fact it looked exactly as it always had. Nevertheless, she shuddered at the sight of it. "I think you can get rid of that entirely."

Julia picked it up by her fingertips with her arm straight and carried it away, while Laura let Jeremy lead her to a chair, the one in which he'd been sitting last night. The chessboard was still laid out, though some of the pieces had toppled over in the scuffle. He began absently to set them to rights, then bent and picked up the knight that had fallen from his hand and rolled under the table.

As he reached to place it in its proper place, he froze, looking from the board to the piece and back again. "Could it be?"

"Could it be what?" said a voice behind him.

Laura looked up to see Colonel Millrose standing there. "I apologize for walking in. The door was open, and I don't think anyone heard my knock."

"Sir," Jeremy said, startled from his reverie. "We've got Thornton."

"Yes, I know. One of the guards alerted me that he'd been captured."

"No, I—I mean, we've got him," he said and held up the black knight. "The cypher for the letter—it's *The Noble Game of Chess*." And he began explaining what he had discovered to Colonel Millrose, something about the pattern, alternating moves, the reversal of the board.

To Laura it might as well have been Greek, but Millrose looked impressed. "By God, I see what you mean," he exclaimed. "Excellent deduction, Addison. But you've just made us a hell of a—forgive me, Miss Hopkins—a great deal more work. We're going to have to turn Thornton's library inside out, and—"

"I beg your pardon, Colonel Millrose," she said. "But I'm afraid Lord Sterling is going to be busy. We're getting married this morning."

"This morning? Well!" The colonel stretched out a hand. "My felicitations to you both. Scott's going to have my head, you know," he said, and laughed as Jeremy shook his hand. "Does that mean you intend to give up your commission?"

"I—I don't know," Jeremy said, giving her a bewildered look. "We hadn't really discussed it."

She smiled up at him. "There's time for that decision, I hope. But more immediately, we'll be on our way to Bath, my dear."

"We will?" Jeremy said.

"Yes, to call on my Aunt Mildred. I think she deserves to hear the announcement in person. We can stop on our way to Everham."

His eyes widened further and his lips parted, though he did not speak.

"My goodness, is that Arthur Remington I see over there?" said Colonel Millrose. "I haven't spoken with him in an age."

As the colonel slid away to allow them to talk, Jeremy sank down in the chair opposite and leaned toward her to say in a low voice, "And why are we going to Everham?"

Nervously, Laura picked up one of the chess pieces, realized she might have disrupted whatever arrangement had led to Jeremy's revelation regarding the cypher, and just as nervously put it back. "Well, I had an idea. I've wished for some time that there was somewhere I could send the girls and women that Lady Sterling rescues, a safe place, where they could heal their spirits, lie in if necessary, even receive training to find new and better posts. And from what you said, Everham sounds ideal for such a purpose, just sitting there in the middle of nowhere, empty…"

As she spoke, he reached for her hands and surrounded them with his, his knuckles as battered as his jaw. Chafing the delicate skin on the back of her hands with his thumbs, he listened patiently to every word, a growing amazement on his face. "As a practical matter, would we be staffing the household entirely with women?" he asked, when she paused.

"Oh. Well, I hadn't really thought about—"

"Because," he continued, "if menservants are permissible within your scheme, it occurs to me that Mr. Remington might know of some former soldiers in need of a similar place to recover from their war injuries and learn new trades in the bargain."

Tears sprang to her eyes again. Nothing she had ever heard or read or seen about falling in love had prepared her for the amount of crying involved, the overflowing tears of joy. "That sounds perfect, my darling," she said, snuffling. "Every plan I have, you manage to make better."

He reached up to draw the pad of his thumb along her cheekbone, whisking away a trace of moisture. "But will this venture mean the end of your thief-taking days?"

She managed a watery smile at his question—not a demand. He truly meant to let her choose? But of course he did. She could not have fallen in love with a man who wanted to change her. "I'm not sure," she said honestly. "I do have one or two promises I must keep. But the most important promise is the one I made to you last night, to be your one and only Lady Sterling."

Leaning forward, he brushed a soft kiss across her lips. "The part you were born to play, my love."

Epilogue

A few weeks later

Jeremy leaned forward, the better to see what lay ahead as the road curved and the first hints of Everham peeked above the treetops. Wordlessly, Laura entwined her ungloved fingers with his and squeezed.

"You mustn't expect much," he reminded her, for perhaps the tenth time since the carriage had been announced that morning and he had risen reluctantly from the breakfast table in Mrs. Hayes's—Aunt Mildred's—house in Bath.

"So I've been told." He could hear the smile in Laura's voice, though he did not turn to look at her. "But I can't help myself—you see, I expect I'll be very happy here. Because I'll be with you."

Happiness. A month ago, it had been entirely out of his reach, or well-hidden at least, behind what had seemed an insurmountable wall of secrets and headaches and debt. He returned the pressure of Laura's fine-boned fingers, admiring their surprising strength. She had sized up that wall, more than capable of scaling it if necessary. Then she had laughed, landed a well-placed blow to its foundation, and sent it tumbling and crumbling into dust.

Where, he feared, it had joined whatever remained of Everham.

"The roof line looks mostly solid from here." He craned his neck until his forehead met glass. Surprise creeped into his voice. "Still standing, it would seem. Though of course you mustn't ex—"

The fingers of her other hand curved around his jaw, turning him away from the window and stopping the rest of the word with her kiss. When she pulled away, her eyes were molten steel, a seductive scold. "Fortunately, I have Mr. Remington's most recent update by heart. No significant structural damage," she began reciting the list, punctuating each item with a swift press of her lips to his. "A few broken roof slates—replaced. Cracked windows—reglazed."

His newly-discovered father possessed an extraordinary range of talents. More quickly than Jeremy had imagined possible, and on the heels of his own wedding, Remington had gathered up a crew of former soldiers—men with strength, eager to learn new trades, and men whose injuries had left them weak, but who were still capable of teaching and training—and set out with them for Wiltshire. He had sent regular, reassuring updates, insisting that work on the main house had progressed so quickly that most of the men had now turned to fixing up the tenant cottages where they would eventually live. In his last letter, he had even reported spending some time tutoring two of the men who'd expressed interest in becoming gentleman's valets, the capacity in which Remington himself had at least nominally served Lord Ashborough.

"Plaster work—underway," Laura continued, then paused for a deeper kiss that succeeded in driving back his worry. "Lord and Lady Sterling's suite—ready for occupancy."

"Mmm, yes." He cupped her cheek in his hand and met her simmering look with one of his own. "Now that you mention it, I do seem to remember something to that effect. But scant furnishings. Only one bed, as I recall..."

He felt the wicked curve of her smile against his lips. "And if Mr. Remington is as clever as I think he is, he'll never find another."

And suddenly an interminable journey, one that moments ago had seemed filled with dread, was now too short. Not nearly enough time to remind her of the innumerable pleasures that might be had with no bed at all.

When the coachman tapped on the roof of the coach to announce their impending arrival at Everham, Jeremy ran his hand along Laura's thigh and promised with a saucy wink that he would not forget where he'd left off.

Then the crunch of a gravel drive beneath the coach wheels made his heart hammer for an entirely different reason. Rather than look to the window, he looked to his wife.

Her cheeks were pink, and though he thought he might reasonably take some credit for that fact, her gaze was at present focused past his shoulder, beyond the confines of the coach. "Oh, Jeremy. It's..." Tears glittered in her eyes. "It's home."

Torn between wanting to see what she saw, and having eyes only for her, he turned slowly, drawing her with him, as the door of the coach swung open and Everham rose before them.

Gray stone walls. White pillars. Windows marching in rows across the façade. He could take it in only in pieces. *Home. Their* home. And the home they would make for all those seeking shelter and peace.

As he helped Laura down, a young man limped forward, the left half of his face blurred by scars. He paused before them and gave a stiff bow. "Welcome, milord. Milady. Sorry to say, Mr. Remington isn't here. He wasn't expecting you for another hour."

"That's all right——" Laura said, her pause prompting the man for his name.

"Babcock, milady."

"Oh, yes. Mr. Babcock," she repeated, and smiled. The young man, a former sergeant, now served as foreman. "He spoke of you in his letter."

"Will I show you around the place?" he asked.

"Thank you, Mr. Babcock," Jeremy said, reaching for Laura's her hand, "but I shall do the honors myself."

His memories of Everham were sketchy; he'd visited only once before. But as he led her inside, trepidation fell away, to be replaced by a curious mixture of gratitude and pride. Without Laura's dowry—and without General Scott's interference before that—Everham would still be a rambling wreck of a house. But now it was on its way to becoming—

"Beautiful," she breathed, looking up at what remained of a mural of the summer sky that adorned the high-ceilinged entry hall. Every surface that could be was covered by coarse holland cloth, with a thick layer of dust atop that. But it took very little to imagine what it would be, someday soon.

"We'll use this space for celebrations," Laura predicted as they stepped into what had probably been an elegant ballroom.

"A harvest supper," he agreed. A wall of windows gave way onto a stone terrace and the remnants of a glorious parterre garden, now mostly weeds. "When there's a harvest."

"Next year, then. Think of it. The gardeners we'll be able to put to work. The women busy in the still room, making up recipes and remedies, healing themselves as they learn to heal others."

As they walked up the stairs, down the corridors, peeking into rooms here and there, her vision came alive. The bustle of people at work and leisure, recovering from past traumas, learning new skills, rebuilding a house—and lives—that had been abused and nearly abandoned.

"I wish to hire Miss Godfrey," she told him on the threshold of the schoolroom.

Some of the mistreated serving girls who would come to them would be expecting, like Betty, he knew. "But it will probably be some years before we will be in need of a governess," he pointed out.

"I am determined that *everyone* who comes to us for help will leave at least knowing how to read and write and figure." Her voice was firm, as if she expected an argument. "Educating servants is not without controversy, I know, but—"

"It is the right thing to do. Will we put Betty in charge of the nursery, then, my dear?" he asked, nodding across the way.

"It is her fondest wish to be trained in the styling of ladies' hair." Laura's eyes sparkled as she tossed her short curls. "But I wonder what you would say to having the Pratt girls as nursery maids?"

"Dinah? And…Dora?" He could still picture the coffee pot tumbling from the tray as it slipped from the girl's hands.

"I don't believe she is naturally clumsy. I would trust her with—why, with a baby of my own."

"Your…own…" Excitement and hope bloomed in his chest. "I wasn't sure whether you wanted…"

"I can't promise to be the most conventional mother," she warned him, "but I—I like children. And I love you. And if I"—a flush of color suffused her cheeks—"*we* go on loving one another as we have been, I cannot think it will be long before a little blessing comes to join us."

The swelling sensation in his chest rose into his throat. He would be a father? Another part of a future he had never before been able to envision for himself. A child, children, running on the stairs, picking flowers in the garden, and playing hide and seek behind the statues in the gallery.

As she spoke, they walked down the wide staircase and entered the library. He could picture the nearly empty shelves filled with Richard Addison's books, every volume he had rescued from the rectory, his real inheritance from his papa—a legacy of knowledge, and compassion, and love. "The latest in a very long line of blessings," he told her, when he could speak again. Blessings that had started, ironically, with words that at the time Jeremy had regarded as a curse.

I want you to marry her.

Thank God for General Scott.

"And here, I suppose, is where you'll work," Laura ventured, tracing the corner of a large desk beneath a dusty cloth.

"Yes. Estate business. Leases. Bookkeeping." Those mundane tasks would be a pleasure, now.

"And…code breaking?" she ventured.

"I—" The world of the Underground had seemed very far away from Everham, until they had stepped into this musty, dim room. Too dim to read her expression. "You do not wish me to give it up?"

"That decision is not mine to make. Do you wish to give it up?"

He weighed his answer for a moment, though he knew it would not change. "No. I don't." He took a step closer to her, picked up her hand and chafed his thumb across her knuckles. "It's become a part of me. But I thought you might not want—"

She lifted her eyes to his. "Do you forget? I fell in love with an intelligence officer."

He smiled in spite of himself. "Millrose will be relieved."

"I daresay. And will you be very troubled if—" Her gaze fluttered down to their joined hands. "If, on occasion, a letter should come from the Underground, or from wherever such things are sent, addressed not to you, but to me?"

"To...*you*," he echoed. "You mean, you're willing to go along with Scott's scheme?"

In the silence, he heard her swallow. "Lady Sterling does know...one or two things that might prove helpful to the war effort."

"Still eager to play a part, I see," he teased. "But are you prepared, my dear, to juggle all of it? Home, family, your enterprise here, and..." He wrapped his arms around her and snugged his hips against hers. "A secret agent on the side?"

"It sounds like the plot of one of those ridiculous plays Aunt Mildred and Julia adore."

"It sounds," he said, pressing a kiss against the top of her head, "like a happy ending."

* * * *

General Zebadiah Scott closed his eyes and muttered a few indistinct words, but when he looked again, the pile of correspondence on his desk hadn't disappeared. In fact, it appeared to have grown larger—or at least, some of the mountain had given way in a sort of avalanche and now covered more territory. If he hadn't known better, he would have thought himself in his office at the Horse Guards and not at home.

Thus was the indulgence of almost a month at the seaside with his wife to be punished.

Heaving a sigh, he set himself to the task of sorting. The landslide—or rather, letterslide—had undone whatever order Highsmith had tried to impose. But as he reached for his spectacles and prepared to begin, he spied a calling card peeping from between two thick letters. With one fingertip, Scott slid it from its nest.

the Lady STERLING
thief-taker

Much had happened in his brief absence. A courier had delivered Colonel Millrose's regular reports to Brighton, including one on Lieutenant Hopkins's sister's unexpected arrival at the Underground, and her subsequent claim to be the notorious pickpocket, Lady Sterling. More recently, Scott had read with satisfaction the newspaper's announcement of Captain Addison, Lord Sterling's marriage to Miss Laura Hopkins.

But even he had not expected this.

A line had been drawn through the words *thief-taker*. And in delicate script, someone had inked a single word to replace them: *spy.*

He picked up the card and flicked one corner with his thumbnail, a half-smile curving his lips, his thoughts far away. Then he tucked the square of stiffened paper into his pocket and set himself once more to the task of sorting his correspondence, this time with interest. The next item that fell beneath his glance was a note from an old friend, musing on the failing health of the elderly Duke of Hartwell. Scott was considering what reply to make when his wife, Helen, entered the room, a letter clutched in her own hand. Evidently, she had been similarly occupied.

"It's from Lady Chesleigh, thanking me for my friendship during our stay in Brighton," she explained as she perched on the corner of his desk, shaking her head. "The poor girl. She must be terribly lonely, to miss having me for a partner at whist." Her voice dropped to a confidential whisper. "She told me that her husband has been away for nearly six years."

"He will be home soon enough," Scott replied, laying his fingertips on the letter and turning it slightly so that his wife could read it. "His grandfather is on his deathbed."

Helen's eyes narrowed. "Is Lord Chesleigh one of yours?"

"I can't answer that. Not," he hurried on, forestalling her protest, "because I am foolish enough to try to keep secrets from you, my dear, but because I'm no longer sure whose side Lord Chesleigh is on. Once I thought that a pretty young bride would be just the thing to soften his rougher edges, perhaps even to keep him in England. But then he returned to France, and…" He lifted his shoulders in a shrug.

His wife's eyes narrowed. "*You* made the match between them?"

"I might have nudged things in that direction, yes," he confessed with a glance toward Lady Chesleigh's letter, where it now lay atop the pile of his own correspondence. "But it would seem that I made a mistake."

"Then you must fix it," Helen declared, hopping to her feet again. "I had planned to suggest that I could find a companion for Lady Chesleigh so that she would not need to spend another winter alone. But the way you speak of Lord Chesleigh makes me wonder whether she might not be equally in need of companionship if he returns."

He nodded, contemplatively at first, and then with eagerness. "An excellent suggestion, my dear. Fetch a bonnet."

One brow rose, still dark despite the silver streaks in her hair. "But we've only just got home. Where are you taking me?"

"Oh, not far. I have the perfect companion in mind for Lady Chesleigh," he said, tucking away his spectacles as he stood. "But I'll want your help in persuading Mrs. Drummond to accept the assignment."

AUTHOR'S NOTE

Sometimes, "research" looks a lot like luck. When the codebook made its first appearance in *One Thing Leads to a Lover*, I described it as a French cookbook, mentioned its recipes for "elaborate pastries," and figured that would be the end of it. When I realized details from the book would play a significant part in *Better Off Wed*, I crossed my fingers and went in search of a real book to match the one I'd described. Pierre La Varenne's *Le Cuisinier françois* (1653) was the first French cookbook published in English (*The French Cook*, 1653); it introduced a number of now-staple French cooking terms into English and remained popular through the start of the nineteenth century—so popular that copies were often destroyed through use (a fact I turned to my favor in the plot). But what about my offhand reference to pastries? For that, La Varenne's *Le Pâtissier françois* (1653) seemed the more likely model. Unfortunately, its translation into English—Marnettè's *The Perfect Cook* (1656)—didn't quite match my earlier description. Fortunately for me, the book refers to itself (everywhere but on the title page) and people at the time would have known it as *The French Pastry-Cook*.

Having learned, at least temporarily, not to leap without looking, I researched chess guides *before* adding that element into the story. Chess master Philip Stamma pioneered algebraic notation in *The Noble Game of Chess* (first published in French in 1737 and translated into English in 1745). Though (as Jeremy notes in the story) his style of notation fell out of fashion in the later eighteenth century, it is very similar to the style used today. The pages and columns of numbers and letters (viewable in Google Books) struck me as the perfect hiding place for a cypher.

Better Off Wed's books, then, are real. The plays mentioned by Laura and Jeremy are not—though a few plot details bear some resemblance to various bawdy Restoration comedies. The Love and Let Spy stories are all inspired, to one degree or another, by television shows from the 1980s, and the invented plays are my nod to *Remington Steele*. The con artist hero of that show loved film noir and always found a way to connect the mystery at hand to his favorite movies. For my charming heroine in 1808, the play's the thing!

Printed in the United States
by Baker & Taylor Publisher Services